the SONG of EMBERS

STARFELL BOOK FIVE

JESSICA RENWICK

Published by Starfell Press

Starfell Book Five
The Song of Embers

Contact the author at www.jessicarenwickauthor.com

ISBN (hardcover) 978-1-989854-26-6
ISBN (paperback) 978-1-989854-25-9
ISBN (eBook) 978-1-989854-24-2

Cover design by Ebook Launch, www.ebooklaunch.com
Edited by Talena Winters, www.talenawinters.com
Author Photo © Bonny-Lynn Marchment. Used by permission.

Printed in the United States of America, or the country of purchase.

The Starfell series:

The Book of Chaos

The Guitar of Mayhem

The Bow of Anarchy

The Curse of the Warlock

The Song of Embers

The Star of Truth (2023)

Other works by Jessica Renwick:

The Haunting of Lavender Raine

Lavender Raine and the Field of Screams

The Witch's Staff (part of the Mythical Girls anthology by Celticfrog Publishing)

"You write your life story by the choices you make."
– Helen Mirren

Please note: I have put together a glossary of unfamiliar words, names, and world-specific terms that is located at the end of the book.

PROLOGUE

Only by a spell-consuming flame can magic be destroyed . . .

Endora Nuthatch jabbed the illuminated page before her with a pointed nail. Her magic sparked. The lamp on the desktop flickered, sending dancing light across the bookshelves in her dark library. *What does that even mean? This blasted book and its twisted messages!*

When she'd had her ex-henchman Arame steal *The Magic and Lore of Starfell* from the Ministry of Mistford, Endora had assumed it would hold the knowledge of all the magic in Starfell. But a year of scouring through its cryptic contents and secretive language had done nothing but confuse her.

Another line formed in the page's margin—*As usual, Endora Nuthatch responds with rage instead of intellect. If she doesn't clear her head, she'll never understand the key to her own creation.*

With a snarl, Endora slammed the book cover

shut and thumped it with her fist. "You think you're so smart, book. But you'll see. I'll find a way to leech *your* magic."

She gazed into the mirror above her desk, her cheeks growing even redder as she took in her furious image. Her sleek ebony hair was pulled into an intricate twist, and her pale skin was smooth as silk. All thanks to the new life she had drained from one of her bewitched portraits that morning. Only her new fangs marred her image. She pressed her crimson lips together to hide the gift from her immortal patron, Halite—the dragon whose bond Endora was desperate to break.

"But how?" she murmured, tapping her chin. "I thought this book would hold the answers, not riddles and word games. A spell-consuming flame. Surely not Halite's fire." She snorted, thinking of the dragon's fiery roar that night in the Oakwrath when she'd foolishly bonded with the beast. "And definitely not a firehawk's. What else produces fire that could possibly destroy warlock magic?"

White-hot pain pierced the back of her mind. She let out a cry and grabbed both sides of her head, trying to squeeze the pain away. As if her patron had been reading her mind, a gravelly voice echoed inside her head—*Return to the Oakwrath, warlock. I command you!*

Wincing, Endora stumbled to the plush chair at her desk and conjured a barrier of black magic in her mind to block the dragon's call. It was only slightly effective, muffling Halite's voice as if she were in another room. But it was better than the stabbing pain from before.

Why was I such a fool? As if that winged salamander's magic could be better than mine! At the time, Endora had thought the dragon's power would make her stronger. That it would give her the means to overpower her bonds to the life-sustaining portraits on her walls and make it possible for her to leave her mansion without her power slowly draining. She had hoped she wouldn't need the Blood Star to free herself after all.

But when her bratty great-granddaughter, Fable, had shown up at the portals, Halite's magic had barely sparked. Endora had found out later that the Life Tree that gave the immortals their powers was dying. And if she didn't find a way to break her bond to Halite, her power might weaken too.

The dragon's muted cries rattled against the wall in Endora's mind. *Lich! Warlock! Lowly magician of Starfell!* Endora gritted her teeth, ignoring the dull throb in her temple. After a moment, the calls quieted, and her jaw relaxed.

She turned to the book. Its pages curled as if in a mocking smile. *Do the bonds break when an immortal dies? Maybe I need a dragon slayer instead of this stupid book.* With a sigh, she leaned her elbows on the desk and flipped it open to a random page. A crudely drawn picture of a falling star peered back at her, captioned *The Blood Star* in curly script.

"Is this a joke?" Endora's nostrils flared. For a second, she was afraid they'd blow smoke the way Halite's did. She patted her nose, relieved to find no hint of vapour.

In the top margin of the page, a new sentence formed—*If the lich could ever cool her hot head, she would see the answers before her.*

Endora slammed her fist on the desk. "Don't be cute with me, you dusty tome. I created the star. Its power is rightfully mine!"

The book leapt at least four inches off the table and landed with a *thud*. The pages quivered, as if demanding to be read. The ink of the paragraph at the bottom grew bolder:

June of the year Five Thousand Thirty-Three: During a great battle with Endora Nuthatch in the Oakwrath Thicket, her great-granddaughter Fable connected to the Blood Star. If one remembers correctly, the creators cast a protective spell on the star so that only those with good intentions can use its powers.

Endora's spine stiffened. Why had she and her son, Stirling, put that blasted spell on it? *Because I was a do-gooder then. I hadn't had a taste of real power and what it truly means—youth, beauty, control . . .*

She clenched her teeth and hissed at the book. "There's an antidote. I made the Blood Curse myself, years later. It will lift the protective spell from the star."

Black ink scrawled across the bottom of the paper—*We're getting there. Turn the page.*

Begrudgingly, Endora did as the book instructed and came to the list of ingredients for the Blood Curse. She scanned it, her chest tight with longing. "I have almost everything. The only two left are the tears of a sleeping squonk and a firehawk's last breath, and I already have several firehawks waiting."

The flock of five birds sat cowering in her stable, ready for the moment when she could harvest their last breaths. If only she could find the elusive squonk. None had been seen for years in Starfell, not since before the accident that had killed her family—her son and grandsons.

Her breath hitched. Stirling and his boys, Morton and Timothy, had found her in Sleepy Valley in the

Windswept Mountains, hunting for souls for her portraits from the now-destroyed village there. In her desperation to show them what her lich powers could mean for their whole family, her magic had gone off without warning. It had ricocheted against the cliff wall, causing the rock slide that took their lives.

Of course, Morton's wretched wife had been there too. Endora's gaze drifted upwards to the top floor of the mansion, where the portrait containing the woman's image was hidden away. Unable to handle Faari's constant banging against the glass, Endora had made her henchman stash it up there years ago—out of sight and out of mind.

Smugly, Endora licked her lips. *She made a deal, and I kept my end of it. How could she have been surprised when I collected the payment she owed?*

Endora's perfectly groomed brows furrowed. *Besides, that woman ruined my chances at a relationship with my grandchildren. The only time I saw them, they were hunting me down to force me to stop making my portraits. Didn't they know that would have killed me? I wanted to be together forever, and they wanted me to die!* Tears sprang to her eyes, and she clenched her jaw, blinking them back. *None of them, not even Stirling, understood what we could have been as a family. The power we could have had together. We could have taken over the government in Mistford. Practically become royalty.*

But no. They spurned my magic. They rejected me.

A scarlet ball of crackling energy snapped to life inside her, fuelling her rage. Directing its flow into her hands, her palms began to burn. She thrust them onto the open book, and the paper steamed and hissed as the pages blackened and curled.

"Show me the answer, you nasty trickster!" Endora bellowed, pressing her hands firmer onto the pages. The book's hiss morphed into a pained howl, and she jerked her hands away, panting. "What can break a warlock's bond to an immortal?"

The shrivelled paper held two blackened hand prints. With a crinkle, the pages flopped weakly to the next section. New words scratched across the blank page, as if exhausted. Or, more likely, afraid.

Phoenix fire can destroy an immortal's magic. Their curses. Their amplifiers. Their bonds. Everything.

Endora gave the book a satisfied smirk, placing her now-cool hands on her hips. "That wasn't so hard, was it?" She tapped her chin, her chest loosening. "Phoenix fire. That Folkvar I collected in a frame a few months ago had been searching for a phoenix in the Windswept mountains." She glanced at the mirror again. "And I have a connection there. I'll send Doug to speak with him about tracking it down."

A flash of red in the mirror made her whirl around. Her magic snapped to life, crackling inside her, and she raised her arms to attack the intruder. A coal-black hound the size of a pterippus foal huddled in front of the far wall of books, its eyes glowing crimson. Under her stare, it bristled and crouched to the floor.

How did that vile creature get in here? Endora kept dozens of the beasts outside to patrol her mansion's grounds and scare off anybody who dared to pry. But they slept in the forest or, if they were lucky, in the stable with the boars. Her lip curled at the thought of the hound's hair all over her pristine furniture.

That new servant must have let it in—the wild-haired young woman who had escaped from the frame above Endora's library fireplace. She'd allowed the girl to keep her life in exchange for looking after the mansion. Cooking, cleaning, feeding the hounds. Endora had seen her outside that morning actually *petting* one of the foul beasts. *The nerve! These hounds are supposed to be dangerous and cruel, not house pets. I will have to punish that girl before she tames them all.*

She strutted to the door and pulled it open, baring

her fangs at the cowering creature. With a thrust of her arm, she pointed into the hallway. "Get out!"

The hound bolted through the door with its tail tucked between its legs. As it scampered away, a smell that reminded Endora of a rotting corpse wafted over her. Before she could slam the door, a man built like a garden rake with greasy hair that fell to his shoulders darted into the room. Putrid brown mist trailed behind him.

Endora scowled. "Doug! What have I told you about transporting inside? I can't stand the smell!"

He gave her a bewildered look. "I transported into the hallway instead o' this room."

Endora waved her hand in front of her nose. "Outside! Do it outside. And leave the stench out there."

"Er—"

"Can you not understand simple instructions?" She ground her teeth. "Never mind. Why are you here?"

He gave her a quick bow, causing his stringy hair to fall forward. After straightening, he slicked it behind his ears. "Well, Ma—Mistress. It's the fire'awks."

"What about them?"

"They're gone."

Her chin jerked up. "What do you mean, they're gone?"

Doug tugged at his filthy collar. "They're not in the

barn. Somebody busted 'em lose."

"Who?" Heat flared up Endora's neck, and she gripped the back of her chair to steady herself. Her pointed fingernails scraped the wood. "Who could have come onto my estate without my guards or the hounds noticing?"

"I—I don't know, Mistress." Doug's face paled, and he glanced around the room as if looking for somewhere to hide. "I was out spying on them there kids like yeh asked." His knees buckled. He let out a cry of anguish and pressed his palms to his forehead. "And this dragon won't leave meh alone!"

Blasted Halite. "Block her." Endora rounded on him. She grasped his shoulders and held her face mere inches from his, willing him to ignore their patron's voice. "Do not listen to her. I told you, we are not obeying her."

Doug winced with pain, holding the side of his head. "I'm trying!"

"Try harder!" Endora spat the words, gripping his shoulders tighter.

Doug gasped and wrenched away from her, falling to his knees.

Endora stood over him. She couldn't allow him to let Halite take command. The only reason Endora kept him around was because he had strong portal magic. Strong enough to enter the Oakwrath, where the wretched lizard lay waiting. What if he was powerful enough to let Halite out of the thicket and into Starfell? The thought of that dragon descending onto her mansion sent a shiver throughout Endora. *I can't allow that to happen. She will kill me for disobeying our bond.*

She nudged the cowering man with her pointed-toe boot, then crouched next to him and grasped his arm. "I am your mistress, not that beast. Do you understand?"

Doug gave her a shaky nod, his eyes rimmed with red.

"Good." She straightened, then smoothed the skirt of her satin dress. "Now, I have another mission for you. I need you to find a phoenix."

Skyview Astronomy Tower

A warm summer wind tickled Fable's cheeks as she made her way up the winding path towards the stone tower at the top of the hill. The silver light of the full moon made it easy to keep an eye on Brennus's black hooded sweatshirt and Nestor's tweed hat ahead of her. Behind her, Fedilmid let out a sigh, marvelling at the orange flowers shaped like paint brushes along the sides of the trail. Her grandfather's gravelly voice grunted in reply. Light filled the lone tower window, as if guiding the way for the group from the Thistle Plum Inn.

Skyview Astronomy Tower. Fable shifted her book bag behind her, then gazed at the star-dotted sky, wondering if the astronomers inside the tower were looking at the heavens too. What kind of discoveries might they be making?

"Did you see that?" Brennus asked from up ahead. Fable tore her gaze from the stars to peer at the wavy black hair of her lanky fourteen-year-old friend. Next to him, Nestor turned his wrinkled face skyward. The old man barely came up to Brennus's shoulder.

A flash of gold shot across the sky. Brennus pointed in its direction, letting out another excited shout.

A shooting star. Just like when the Blood Star had fallen last autumn. Fable reached into her pocket. Her fingers brushed the rough surface of the star, catching on its jagged crack—the blemish caused by her magic combining with Endora's about a month ago in the Oakwrath Thicket. She hadn't been able to tap into its magic since. Not even for simple spells to heal a dying house plant or to create a protective barrier around Alice's herbs to block a hail storm. Sure, she'd managed the enchantments on her own. But it should have been easier. She should have felt the star's power guiding her.

Brennus looked down at Nestor with a wide grin. "That's the second one in a row!"

"Isn't that interesting?" Nestor adjusted his hat, still gazing upwards. "When we return to the inn later tonight, be sure to make a note in your study journal before going to bed."

Despite her melancholy thoughts, Fable smiled to herself. Since she and her friends had returned to the Thistle Plum Inn from Stonebarrow, the squat astronomer had taken Brennus under his wing, teaching the teen how to use the inn's telescope and to read the star charts in his study. Fable was relieved Brennus had taken an interest in astronomy. For a while, he had longed to become a warlock to gain magic to help his parents, who were bound to a store cursed to travel around Starfell. But that came with its own chains—a lifetime commitment to an immortal being. Better a lifetime passion for studying stars than a lifetime of bondage to an immortal, no matter how powerful it might have made him.

Fedilmid's cheerful voice sounded behind her. "We're almost there, Stirling. Only a few more minutes, and we'll be over this rise and onto flat ground."

"Hope we get there before my legs give out," Stirling wheezed. "Whose idea was it to make me climb all the way up here? I'm too old to climb mountains. I should be sitting in Alice's parlour, smoking my pipe and doing my daily crossword puzzle."

Fedilmid chuckled. "You're not much older than me or Nestor. Besides, there's no rush. Antares and Carina will be there all night. Hopefully with hot tea and strudels waiting. You'll love Carina's apple strudels. They are to die for."

Fable glanced over her shoulder. Her mentor,

Fedilmid, had his arm looped through the other man's elbow as they shuffled up the steep path. His blue eyes crinkled with mirth behind his half-moon spectacles.

"I don't care about strudels." Stirling's shoulders slouched as he gripped Fedilmid's forearm. His wispy white hair caught in the breeze, and he flattened it with his grizzled free hand. "And I don't care about this tower either. I told you; I don't remember working there. I can't recall being an astronomer at all."

Fedilmid patted his shoulder. "Perhaps this visit to the old tower will wiggle some memories loose."

"It won't. My mind doesn't work right." Stirling huffed. "It's no good anymore. Whatever my mother did to me—"

He snapped his mouth shut, then glanced up and caught Fable's gaze. His amethyst eyes glinted in the moonlight, matching her own perfectly. Fable's heart hitched. She stumbled over a rock and let out a soft yelp, but managed to right herself.

"You alright there, Fable?" Fedilmid called to her.

She took a deep breath and rolled her shoulders. "I'm fine. Just clumsy."

Fedilmid gave her a wry grin. "Something else you have in common with your grandfather."

My grandfather. Fable couldn't quite believe the

words. Her whole life, she'd thought Aunt Moira and Timothy were her only family. When Aunt Moira had gone to Larkmoor last month, Fable had been afraid her aunt was planning to move back to that dreadful place where her magic was so unwelcome. Instead, Aunt Moira had returned to the Thistle Plum with an old man from the nursing home where she'd once worked. Even more surprising was when she'd revealed that the man was Fable's and Timothy's grandfather, Stirling Nuthatch. But it wasn't exactly a joyous family reunion. Stirling couldn't remember anything from before he woke up in the nursing home ten years ago, not even the rockslide that put him there. A rockslide caused by his own mother, Endora.

The Blood Star weighed heavily in Fable's pocket. Endora and Stirling—mother and son—had created it together. According to a book in the Mistford library, they had made it with the power of a mother's love.

Try as she might, Fable hadn't been able to wrap her head around that. If Endora knew anything about *love*, why was she so determined to destroy Fable's life? First, the vile woman had tried to trap Fable with the *Book of Chaos*, even though she'd ended up kidnapping Fable's cousin Timothy instead. And then, she had attempted to steal Fable's magic with an evil spell. Not to mention all the innocent people she'd trapped inside her cursed frames to steal their lives.

And now the lich was also a warlock, bonded to the Dragon Queen, who was bent on destroying the city of Mistford. Fable shuddered as she thought of Endora's sharp new fangs, the trait she'd inherited from her patron.

The only thing that could help Fable stop them lay splintered inside her pocket. The Blood Star. *It enhances my magic to cosmic levels. Or, at least, it did. Before I broke it.*

Brennus stopped, waiting for Fable as Nestor continued up the trail. She jogged to catch up to him. He grinned at her, revealing the dimple in his russet-brown cheek.

"I bet when we get there, Antares and Carina will be ready to head out to look for those fallen stars." He pointed to the tower. Now that they were closer, Fable could see a glass dome roof on the top. "Nestor says Antares is always glued to their telescope. There's no way he didn't see the stars fall. I wish we could go with them. Do you think they'll find the stars?"

Fable's chest warmed at her friend's enthusiasm. "I wonder why they didn't go after the Blood Star when it fell?"

"They probably did, but we got to it before they could find it. Remember, we were right there on Squally Peak when it fell." He ran a hand through his hair. "If we arrive in time, maybe they *will* let us go with them."

"Maybe," Fable replied. "But remember, we're only going to Skyview for Stirling and to find out when that phoenix is going to change."

Brennus's expression grew sombre. "Do you think the Folkvars are right about when it's going to burn?"

"And then rise from the ashes." Fable's stomach grew queasy. She'd rather think about phoenixes emerging from the ashes as baby chicks than them bursting into flames. "The Folkvars know a lot about the mountain range and its wild creatures, and Vetch is their best ranger—"

"All he does is record what's happening in the wilderness." Brennus scoffed. "Thorn said he doesn't have magic. None of the Folkvars there do."

Fable gave him a sideways look. "Magic isn't everything. And Juniper told Thorn that Vetch has kept tabs on the phoenix in the Windswept Mountains for years. He thinks it's going to change life cycles soon, and he knows the bird better than anyone else."

Brennus raised a brow. "Better than an astronomer who can literally read the stars?"

"Nestor says it isn't a precise science. You know that."

Brennus pressed his lips together. "I only want to be sure. If we want to heal your star and free my parents from Ralazar's shop, we have to be there when it burns."

Fable brushed his forearm. "I know. And we will. Fedilmid and Nestor are doing their best to figure this out."

He gave her a weak smile, his brows still knit with worry. The phoenix's ashes could heal anything, including Stirling's amnesia and the broken Blood Star. So naturally, its flames could destroy anything too—including magic. Even a warlock's curse, like the one Brennus's parents were under. If Brennus could use the bird's fire to burn Halite's amulet, which the dragon's other warlock, Ralazar, used to trap the Tanagers inside the store, perhaps his parents could finally be with him again.

The group came to the top of the hill. The lamp next to the tower's door shone over them like a lighthouse guiding them home. Thick green moss grew along one side of its stone walls. The entire structure tilted sideways as if about to lurch over the cliff. Nestor had told them this place was the pinnacle of astronomy research. Fable hadn't imagined it would be so—well, ramshackle.

"Ah, Skyview Tower." Fedilmid led Stirling over to Nestor, who stood at the moss-covered door. "I haven't been here for ages. Ready to go inside and see the astronomers?"

Stirling eyed the building suspiciously. "I worked in this shack for twenty years?"

Nestor nodded. "Twenty-one, actually."

Brennus scrunched his nose, looking the tower up and down. "Is it, uh, safe to go in there?"

Fedilmid puffed his chest. "Of course it is. For someone who has no issue rushing into a building that shifts around Starfell unexpectedly, you're being a tad judgmental."

Brennus flushed and shoved his hands into the pockets of his hooded sweatshirt. The Odd and Unusual Shop where his parents worked was named that for more than one reason.

"I assure you, it's perfectly safe," Nestor said as he pushed open the door. He gave Fedilmid a sidelong glance. "I heard it on good authority that the Fey Witch provided magical supports to it about a decade ago."

Fedilmid lifted his chin. "That's right."

Fable covered a smile and exchanged glances with Brennus. Despite the Fey Witch's far-reaching reputation in Starfell, the residents of the Thistle Plum

Inn were among the few who knew the witch as one and the same as Fedilmid. It was how Fable, Brennus, and their friend Thorn had met Fedilmid in the first place, when they'd joined forces to find their families over a year ago. Families taken from them by Endora's wicked magic and trapped inside the lich's portraits to unnaturally extend her life and youth.

Fedilmid stepped into the dark tower and held out a hand to Stirling. "Watch your step. The landing's a bit soft from the mould."

Brennus cocked a brow. "You'd think the Fey Witch would have taken care of that too."

Fedilmid gave him an amused look. With a grunt, Stirling brushed aside the witch's hand and entered the tower with a shaking step. Nestor and Brennus followed. A damp chill settled over Fable when she closed the door behind her. Water pooled in the crevices of the stone floor, and a dripping sound echoed around them. In the middle of the room, a spiral staircase ascended to the rough wooden floorboards of the second level. Light filtered between the slats.

Stirling craned his neck to look through the hole above.

Fable followed his gaze. "Do you remember this place?"

"No," he snapped. "I already told you. I remember nothing from before I woke up in Larkmoor."

"I just thought—"

"You thought wrong. You all did." He hunched his shoulders, then began to climb the stairs. Fedilmid rushed to help him, but he pushed the witch's hands away again. "I can do this myself."

Fable swallowed and adjusted the strap of her book bag on her shoulder. Over the last few weeks, Stirling's temper had grown shorter and shorter. Fable tried to be sympathetic. After all, it must be scary to lose your memory. While he remembered Aunt Moira as his nurse from Larkmoor Manor, he'd had no idea she was his daughter-in-law until she'd brought him to Mistford.

Another one of her secrets. Fable's jaw tightened as he followed the group up the stairs. Her aunt had hidden Fable's family history from her for years. Her parents' magical life outside the boring village of Larkmoor. That they'd left Fable with Aunt Moira that fateful night they'd set out to confront Endora. How they had died. *No wonder he's cranky. I know exactly what it's like to be lied to about who I am.*

Fable followed Stirling into a bright room bathed with warm light from dozens of little bulbs set into the stone walls around them. Free-standing wood-framed cork boards with wheeled legs stood haphazardly around the room, their surfaces cluttered with black maps and charts criss-crossed with glittering gold lines. A handful of tables sprawled between them, piled with books, loose papers, rulers, protractors, and other tools Fable didn't recognize. But the centrepiece of the room was the huge telescope the size of a tank. A cylindrical barrel as big around as Fable herself pointed towards the glass dome above them, supported by what looked like eight metal spider legs.

A round man with frizzy black hair sat on a mechanical chair in front of the telescope with his back to them. He leaned forward, squinting into a smaller tube that led into the machine at right angles.

He spoke without looking up. "They're both drudgers. Not even a glint of magic in either of them. They came from the Oberon constellation, I think. Check location three million twenty-four. That one looked a bit wiggly last week." He waved in their general direction, keeping his eye on the eyepiece.

Fable didn't even think he was speaking to them, which was confirmed when a head with two curly black buns popped up from behind a stack of books near the telescope. The woman had rich brown skin and looked to be in her mid-twenties. She peered at the man through a pair of unusual glasses. The arms held several layers of round, metal-framed lenses that could swing up and down as needed. At the moment, the lenses were all down, which made the woman's eyes look as bulbous as Arame's, the toad-like man who had helped Fable and her friends escape Endora's mansion the summer before.

"Oberon! Drudgers or not, that's still interesting, Antares." She jumped to her feet and rushed to the closest chart. "Nothing has fallen from there for six years. I wonder what happened? It couldn't be age, that constellation is only one thousand and thirty-two years old. I wonder what could have called them down. Perhaps a fae creature—"

"Why would a fae creature want an old rock with no magic?" Antares spun the mechanical chair around, and his scowl faded as he took in their visitors. "Nestor! Fedilmid! I wasn't expecting you until Thursday."

Nestor pushed back his tweed hat. "It is Thursday."

Carina let out a squeak, then flipped up the top lens from her glasses and checked her watch. "He's right. It *is* Thursday. You'll have to forgive us, Nestor. We haven't been sleeping well."

"You mean *you* haven't been sleeping well." Antares pressed a button on the arm of his chair, and it lowered to the hardwood floor. He lumbered to his feet and made his way over to the group. "She insists on having morning coffee once we get off work. I don't join her though. It's ridiculous to have caffeine at bedtime."

Fedilmid stroked his beard, grinning. "May I suggest chamomile tea instead?"

Carina rushed over to them, her buns bobbing in time with her upturned lenses. She pushed one down, causing the image of her eyes to warp and bulge. She grasped Stirling's hand, trembling. "Stirling Nuthatch? Is it really you? When we heard you were alive—"

"Carina!" Antares hissed at her.

Stirling pulled away from her, a frown deepening the wrinkles on his forehead. "Er—"

"We know everything about you! Studied every one of your books," Carina gushed, holding her cheeks. "My copy of *A Stargazer's Guide to Space and Time* is so tattered the pages are falling out. Oh, would you sign it for me? Please? I know it's around here somewhere."

Antares rubbed his forehead. "I'm sorry, sir. She's just excited to meet you. I mean, you invented the Starfinder telescope—"

"Which we still have!" Carina looked nervously at the enormous telescope. "Well, we have a Cometseeker now, but that doesn't mean the Starfinder is obsolete. In fact, your design set the bar for all future star-seeking technology."

Stirling's face grew ghostly white, and he took a step away from them. "I don't remember any of this. I'm sorry."

Carina's expression fell. She flipped up another lens, shrinking the image of her eyes to normal. "What do you mean, you don't remember?"

Fedilmid put his hand on Stirling's shoulder. "Unfortunately, Stirling has a rather severe case of amnesia. We were hoping this place might trigger some memories for him. But alas, it doesn't seem to have worked. It's alright though. It was worth a try."

"I'm sorry, sir," Antares said.

"Is there anything we can do to help?" Carina wrung her hands. "You're welcome here any time, of course. Maybe a visit to the storage facility in town where we keep the Starfinder would help?"

Stirling took another shaky step back. "I—I'm not sure."

"We'll think about it and let you know." Fedilmid gave Carina a kind smile. "Now, we are here for another reason too. Perhaps you can help us with something."

Antares leaned his ample hip against the table behind

him, crossing his arms. "What kind of something?"

Nestor moved to the nearest star chart and traced one of the lines with his finger. "Fable has a broken spectral. Its magic doesn't work anymore. We'd like to fix it, and we have word that a phoenix is going to cycle soon."

"Spectral?" Fable had never heard the term before.

"A magical star," Brennus replied, and Nestor gave him an approving nod. "The opposite of a drudger. The Blood Star definitely counts as a spectral."

Antares grabbed the edge of the table. "The what?"

Carina flipped down two lenses and stared intently at Fable. Her eyes looked so warped they were almost crossed. "Did you say the *Blood Star*?"

Fable gulped and took the star from her pocket. She held it up for Carina to see. "I cracked it about a month ago."

"*You* cracked it?" Carina looked to Fedilmid. "How could she have cracked it? Only its creators can break it. No offense, Fable, but there's no way you could have made it. You're what, ten years old?"

A hint of annoyance sparked inside Fable. "Thirteen, actually." Why did she have to be so short? She'd been hoping for a growth spurt like her friends and Timothy had all experienced, but she'd had no such luck yet.

"Still, much too young to have created the Blood Star," Antares said.

"It's a long story, but one of its creators was involved," Nestor assured him. "It's from the Gaea constellation, I believe."

Antares frowned. "That is correct. We saw it tumble from the sky last autumn. We looked for it, but we never found it. How did you end up with it?"

"That's another long story," Fedilmid replied. "But we'd like to fix it with a phoenix's ashes. Are you able to read the stars regarding the phoenixes in Starfell? Since they are celestial beings, we hoped you'd be able to pinpoint their life cycles."

"Of course," Carina said, returning her gaze to the star in Fable's hand. "But I don't know if phoenix fire can heal the Blood Star. Like you said, Nestor, it's from *Gaea*."

Nestor frowned. "A phoenix's ashes can heal all types of magic."

"But Gaea is the mother constellation," Carina replied.

Antares nodded. "From our studies over the last couple of years, we think Gaea holds the most powerful of all the spectral stars. And the Blood Star . . ." His voice grew to nearly a whisper. "It's the most powerful star that's ever fallen. We were devastated when we couldn't find it. Thought for sure the police from Mistford must have snatched it."

Carina raised a finger. "What he means is, we don't know if phoenix fire alone can heal it. It's written in the constellation that a mother's love created it. Which means—"

Brennus lifted his head. "Endora."

Fable's stomach clenched, and she clutched the star to her chest.

Carina joined Nestor at the star chart, then pointed to a line of glittering geometric drawings in the centre. "She's the mother in the Blood Star story, right? It's only a theory, but if only she can create or destroy the star's magic, I think you'll need her to heal it too."

TWO

A Star's Destiny

Fable's tongue felt like it was glued to the roof of her mouth. She swallowed, forcing herself to speak. "No. Endora would only heal the star so she could connect with it. So she could use the Blood Curse on it to destroy her bind to her portraits. We can't let that happen. She'll hurt even more people."

Carina chewed her lip, looking at Nestor. He scrubbed his face with his palm. "Fable's right. We can't let Endora anywhere near the star. Are you sure phoenix ashes won't heal it?"

Carina pushed her glasses higher on her nose. "Nothing is for sure. You know how these constellations can be. They're always a riddle to figure out."

"My sister is usually right, though." Antares joined them, staring at the chart of Gaea. He traced a finger along one of the golden threads. "But it doesn't say anything about phoenix ashes not working. If you have a way to get some, I say try it." He paused, glancing at the telescope. "I might be able to find you a phoenix, but how are you going to reach it? Much less right when it's ready to cycle?"

Fedilmid stroked his pointed beard. "We know where one is already. We have connections with the Windswept Folkvars, and their lead ranger keeps tabs on a phoenix near their colony. He thinks it's going to start its next life cycle soon."

Antares's brows shot up. "The Windswept Folkvars? Do they trust you? They usually keep to themselves."

"We have an inside source."

Antares made his way to the telescope. He climbed the metal steps and took a seat in the chair. "Well then, let's take a look to verify when this mountain bird will burn. For your sake, I hope it's sooner than in a few decades. Carina, check the Paragon chart."

Carina skittered across the cluttered room, dodging through the charts and tables. She stopped at a black map with gold dots and lines in the shape of a bird with outstretched wings. She flipped down four lenses this time, making Fable wonder just how terrible the spritely woman's vision must be.

Carina pulled a pencil and a tattered notebook from the front pocket of her vest. "I'm ready, Antares. What do you see?"

He peered through the eyepiece of the telescope,

swirling the knob above it. "Hm . . . Point twenty-six-thirty-two has brightened, and it's now only two dots left of its last trajectory with point forty-eight-zero-three."

Carina's already bulbous-looking eyes widened. She tucked the pencil behind her ear, placed her free hand on the chart, and began to measure with the width of her palms. After a moment, she took the pencil and scribbled in the notebook.

"That's in only six or seven days."

Antares twisted a gear on the other side of the eyepiece. "That sounds about right. Maybe eight, depending on the weather. Wow." He looked over his shoulder at the group. "You got lucky with the timing."

"There's another phoenix in the Burning Sands," Carina pointed out. "But it's not due to start a new cycle for at least a century."

Fable tightened her grip on the star. *Six days?* They would have to leave the Thistle Plum right away. Vetch had told Juniper that it looked like the phoenix was preparing to start its new life—the vibrancy of its feathers was waning, and it had been building a new nest and gorging itself on the peaches and berries that grew in the valleys. He'd said those were sure signs it was getting ready to change.

Fedilmid and Nestor huddled together, speaking in

hushed tones. Stirling had taken a seat at one of the tables and was flipping through an astronomy book, his forehead wrinkled in concentration. Fable hoped something in it would trigger his memory.

She pocketed the star and approached Carina to get a better look at the map of Paragon. Brennus followed her and peeked over the astronomer's shoulder at her paper.

"How did you come up with that equation?"

"Oh, it's easy." Carina flushed, looking pleased. She pointed to the zig-zagging lines on the chart. "Star number twenty-six-thirty-two represents the phoenix. Its position around forty-eight-zero-three shows its lifeline. This chart showed where the bird was when it last burned, so I measured the distance."

Brennus raised his brows. "How do you know to do all that?"

"Um, books. I guess."

"And four years of an apprenticeship with me, plus another few years of experience," Nestor said, looking up from his hushed conversation with Fedilmid. "She was one of my best apprentices."

"And your last." Carina's voice was tinged with sadness. "Everyone in the Astronomers' Guild was disappointed when you retired."

"I may be coming out of retirement." Nestor nodded at Brennus. "For a short time and to work with Brennus here. He's shown great interest and aptitude for the science. We've had some lessons with my materials at home."

Carina's face lit up, and she popped up what must have been at least five lenses. The image of her eyes shrank with every one. "You want to become an astronomer?"

Brennus shoved his hands in his pockets. "I don't know for sure. I have some other things to deal with first, but I'm thinking about it."

"In that case, take these to further your studies." She grabbed an armful of rolled-up papers from the table beside them and thrust them into his hands. "They're charts of Rugen, Yellin, and Panthera. They're the constellations closest to Starfell and the simplest to learn about."

"But don't you need them?" Brennus asked, organizing the rolls in his hands.

"We have more copies in the back." Carina swept her arm towards the far wall behind them, which was lined with dark wooden cabinets. She beamed at him. "I hope you'll come work with us one day."

"Oh, well, thank you." Brennus hugged the charts

awkwardly. "Erm, do you have a bag I could borrow?"

"Oh, silly me! Of course." Carina swept aside a pile of papers and some kind of triangular ruler, then picked up a ratty olive-green tote. "Here you go. Keep it."

She held it open and Brennus placed the maps inside, then took it from her.

Fable placed her hand on the map of Paragon. The paper felt silky beneath her touch. "Carina, do you think you could show me the map of the constellation the Blood Star came from? Gaea, right?"

"Of course," Carina replied warmly. She glanced at her brother, who still sat peering through the telescope's eyepiece. "Antares, do you need any more help?"

He gave her a thumbs down, not taking his eyes away from the telescope. "Nope. I just saw a flicker near point sixteen-thirty-three. I'm trying to see if the full moon is shifting or if its merely a mosquito on the dome."

Carina beckoned for Fable and Brennus to follow her, leaving Fedilmid and Nestor in an intense conversation. When they reached the map of Gaea, Fable craned her neck to study it. The shimmering gold lines formed the shape of two hands clasped together.

Carina slid down a lens, pointing at the outline of the interlaced fingers. "According to one of Mr.

Nuthatch's old books, this symbol means: *The star will reunite the mother and child, and peace will come to Starfell.* I'm guessing that means the Blood Star. And that this reuniting would fix its magic, no problem."

Brennus glanced in Stirling's direction. The old man turned the page in the book before him, absorbed in whatever he was reading. "I can't believe he doesn't remember any of this. Can you tell when they're supposed to reunite?"

Carina tapped her chin. "I'm not sure. It appears to be destiny. And we all have free will, don't we? The choices we make can change fate or avoid it altogether."

Fable's throat tightened. "What happens if the mother and son avoid this destiny?"

"The opposite of the destiny. Chaos instead of peace, I'd wager."

"Chaos?" Brennus asked.

Carina pursed her lips. "You know. Floods. Fires. War. The usual. If Endora's involved, I'd bet on some kind of war."

Fable swallowed, thinking of the lich's new alignment with Halite. If they decided to work together, she didn't want to imagine the kind of chaos they would bring to Starfell. But if Fable could heal the Blood Star and use its magic again, she could put a stop to them.

Destiny or no destiny.

She met Carina's gaze. "And you don't think the phoenix ashes will work to heal the star instead?"

"I mean, the reuniting of a mother and child is a pretty strong path." Carina shrugged. "But the ashes would work with most other broken spectrals. So maybe I'm wrong." She traced a finger along the bumpy lines that formed the knuckles on the constellation's hands. "It doesn't say anything here about what to do if the star gets damaged." She flicked her gaze to Fable, her expression softening. "Tell you what; I'll head over to Skyward University in Mistford—the astronomy school—and check their archives. There might be more information about stars from Gaea in there. I'll let you know what I find."

The tension in Fable's chest eased. Maybe there was more to this destiny than what Carina knew. Maybe it could be avoided without causing any chaos. "Okay. Thanks."

"Hopefully, the ashes will work." Brennus shifted the tattered bag beneath his arm. "Because we can't put Stirling in danger. Endora's off her rocker."

"The ashes won't heal the root of the problem," Carina replied, "and that's 'why did Endora go bad? Why did she choose to become a lich in the first place?'"

Fable's heart sank. Any time she'd faced her great-grandmother in the past, there had never been any kind of empathy in the woman's amethyst eyes. She'd never even hesitated to attack her own family.

"There's no healing Endora. The best we can do is confine her to her mansion and destroy every one of her horrible portraits so she can't hurt anybody else."

An hour later, Fable sat wedged between her grandfather and Brennus in the back seat of Fedilmid's van, bouncing along the cobbled streets of Mistford towards the Thistle Plum Inn. Brennus poured over one of the maps Carina had given him. And even though it was well past midnight and Fable should have been exhausted, her mind and magic both whirled inside her. She fidgeted with the Blood Star, wishing to feel even one ounce of the energy within it. But it lay cool beneath her fingers, just as it had ever since she'd cracked it.

She squeezed it tighter, musing over Carina's words about the star's destiny to reunite Endora and Stirling. Her grandfather slumped against the window, staring silently into the night. He was so thin. So frail. Even if he wanted to, there was no way they could let him meet with Endora. She may have once been a loving mother, but now, there was no trace of kindness within her. She didn't care about her own great-grandchildren. Would she even recognize her now-elderly son?

And without the Blood Star's magic, could Fable keep him and everyone else safe? Sure, she and her friends had escaped Endora's attack in the Oakwrath. But that was because Halite had turned on the hag, distracting her. Even with the Blood Star's power, Fable had only managed to slow Endora down.

Without the star, I can't protect anybody. Much less the son Endora tried to murder once already. They needed to get those phoenix ashes. And Fable could only hope the ashes would work.

Fedilmid stopped the van on the street in front of the Thistle Plum. Everybody got out and began to make their way up the stone walkway. As she surveyed the familiar Victorian-style inn, Fable's worries eased. She'd lived there with her cousin and friends for several months now. Even with its peeling purple paint and faded pink shutters, this place had come to feel like home for her. And Nestor and Alice Serpins, the inn's owners, had become like grandparents. It was hard to imagine that she, Aunt Moira, and Timothy would be moving into their own house soon—the one she'd inherited from her parents.

They reached the sagging front steps, and Stirling gripped the rail to heave himself up.

Fedilmid grasped his elbow. “Here, let me help you.”

Stirling grunted and shrugged him off. “I told you before, I don’t need help.”

“Come, now,” Nestor said kindly. “We only want to make it easier while you build your strength.”

Stirling puffed his chest, shifting his gaze between the two men. “Neither of you are much younger than me. Moira sprang me from that old person’s joint because I was miserable there.” He jabbed a wrinkled finger in their direction. “And I don’t want to relive the experience here.”

Fable shifted her bag, glancing at Fedilmid. That wasn’t exactly what Aunt Moira had told them. According to her, he’d been causing trouble at the nursing home. Apparently, he’d tried to break out twice and had started a food fight in the cafeteria. And, of course, he’d been giving the other care workers at the home a hard time too. Much like he was doing to Fedilmid and Nestor now. The managers had contacted Aunt Moira and told her to come get him before they tossed him out.

Leaning heavily on the rail, Stirling thumped up

the steps with a jerky stride. He lifted his chin, giving them all a smug look. “See? I can manage on my own.”

Fable bit back a smile. Her grandfather’s stubborn nature reminded her of her cousin, Timothy. As she followed him inside, she wondered if her father had been like that too—determined and strong-willed. She wished she could ask her grandfather about him, but it would be pointless.

Stirling and Nestor shuffled towards the inn’s kitchen, probably for a cup of tea to help them settle down for the night. Beside her, Brennus covered his mouth as he yawned. Fedilmid lay a hand on Fable’s back, directing her towards the stairs that led to the room she shared with Thorn.

“Have a good sleep, kids,” he said. “Remember, tomorrow we have another important mission—checking on Eighteen Lilac Avenue one last time before we leave for the mountains. I’ll talk to Moira tomorrow morning, but after what Carina and Antares told us, I think we’ll have to head out shortly. Perhaps the day after tomorrow.”

Fable’s heart lifted. Eighteen Lilac Avenue was the address of her family cottage. It had sat empty for almost a decade and needed a lot of work before she, Aunt Moira, and Timothy could move in. Fedilmid and his husband, Algar, had been in charge of the renovations, and after months of organizing contractors and even hammering a few nails themselves, the two men were close to making the house a home again.

"Oh, right!" Brennus replied with a sleepy grin. "I can't wait to see what they did with Timothy's room. He told me he asked his mom for a big screen TV and the new Ultra Z video game console."

Fedilmid quirked a brow. "Do you think Aunt Moira approved that request?"

"Probably not. But maybe she agreed to getting it for the living room."

Fedilmid chuckled. "We shall see. Alright, off to bed. It's late, and you know how Aunt Moira feels about sleeping in."

Brennus gave him a salute and started up the stairs. Fable followed him. The star lay heavy in her pocket, and her mind turned to Endora. It seemed strange to get excited about Eighteen Lilac Avenue while the lich was still out there, plotting and planning.

If we find the phoenix ashes, at least my grandfather will have his memories back. But what if Carina's right and they don't heal the star? What if the only way to fix the Blood Star is for Endora and Stirling to reconnect? Fable's neck stiffened. She couldn't defeat Endora without the Blood Star's power. But Endora could easily tear Fable's grandfather away, exactly like she'd done to Fable's parents.

They reached the landing and Brennus gave her a quick wave before heading to the room he shared with Timothy, who was probably fast asleep. Brennus opened the door quietly and tiptoed inside, and Fable continued to her door, her mind on anything but sleep. If the phoenix ashes failed to heal the star, she would have to find another way to fix its power.

If she wanted to defend the people she loved from Endora, she had no other choice.

THREE
Something Dead in the Basement

If Fable squinted hard enough, she could envision her quilted bed from Rose Cottage below the window in her soon-to-be bedroom at Eighteen Lilac Avenue. The pink shades of the blanket would match the plum-coloured walls perfectly. She imagined her old oak bookcase in the corner with the olive-green rug in front of it. She'd never had her own bedroom before. At least, not that she could remember. Would Aunt Moira let her have the bookcase in here? Or would it be better in the living room where Timothy could use it too?

Thorn's voice came from the hallway. "Hey, Fable."

Fable turned around, and Thorn gave her a wave from the doorway. The blue-skinned Folkvar girl's copper braid hung over her shoulder, nearly reaching her waist. She ducked into the room, holding a blue glass vial filled with clear liquid in her long, thick fingers.

"Hey, Fable. I brought this oil for your room." She wiggled the tiny bottle, then pulled out the cork stopper and dabbed the oil on her fingers. A sweet flowery scent hit Fable's nose as Thorn turned and began to rub it on the top of the door frame. Standing a foot and a half taller than Fable, she didn't even need to stand on her toes to reach the frame.

Fable made her way over the hardwood floor to her friend's side. "What are you doing?"

Thorn glanced at Fable, her moss-green eyes catching the soft light coming through the uncovered window panes. "Greencraft. Alice made this with althaea, which is a flower that has magical protection properties."

Thorn had been learning greencraft from Nestor's wife, Alice. For months, Thorn had been wearing vial necklaces for communication, creating satchels for pleasant dreams, and rubbing herbal oils all over the place. Fable wasn't sure if or how greencraft worked, but Alice was a well-respected witch, so the plants must hold some sort of magic.

The Folkvar girl placed the cork lid into the mouth of the jar and stuffed it into the pocket of her beige canvas pants. Placing her hands on her hips, she gave the frame a satisfied nod. "This should keep your room safe from anything that could hurt you, and it'll probably help with fighting off nightmares too."

"Thanks," Fable replied, not wanting to remind Thorn that she had her own protection—the magical shield she had used before to keep her and her friends safe from Endora's guards. "You've been practicing a lot with Alice lately. I guess you want to learn as much as you can before your move, huh?"

Her heart pinched. Thorn and her sister, Orchid, were moving to the Windswept Folkvar colony at the end of the summer. Their aunt, Juniper, had tracked down the girls the month before and offered them a home. While Juniper had promised that Fable could visit often, Fable was going to miss her friend. They had shared a room for almost a year now and spent every day together. Sure, Fable was excited to have a permanent home in Mistford and for Thorn to have found her aunt. But she had mixed feelings about all the changes that were looming ahead.

Thorn wiped her thick hands together, glancing at Fable. "I'm getting pretty good at greencraft. That oil Alice helped me make for my meditations even worked. I used it the other day to keep my cool when Timothy pranked me with one of Alice's seashells. We were making candles with them, and the one I was holding *bit my finger*. But one whiff of that oil and my anger totally went away. Timothy said my eyes didn't even turn yellow."

"That's impressive. But your temper isn't always a bad thing. It has helped get us out of some bad situations before."

Not long after Fable and Thorn had met, Thorn had managed to focus that temper into saving Brennus from a terrible punishment at the Buttertub Tavern—and that was only one example of the many times Thorn's temper had helped them.

Thorn pressed her lips together. "But it's not always a good thing either. Anyway, I was excited about getting better at greencraft and having something other than my strength to be proud of." She frowned. "But Aunt Juniper told me that the Folkvars in the Windswept Mountains don't like magic."

"What do you mean? Why wouldn't they like magic?"

"She said they think it's dangerous," Thorn replied. "I wonder if that attitude came from Larkmoor. The Windswept colony isn't far from there."

Fable's stomach knotted. It was true. The townsfolk in Larkmoor hated magic, which was why Fable never wanted to go back.

"I thought you said the people in the Greenwood worked with the earth's energy. That seems a lot like greencraft to me."

Thorn's frown deepened at the mention of her old home, the Greenwood Forest. When she and Fable had first met, a fire had recently destroyed it, killing or driving out most of the life in the woods. Many of the surviving Folkvars, including Juniper, had moved to the colony in the Windswept Mountains.

Thorn pulled out her necklace from under her shirt collar, revealing the glass vial pendant filled with herbs. "They used nature as medicine. But yeah, their methods are related to greencraft. In fact, I think they were using plant energy in the same way Alice does. They just didn't think of it as magic." She took a deep breath. "Chamomile tea to calm your nerves. Plantain leaves for healing wounds. Thyme at your bedside for a peaceful sleep. It's all the same, only thought about differently." She grasped the vial and took a deep breath. "Maybe once I show them, they'll come around."

Fable gave her friend a sympathetic look. "I'm sure they will. It sounds the same to me. And the people in Larkmoor basically shut themselves off from the world, so their fear of magic can't have spread that much."

Thorn sighed and tucked the vial beneath her collar. "I just hope they'll like me."

"They will. What's not to like about you?" Fable

squeezed her friend's muscular arm affectionately.

Thorn had been longing to leave Mistford ever since they got there last fall. While the city had seemed like an enchanting fortress of acceptance for Fable, it hadn't been that way for Thorn. People treated Thorn differently, often pointing at her bulky frame and whispering behind her back. Thorn had even found a book in the magic shop that said Folkvars were dangerous. It was no wonder she wanted to move. Fable only wished she could make others see Thorn for who she truly was—the kindest, bravest, most loyal friend anybody could ask for.

"I guess we'll see in a few days," Thorn replied. That morning at breakfast, Aunt Moira had announced they would leave for the Windswept Mountains the next day. "I can't wait to see my future home." She gestured to Fable. "And to finally end this toxic situation with Endora and the Blood Star."

Fable patted her pocket, comforted by the star's lump. But Carina's words from the night before weighed on her mind. "The astronomers aren't sure if the phoenix ashes will heal the star. I don't know how they can tell, but they read the constellation the star came from and think it has some kind of destiny."

"Destiny?" Thorn raised her brows. "What did they

mean by that?"

"Carina said it was destined to reunite the mother and child who created it. She thinks that will somehow fix the star's magic."

Thorn huffed, scrunching her nose. "You mean Endora and Stirling? Letting Endora see him doesn't seem like a good idea. Didn't she try to kill him once already?"

"Yes. And with her being bonded to Halite now . . ." Fable cringed at the thought of Endora's new sharp-toothed smile. "We can't confront her without the star's magic. Without it, there's no way I can keep everyone safe. I need its power to destroy those portraits and to bind her inside the mansion again."

Thorn rubbed her chin, looking at Fable from the corner of her eye.

"What?" Fable asked.

"You've defeated her before without the star's magic."

Fable crossed her arms. "No. I've only managed to blast her off or sneak us away from her. And if it weren't for Halite turning on her in the Oakwrath, we would probably be in a portrait on her wall right now." Fable's voice hitched. "And even then, I had the star's magic to hold her off, remember? Before I broke it."

Thorn held up her hand. "That's not how I remember it. First, *Endora* broke it. Not you. Nestor said only the star's creators can do that."

"But if it weren't for me—"

"Second," Thorn counted her next finger, "you held her off even before you connected with it. And you guided us out of there after it broke. What about all those times you beat her before? At the Bottomless Sea, on Squally Peak, in her own library . . ."

Warmth crept over Fable's cheeks. "I had help every time."

"And you have help now." Thorn clasped her shoulder. "You're stronger than you think, especially with all of us on your side."

Fable's throat tightened. She didn't know what to say. Her friends could never understand what it was like to have an evil great-grandmother. A horrible lich who hurt people to keep herself young and alive forever. A monster only Fable had the power to stop.

And without the Blood Star's energy, she wasn't strong enough. That feeling when she'd connected with it in the Oakwrath—she had never experienced anything like it. That grounding. That peace. That *home*. It was like the star's magic had made her whole, filling every crack and broken piece within her.

And then, she'd let Endora smash it.

She blinked back the frustrated tear threatening to spill.

The sound of footsteps pulled her attention to the hallway. Her cousin, Timothy, bounded into the room with a wide grin. His mousy hair fell over his eyes. At nine years old, he was almost as tall as Fable and was still growing like a weed. Just the other day, Aunt Moira had said he would probably be taller than her by Yule.

He pointed towards the stairs at the other end of the hall, rattling the bone bracelets on his wrist. "There's something dead in the basement."

Thorn groaned. "Please tell me it's not a person."

He giggled, shaking his head. "If it was a person, don't you think I'd get Mom to call the police? I'm pretty sure it's only a mouse."

When his unusual powers of controlling dead things like bones and shells had first manifested, Fable hadn't known what to think about it. But after talking to him and letting him show her what he could do, she had come to embrace his new gifts.

"So why are you telling us instead of getting an adult to clean it up?" Fable asked.

"Because when Brennus and I went to check it out, we found something else," he said, looking directly at

Fable. “Something with your name on it.”

Fable’s chest tightened. This had once been her parents’ home. In fact, the room they were standing in was hers for the first few years of her life, before Endora had ruined everything.

“What is it?” she asked him.

“A box,” he replied. “We didn’t open it. We thought you’d want it, though.”

“I do!”

Fable and Thorn followed him from the room. They thumped down the stairs and past Fedilmid and Algar, who were inspecting the new windows in the living room, then headed down into the dimly lit basement.

When they reached the bottom of the creaky steps, Brennus glanced up from the back corner of the room where he was sweeping the concrete floor. He gestured to a ragged-looking dresser against the wall. “Timothy brought me down here to look for a dead rodent. He sensed it in there, and when I opened the drawer, we found a box. Your name’s on the lid.”

Fable crossed the cold floor and pulled open the top drawer of the dresser. Inside the dusty compartment lay a tiny rodent skeleton and a wooden chest about the size of a shoebox. Her name was engraved on the metal plate on the lid.

"What is this? A jewelry box?" she asked.

"Hang on." Timothy peered into the drawer and curled his fingers inward. The mouse skeleton jerked to its feet. Moving stiffly like a zombie, it jumped to the floor and marched over Fable's shoes.

"Ew! Timothy!"

His eyes squinted with laughter, and Brennus's chuckles joined in from behind them. The mouse scrambled over to him and collapsed at his feet in a pile of tiny bones.

Thorn caught Fable's eye and shook her head with a wry smile.

Timothy gave them an innocent shrug, still giggling. "I was helping you so you didn't have to touch the mouse."

"Thanks," Fable replied dryly. She turned her attention back to the drawer, then swatted aside a cobweb and pulled out the box. A tingle of excitement ran through her. Had her parents left this here? Why was it in this dresser?

Timothy and her friends crowded around her, trying to get a look.

"What is it?" Thorn asked.

Brennus cocked a brow. "A box."

Thorn snorted. "Obviously."

"Open it!" Timothy urged Fable.

"Give me a second." Fable's heart raced as she wiped the dust from the plate bearing her name. What could be inside it? Its dark brown wood was smooth beneath her fingers. Her hands trembled as she fumbled with the metal latch and popped the lid open.

Her breath caught. It wasn't a jewelry box, but inside lay an assortment of trinkets that must have been hers. A photo of her parents holding a baby with rosy cheeks, a swirled lock of black hair, and deep purple eyes lay on top.

She picked up the photo and showed it to the others. "It's me. And my parents."

Before she could delve into the other contents, a familiar song sprang to her lips. She didn't know what the words meant, but it was the chant she used to create her protective barrier. The one Aunt Moira used too. The magic inside her flickered to life, reaching for the photo.

Timothy tilted his head. "Fable? What are you doing?"

His voice was muffled, as if it came from far away. Fable blinked, looking at her friends as she continued to sing. A golden aura swarmed the edges of her vision.

Thorn gripped her forearm, shooting Brennus a

nervous look. "What's happening to her?"

Fable's tongue froze as the golden light blurred her vision entirely. Dizziness came over her. Her knees buckled, and she began to fall.

She opened her mouth to scream, but nothing came out.

FOUR

The Darkness Within

The golden light gave way to a hardwood floor careening towards Fable. She closed her eyes, bracing for the impact. But instead, she felt . . . nothing. She peeked one eye open, and a familiar room came into focus around her.

One glance out the open window at the magnolia tree, its branches holding the last remnants of fall's red leaves, told Fable she was in her bedroom at Eighteen Lilac Avenue. But it was different. The walls were light pink, and soft musical notes of a nursery rhyme floated over her. She turned from the window, and a man with shaggy black hair that reached his shoulders stood huddled over an oak crib. A mobile spun perfect yellow stars above it, playing the soothing music. Next to him, a woman with wavy brown locks and plum-like cheeks lay a soft yellow bundle that could only be a baby inside the crib.

Those are my parents. So that must be me. Fable's chest hitched. Did she go back in time? Was that box a time machine?

As her mother lovingly adjusted the blankets around the baby, Fable took a tentative step closer. "Hello? Can you hear me?"

Morton put his arm around Faari's shoulders, gazing at the baby and paying thirteen-year-old Fable no mind.

"I guess you can't," Fable whispered, entranced by the scene. She reached out to touch her mother's shoulder. But her fingers went right through the woman's peach-coloured cardigan, almost as if Fable was a ghost.

Am I astral projecting into the past? She'd astral projected before, thanks to Brennus's guitar and its magic. If you strummed the right chords and concentrated on where you'd like to go, the instrument could send your consciousness anywhere in Starfell. It could be erratic, sometimes taking you places you didn't want to go, but she'd never had it pull her into the past before.

With a happy sigh, her mom reached into the crib again. Fable peered over the bars at her sleeping younger self. A perfect curl of ebony hair lay against her forehead, and her dark lashes fluttered with her tiny breaths.

This is so weird. Fable glanced around the room,

looking for the golden aura that had brought her there. There was no sight of it, but she didn't want to leave anyway. Her parents had died when she was only a toddler. She couldn't remember them. Not like this. Sure, she had photos. But this . . . this was so *real*.

Faari brushed the back of her hand along baby Fable's plump cheek. "Isn't she beautiful, Morton? Even more lovely than I dreamed of. Her soft hair and skin, those chubby little hands and fingers. I can't get enough of her."

Morton nodded, smiling at the baby. "She's perfect."

"Her amethyst eyes. They're just like your father's. And your grandmother's."

Fable flinched. She'd once liked her unusual purple eyes. But since learning she'd inherited them from her horrible great-grandmother, she wished her eyes were hazel like Timothy's instead. Her mother wore an awed expression, as if she was excited about her daughter having something in common with Endora. Fable pressed her lips together, unsure of what to think.

"Her magic." Morton's voice was soft. "Can you feel it buzzing around her? It's emanating from her like a beacon."

Before Faari could reply, a loud pounding at the

door downstairs drew their attention. Morton strode to the window as Faari cooed to the fussing baby.

"Are you expecting someone?" she asked.

Morton frowned as he pulled aside the curtain and peered at the yard below. "I'll deal with this. You stay with Fable."

Faari's eyes widened as the pounding came again. "It can't be!"

"Please." Morton went to her side and gave her a pleading look. "Let me handle her. I don't want her to see Fable. If she notices her eyes—"

"The spell your father gave us!" Faari gave him a wild-eyed look and clutched his shoulder. With her free hand, she pulled a scrap of paper from her pocket and tried to make Morton take it. "If Endora tries anything, use it. You can stop her with it. Remember, you have to say, *optempero*—"

A ball of dread formed in Fable's stomach. *Endora? What is she doing here?*

"No." Morton wrapped his fingers around his wife's hand, enclosing the paper. "You know what I think of that spell. Compelling someone, forcing them to bend to my demands . . . It's no better than what Endora does."

Faari's eyes turned glassy. "Endora *kills*

people, Morton."

He cupped his free hand around her cheek. "Is taking away someone's will any better?"

A muffled high-pitched shout came from outside, and the thumping grew more insistent.

Morton glanced at the window. "I have to go deal with her. Stay here. Keep Fable safe."

Her lip trembling, Faari nodded. Morton kissed her cheek, then strode from the room with his hands clenched. The baby let out a cry, and Faari placed the paper on the dresser, then moved to the crib. She picked up the baby and held her close to her chest.

Fable's pulse quickened. *A spell to take away someone's will? That sounds like dark magic.* She stepped towards the dresser to get a look at the paper, but an all-too familiar voice outside grabbed her attention.

"Open this door at once!"

Her neck tingling, Fable went to the window instead and looked outside. Just as her parents had thought, Endora stood at the front entrance of the cottage, wearing a long satin jacket covered in gemstones. She raised a gloved hand and thumped the door again.

Faari hummed softly to her baby, rocking her back and forth. "It's okay. Your dad's going to send her away. We won't let her scare you."

Fable turned her attention to the yard below, her heart thudding. Endora raised her fist again, and Morton opened the door and stepped outside. Fable could barely make out their voices through the open window.

"Endora," he said flatly. "What brings you to Mistford?"

Endora tilted her head, adjusting the tight twist in her ebony hair. "Morton, darling. Don't you mean Grandma?"

"What do you want?"

Endora gestured at the house. "Why, to meet my great-granddaughter, of course. We are family, after all."

"She's sleeping." Morton ran his hand through his curls. "Look, I think it's best if you leave. You know how Faari and I feel about you coming here."

"I'm family, Morton," Endora replied darkly. "If it weren't for me, you wouldn't even exist. And neither would that baby."

"Like I said, that baby is sleeping. You need to leave."

Morton touched her elbow as if to guide her away, but Endora snatched his wrist and twisted it away from her. Fable gasped, covering her mouth. For a moment, she'd forgotten nobody could hear her. She glanced behind her. Faari paced in front of the crib, trying to soothe her crying baby.

"Have you forgotten who I am?" Endora sneered, drawing Fable's attention back to the scene below. She still held Morton's wrist. "I am the most powerful sorceress in Starfell."

Morton yanked his arm from her grasp. "No, you're a lich. And that was your choice."

Endora crossed her arms, looking her grandson up and down. "I can sense the child's power from here. She's my only descendant to have inherited any worthwhile amount of magic. Tell me, does she have purple eyes like mine?"

Morton glared at her, but didn't respond.

Endora leaned closer to him, her voice so low Fable could barely hear it. "Do you know what she and I could do together? What things we could be capable of? We could give this entire family a whole new life. Let me take her under my wing. When she's twelve or thirteen, she should come into her powers. If I could train her—"

Morton bristled at her words. "We like our life as it is, thank you. And you already had your shot with Dad. What makes you think this would turn out any differently? That she would want to be like you?"

Endora's eyes flashed crimson. Her lip curled with a snarl. "You have no idea what you're talking about. She *is* like me. You think her magic will be shiny and good? Without guidance, the darkness will take her too."

"And you want me to believe that you, a lich consumed by darkness, will guide her to the light? You must think I'm stupid." Morton pointed at the street. "Get off my property!"

Fable's knees wobbled. She went to grip the window ledge to steady herself, but her hand went through it. A gentle breeze ruffled her hair, wrapping around her like a cool hug. The golden aura formed again, blurring the image of Faari and the baby. Fable tried to push against it, her stomach tight.

"No, wait!" she cried. "Please, only a few more minutes. I don't understand. What darkness will take me? I need to hear more!"

But the golden light overtook the room, and the world tipped upside down. Fable squeezed her eyes shut as she began to fall. In a matter of seconds, she was lying on the cold concrete floor of the basement.

With her heart thundering, she opened her eyes and grasped at the hands shaking her shoulders. Timothy stood over her with Thorn and Brennus behind him, all of them with panicked looks on their faces.

"Fable! What happened?" Timothy asked, loosening his grip.

She sat up, rubbing her head. She glanced around the room, disappointed by the dull grey walls and the rafters above her. Her heart ached with loss and confusion. Endora's words echoed in her mind—*She's like me. Without guidance, the darkness will take her too.*

Fable glowered at Timothy. "Why did you bring me back? I wasn't ready!"

His mouth fell open. "You passed out! We had to wake you up."

Thorn put her calloused hand on Fable's forehead. "Are you okay?"

"Your eyes rolled back in your head like you were possessed," Brennus said. "I was half-expecting you to turn into a zombie."

Fable pushed Thorn's hand away and got to her feet. "I'm not a zombie."

But if I'm just like Endora, I might as well be.

She glanced at the box, which lay open at her feet. The photo rested on the floor beside it. She must have dropped it when the magic took effect.

"What happened?" Timothy asked, his face ghostly

white. "You went all stiff and looked like you died. But you didn't." He paused, rubbing his bone bracelet. "I would have known."

Fable picked up the photo, hoping it would transport her back in time again. She closed her eyes, willing the golden light to surround her. But nothing happened.

"What are you doing?" Thorn's voice was laced with worry.

With a frustrated groan, Fable placed the photo inside the box. "I was trying to astral project."

"Astral project?" Brennus asked. "Is that picture magic? Where did it send you?"

"To my bedroom. Here, at Eighteen Lilac Avenue."

Brennus raised a brow. "Wow. Powerful."

Fable met his gaze. "But in the past. I was a baby, just a newborn. Both my parents were there."

"What?" Timothy asked. "What kind of magic does that?"

"You have to show this box to Fedilmid," Thorn said. "I don't know anything about time travel, but it must be dangerous."

Brennus eyed the box with interest. "Your parents must have left it for you. But why would they want you to time travel?"

"I wasn't really there," Fable explained. "It was

kind of like astral projecting, except they couldn't see or hear me. It was weird." She rubbed the back of her neck, trying to ease her tension. There was no way she could tell Timothy and her friends the rest—the awful truth of what Endora had said.

Timothy scratched his head. "I wonder if Malcolm knows anything about this."

Fable pointed at him. "Don't tell anybody. Please. Especially Aunt Moira. I want to talk to Fedilmid first."

Timothy looked at Brennus, as if for help. "But—"

"Promise me."

Her friends exchanged glances, then nodded in agreement.

"Okay," Thorn said. "But promise you'll talk to Fedilmid about it tonight. Remember how long it took you to ask him about the amulet? And then, well, you know. It opened that portal."

A flicker of irritation ran through Fable. "It let us into the Oakwrath to save Timothy."

"Timothy wouldn't have been there in the first place if we'd known what the amulet did," Thorn reminded her.

Fable's annoyance winked out, and heat crept up her neck. "Okay. Good point. But we still needed it to help the Jade Antlers return to Starfell."

Aunt Moira's voice came from the top of the stairs. "Children? Are you down there? Time to come up. We need to head home."

"We are home!" Timothy shouted.

Fable could practically see her aunt rolling her eyes.

"You know what I mean," Aunt Moira replied. "It's time to return to the Thistle Plum." She paused. "There's a surprise waiting there for you."

Timothy dashed to the stairs with Brennus at his heels. "What kind of surprise?"

"Are we stopping at the Drippity Cone on the way home?" Brennus added.

Fable set the photo in the box and closed the lid. She ran her finger over the name plate, wondering why her parents had left this for her. Was it to tell her the truth? The secret of why Endora had wanted Fable so badly . . . the reason the lich had planted *the Book of Chaos* in her bedroom at Rose Cottage all those years ago?

She forced the thoughts from her mind, then tucked the box beneath her arm and glanced at Thorn, who waited for her by the stairs. "Don't worry. I'm going to show this to Fedilmid tonight."

Thorn's expression softened. "I'm sorry. I didn't

mean to sound harsh about the amulet." She looked at the box and tilted her head. "What happened in the projection? Could you talk to your parents?"

Fable shook her head, balancing the box against her hip. "I tried to, but they couldn't hear me. I felt like a ghost. And it was weird watching them and listening to them talk about me."

Thorn's eyes widened. "What did they say?"

Fable swallowed. "Oh, you know. New parent things. They were gushing over their baby."

"Oh, that's nice. Maybe there are more memories like that in the box, and you'll get to know more about your parents."

Fable nodded, unable to speak around the lump in her throat.

"Girls?" Aunt Moira's face appeared in the doorway at the top of the stairs. The high bun on her head bobbed as she rapped her knuckles on the railing. "Are you coming? We have to return to the inn. Alice phoned. There's a surprise visitor waiting for you."

"A visitor?" Thorn asked. "Is it my sister?"

Aunt Moira gave her a coy look. "Let's get moving, and you'll find out."

FIVE

A Surprise Reunion

Fable's book bag thumped against her side as she raced past the group and up the rickety front steps of the Thistle Plum Inn. With the late-afternoon sun warming her back, she swung open the door. As she rushed towards the kitchen, where she assumed their surprise visitor would be waiting, the smell of Alice's pink and orange zinnias in the vase next to the door wafted over her.

The others piled inside behind her. Aunt Moira came in last and closed the door, then let out an exasperated sigh. "Slow down, Fable. There are guests here, remember? They don't need you kids running around causing a ruckus."

Fable stopped in the hallway entrance. "I'm not causing a ruckus. I just want to see who's here. Is it the Jade Antlers?"

Brennus adjusted the star maps poking out of the tattered bag Carina had given him. "Or Grogan?"

"Or maybe Roarke?" Thorn asked, referring to the

messenger raven often employed by the immortals' warlocks.

Fedilmid gave the kids an amused smile. "You'll have to wait a few minutes. Moira, we should head down to Nightwind's stable to check on you-know-what."

Aunt Moira nodded. "Children, wait for us in the kitchen."

"That's where I was headed," Fable said, adjusting her bag. The hard edges of the wooden chest hit her side, reminding her to show it to Fedilmid later.

Aunt Moira put her hands on her hips. "Walk there in an organized manner, please."

"We won't be long." Fedilmid dipped his head, and the adults returned to the sunshine outside.

Fable led Timothy and her friends past the busy parlour, forcing herself to walk. The sounds of murmured laughter and teaspoons clinking on fine china came from the room. The guests must have been having their afternoon tea and Alice's homemade cookies. When Fable pushed through the swinging French doors into the kitchen, the savoury smell of herbs and fresh-baked bread washed over her, along with a wave of heat.

Alice was slicing red onions on the butcher's block island in the middle of the room. Wisps of grey hair had escaped her round bun, and sweat beaded on her wrinkled forehead. The Nuthatches' tawny mastiff, Grimm, sat at her feet. He whined in desperation for any morsels that might fall his way. He was so tall that even sitting, he could easily steal a snack from the counter if someone wasn't looking.

Alice set down her knife and waved a wizened hand at him. "Grimm, you can't possibly want an onion. Don't you know they're toxic for dogs?"

Grimm replied with a happy bark, his tail swishing across the tile floor.

She shook her head, then smiled at the kids. "Hello, children. How's the house coming along?"

"Hey, Alice. It's almost ready for us to move in," Timothy replied. "Mom said we're going to get bunk beds for me and Brennus!"

Brennus smiled tightly, and Fable gave him a sympathetic look. Fedilmid and Aunt Moira had been planning for him to move to Eighteen Lilac Avenue with the Nuthatches. Even though they were hoping to break his parents' curse, there were no guarantees they could do it. And even if they did, his parents would probably need a temporary home too. Aunt Moira had made it clear the Tanagers would always be welcome to stay with her, Fable, and Timothy. But that didn't mean the uncertainty was easy for her friend.

Timothy wandered over to the butcher's block and rested his elbows on it. "Mom told us to wait here. Do you know who's here to see us?"

Brennus rubbed his hands together, his expression shifting as he sniffed the air. "And is that bread for us?"

Alice nudged Timothy's arm. "Elbows off the counter. It's for us to prepare food on, not for young boys to rest on." She wiped her hands on her apron. "If you're good, I'll save some bread for you. And yes, Malcolm's here. I believe he's upstairs in his room."

"Yes! I'll go get him. I can't wait to tell him about that mouse today." Timothy spun on his heel and raced from the room.

"Your mom said to walk, remember?" Thorn called after him.

Grimm leapt up and trotted after his boy.

Brennus gazed at the swinging doors, chuckling. "Actually, Moira told us to stay here. Should I go after him and make him wait with us?"

A gruff voice came from the nook at the back of the room. "He's just excited. Let him be." Stirling sat at the table with a crossword puzzle and a coffee-stained mug. He'd been so quiet, Fable hadn't noticed him when they first came in.

Fable made her way to the table and looped her bag

on the back of the chair across from him, then took a seat. Her grandfather hadn't been interested in going to Eighteen Lilac Avenue that morning. Fable had hoped he would want to see his son's old house. But to Stirling, Morton was simply another forgotten piece of his past. Fable probably knew more about her father than he did.

Thorn approached the herb rack above the sink and inspected the dried leaves hanging from it. "Is Orchid here too?"

Thorn's sister and Malcolm were members of the same warlock order, the Jade Antlers. The only other member was Sir Reinhard, a knight who had helped Fable, Timothy, and their friends escape Endora's mansion last summer. The Jade Antlers had been out on another secret mission for their immortal patron for the last few weeks.

"She and Malcolm got here about an hour ago." Alice picked up the cutting board and slid the onion pieces into a glass bowl. "She's settling the firehawks into Nightwind's stall."

Fable's heart jumped to her throat. "The firehawks?"

Alice's expression warmed, and the lines around her milky blue eyes crinkled. "You heard me right, dear. The warlocks saved them from Endora's stable." She glanced past Thorn and out the window above the sink. "I believe Fedilmid and Aunt Moira are out there adding an extra protective barrier around the barn."

Brennus let out a whoop, and Fable's grin grew so big it hurt her cheeks. *Star is finally safe!* The plucky chicken-like bird had been Fable's first friend outside Larkmoor. Fable had met the talking firehawk in the Burntwood Forest shortly after going through the portal in the *Book of Chaos*.

They'd reunited a few months ago at Mistford's spring festival, but it hadn't been a happy meeting. Star and four of her flockmates had been trapped in a cage, captured by the owner of a travelling zoo for magical creatures. When Fable and her friends had returned to save her, Endora's henchman had already kidnapped them. The lich wanted them for their fire breath, an ingredient in her Blood Curse, which would force the Blood Star to connect with her.

Fable got to her feet and picked up her book bag from the back of the chair.

Stirling rapped the table with his fist. "I believe your aunt said to stay here."

Fable lowered her bag and gaped at him. "But Star—"

With a frown, he jabbed his finger on the table. "Sit down and wait."

That's not fair. He didn't say anything when Timothy left. Fable and Brennus exchanged a concerned look, then Fable swallowed her pride and took her seat. Thorn and Brennus both joined them, sitting on either side of her. Brennus set his bag on the floor beside him.

Alice went to the fridge and got a basket of strawberries, then returned to the counter and began to slice them. Stirling glowered at his crossword and tapped his pencil on the paper. Fable chewed her lip, still stinging from his reprimand. She fiddled with the ties of her bag, wishing she could ask him about the box with her name. Had her parents shown it to him? Before his accident, had he known about the secrets inside it? Maybe it could spark his memory.

She opened her mouth to speak, but his scowl told her now wasn't the right time. *Maybe tomorrow he'll be in a better mood.*

Brennus peered across the table at the crossword puzzle. After a moment, he cleared his throat. "I think three down is *Brawn*."

Stirling raised a grey brow. "Excuse me?"

"*Brawn*." Brennus pointed at the paper. "*An immortal wolf with moon magic*. At first, I thought it must be *warg*, but it doesn't fit. Brawn does, though. That's the name of Grogan's patron, who's a warg." He paused, taking in the confused look on Stirling's face. "Grogan's a warlock we know from Stonebarrow."

Stirling narrowed his eyes at the boy, then silently wrote the letters into the square boxes on the page. Brennus was right. *Brawn* fit perfectly.

Aunt Moira strode through the swinging doors into the kitchen. Fedilmid hustled after her, holding a squat brown bird with mottled feathers.

"Star!" Fable pushed back her chair and raced over to Fedilmid.

Fedilmid placed Star into her outstretched arms, and Fable hugged the firehawk to her chest. "I'm so glad you're here."

"Fable!" Star nibbled the collar of Fable's dress. "It feels wonderful to be free of that old hag and to be here with you."

Fable pressed her cheek against the top of Star's head, then straightened and ran her hand over the firehawk's neck. Thankfully, her friend didn't seem injured from the chain that had prevented her fire breath.

"Are you okay?" Fable asked. "What did Endora do to you?"

Star nuzzled Fable's shoulder. "I'm perfectly fine. I won't pretend it was fun to stay in that wicked woman's stable—especially with those giant boars—but at least there was one kind servant."

Brennus cocked his head. "Doug?"

"Oh, heavens no." Star let out a disgruntled cluck. "That man smelled even worse than the boars, and his temper was nastier too. It was the other one, a girl called Leena. She brought us scraps from Endora's kitchen and cleaned our cage every day."

"Endora has another servant?" Fable's stomach twisted.

Thorn gave Star a skeptical look. "With a name? I thought all Endora had around there were Doug and a hoard of undead."

Fedilmid scratched his beard, looking worried.

Aunt Moira leaned her hip against the butcher's block, glancing at Alice. "I wonder if she kidnapped somebody else."

Star bobbed her head. "Leena didn't tell us much, but I got the impression that she wasn't there freely. She's far too nice to help Endora willingly. She was even kind to those brutish hounds."

"That's so weird," Brennus said. "I wonder why Endora didn't stick her in a portrait and suck the life out of her like everybody else."

Aunt Moira pressed her lips together. "Brennus."

He lifted his chin. "What? That's what she does.

Look at what she did to Thorn's parents. What she wanted to do to Star. And to *us*. She wouldn't keep a servant alive unless they could help her."

"Leena must have some kind of powerful magic," Fable agreed, "or she wouldn't have been walking around there."

"Alive, that is," Brennus added.

Stirling coughed and set down his pencil. He looked at Thorn with a wrinkled brow. "Did my mother have something to do with your parents' deaths?"

Thorn gave him a stiff nod.

Fedilmid folded his hands in front of him. "Perhaps the Jade Antlers can find a way to rescue Leena too." He focused his gaze on the firehawk in Fable's arms. "Star, we're so pleased to have you here. Would you and your friends like to stay until things are under control with Endora? We could send a message to the rest of your flock. She might go looking for more of you, now that she's lost a key ingredient for her curse."

Star let out a soft cluck. "I think that would be best. Thank you, Fedilmid. Speaking of the curse, Leena told me Endora has given up on that for now. Apparently, she's focused on breaking her bond with Halite."

"Good luck with that," Brennus said. "A warlock bond is unbreakable. At least, that's what Sir Reinhard and Grogan told us."

Fable pressed her lips together. "Why would she want to break the bond? I would think warlock powers combined with lich magic would be almost as strong as—well, a connection with the Blood Star."

"The Life Tree is dying," came a young woman's hoarse voice from behind Fable. She twisted around and saw Orchid standing in the open French doors. "That's why Endora wants to break free of Halite's grip." Orchid entered the room with her bow slung around her shoulder and a tired look on her dirt-smeared face. Her copper hair was pulled loose from its braid, and brown stains covered her tunic. "The withering tree is draining Halite's power, so the dragon is useless to her. I imagine she doesn't take well to being bossed around for nothing in return."

Thorn got to her feet and reached her sister in several long strides, then threw her arms around Orchid's shoulders.

"Are you okay? You look exhausted," Thorn said, pulling away. "And how did you get Star and her friends out of there?"

"I'm fine." Orchid gave her a weak smile. "It was tough to hold off those hounds, but we had help from the inside. One of Brawn's warlocks is pretending to work for her."

"That must be Leena!" Star let out a smug cluck and nudged Fable's shoulder with her beak. "That would explain her shaggy mane. I thought she was too young for grey hair. Now, Fable, would you mind putting me down? I'd like to rest."

"She can take Piper's bed for now." Alice nodded at the pet bed next to the wood stove. Piper was an uprooter—a lizard the size of a chihuahua with magical powers of persuasion—who split his time between the inn and the Odd and Unusual Shop.

Fable made her way to the stove and gently placed the firehawk in the bed.

Brennus gave Orchid a wide-eyed look. "Endora's servant is a warlock?"

"Yes, she's one of Brawn's. Endora captured her, but she managed to escape the portrait and convince the lich to let her live as a servant."

"How did she manage that?" Thorn asked. "Endora isn't exactly reasonable."

"Don't ask me." Orchid snorted. "That girl must be extremely persuasive. While Leena was helping us sneak the firehawks out of Endora's stable, she mentioned that she's spying for Grogan's order, the Iron Wolves."

Brennus let out a breath. "A warlock spy! That's so cool."

He gave Orchid's rounded fur-covered ears a longing look. After performing a bonding ceremony, warlocks gained a physical trait from their immortals. Each of the Jade Antlers had received a different deer-like trait from their peryton patron, Estar. Sir Reinhard had short green antlers on his head. Malcolm kept his feature hidden, but Orchid had shared her suspicion that he had a tail. Fable wondered if any of Estar's warlocks ever grew functional wings. That would be pretty cool, she had to admit. But not worth the price of serving someone else for your whole life.

"It'd be cooler if she had never been captured by Endora at all," Orchid mused. "But I guess there's nothing wrong with taking advantage of the situation."

"You look tired, dear," Aunt Moira said. "Why don't you go upstairs and take a bath and have a nap? We saved the room next to Fable and Thorn's for you."

Thorn tugged her sister's arm. "Yeah. And tomorrow, we can pack for our trip to the Windswept Mountains. I talked to Aunt Juniper yesterday, and she said she's ready for us."

Orchid's face fell, and she rubbed the back of her neck. "I'm sorry, Thorn. I won't be going to the colony with you."

Thorn looked as if she'd been struck. "Why not? That was the plan."

"I know, but Estar has another mission for us."

"I thought Estar was going to let you finish your schooling before asking you to work for her."

"It's summer." Orchid's expression softened. "There's no school until fall. Besides, this is about saving the Life Tree. It's what gives the immortals their powers. If it dies, they die too. Like I said, that's why Endora wants to sever her ties from Halite. Because Halite's magic is fading. In fact, I think Halite could be syphoning Endora's powers."

Brennus tapped his fingers on the table. "Like a reverse warlock bond? Is that even possible?"

"Yes," Orchid replied. "But usually, a warlock has no magic before bonding with an immortal. Endora and Halite's situation is unique."

"That explains why Endora wants to break the bond, but how can she? I thought it was impossible," Fable said.

"Well, there's rumour that there's one way to do it." Orchid shifted, adjusting her bow around her shoulder. "But I have no idea what it is and if it's true."

Fedilmid huffed. "If there's a way, I imagine Endora

will try it. But that's good news for us. If she's set aside her worries about the Blood Star, then she shouldn't be a problem while we try to heal it."

"One would hope," Alice agreed. "But that awful lich is good at getting in the way." She glanced at Stirling. "Sorry. No offense intended."

Stirling's sour expression turned even darker. "None taken. I don't remember the woman. And it doesn't sound like I want to."

Fable wished all their attempts to spark her grandfather's memory had worked. Endora must have done something awful to make him turn away from her. In the vision she'd had earlier, her father had mentioned that her great-grandmother had already lost her shot with Stirling. So whatever she'd done, it was before Fable had been born. Brennus once said that to gain a lich's powers of immortality, a magic-caster had to spend years learning dark magic and performing evil acts. And they needed to sacrifice souls to maintain that immortality, which explained Endora's vile portraits. What else was her great-grandmother capable of?

Fable's stomach grew queasy. *What if she had raised me like she'd wanted? Would I be capable of evil things too?*

Aunt Moira's voice cut through her racing thoughts.

“Alright, children. It’s time to wash up for supper. Be back down here in about half an hour.”

“We’re having roasted chicken with baby potatoes and garden salad,” Alice said with an apologetic look at Star. “And some beans for Thorn’s protein.”

“And that bread?” Brennus asked eagerly, gesturing at the oven.

“That’s meant for breakfast.” Alice chuckled. “But, like I said, if you’re good, perhaps you can have a slice or two for a bedtime snack.”

Brennus grinned, then picked up his bag. He, Thorn, and Orchid filed from the room. Fable squatted to give Star one final pat.

“I’ll come visit you before we leave tomorrow.”

Star bobbed her head in acknowledgement. “I’ll be in the stall across from Nightwind.”

Fable straightened, then went to the table and scooped up her book bag. On her way to the door, she stopped beside Fedilmid, her mind whirling. Should she tell him about the box? What if he asked about the vision of her parents and Endora? Or worse, what if he saw it and heard what Endora had said about her?

He gave her a sideways glance as he tried to steal a strawberry from Alice’s cutting board. Alice swatted his hand.

He faked a look of alarm. "Ouch! Alice, have you been working out again? You just about slapped my hand right off my wrist."

Alice rolled her eyes, laughing. "You're as bad as the kids. Now, shoo! You can have some strawberry salad at dinner."

"I suppose I can wait." He tucked his arm through Fable's and led her to the doorway. "You look like you have something on your mind, Fable."

Fable pressed her lips together, still unsure of what to do. She didn't want Fedilmid to know about the projection or whatever it was. But that was the problem. She wasn't even sure what kind of magic the picture in the box had drawn her into. Maybe the vision wasn't even real. Maybe Endora hadn't visited her parents when Fable was a baby.

A spark of hope lit inside her. If Fedilmid could clear this all up, she would feel better knowing exactly what this box was and why her parents had left it for her. She didn't have to let him touch the picture.

She met Fedilmid's gaze. He pulled his arm free, then pushed open the doors. Fable followed him into the dining area.

"Fable?" he asked. "Are you alright?"

"Yes. I'm fine." She patted her book bag. "I found

something at the house I'd like to show you."

Fedilmid's expression brightened. "Is that so? Would you like to meet in Nestor's study after we eat?"

She nodded, then leaned her head close to him. "Please don't tell anybody else about it yet. I want to talk to you first."

"Of course," he replied. "I wouldn't dream of spilling the beans to anyone. Now, go get washed up for supper before Aunt Moira chases you up those stairs."

The tension eased from Fable as she made her way to the second floor. With Fedilmid's help, she should be able to figure out the box and what kind of magic it held. She wondered what significance the other objects inside it had. She hadn't had a chance to go through it thoroughly. At least, not without fear of sparking its power again.

She reached the top of the stairs and turned towards her room. Through the window at the end of the hallway, Fable could see Nightwind's stone stable at the bottom of the hill. Her chest warmed. *The firehawks are safe again, thanks to the Jade Antlers. And that other warlock, Leena.*

And with Endora focused on breaking her bond with Halite, Fable finally had a break from the lich's wrath. Which made her job of healing the Blood Star that much easier. They would leave tomorrow for the Windswept Folkvar colony, find the phoenix, wait for it to do its magic, and then heal the star and Stirling's memory.

For once, things might just go according to plan.

Evocation Magic

The evening sun shone through the windows of Nestor's study, casting a golden light over the book-lined walls and dust motes floating in the air. Fable approached his desk, holding the wooden box, and set it down gently on the cleared surface. She loved the comfort of this room. With its beach ball-sized globe in the corner and the maps and charts hanging from the back wall, it now reminded her of Skyview Astronomy Tower.

The door clicked behind her and Fedilmid strode to the desk, his blue robes swishing around his ankles. They had finished dinner an hour ago, and after helping Brennus and Thorn wash dishes, she had excused herself to show Fedilmid what she'd found at her house.

He stood across from her and pushed his half-moon spectacles up his nose, peering at the box. "So what's this all about?"

"I found this in an old dresser in the basement of my house. Well, Timothy and Brennus did," Fable explained.

He tapped the metal nameplate on the box's lid, making his bejewelled rings glisten in the light. "It was obviously meant for you. What's inside it?"

She opened the box. The photograph that had transported her back in time lay on top of the other items, just as she'd left it. She went to pick it up, a lump in her throat, then hesitated. "When I touched this picture at the house, I astral projected."

Fedilmid stroked his pointed beard. "That's . . . interesting. Did it work like Brennus's guitar? Where did it take you?"

"Well, it wasn't exactly the same as using Brennus's guitar." She let out a breath, trying to find the right words.

Fedilmid had always been understanding, her rock in the stormy sea of her new life outside of Larkmoor. But she'd never heard of anybody time travelling before. Not even in any of Thorn's or Brennus's stories. After visiting the police station in Mistford, she'd learned certain types of magic were banned in Starfell. What if time travel was illegal, like cursing someone to sickness or death?

"How was it different?" he asked gently.

She swallowed, meeting his gaze. "I went back in time."

The whole story rushed from her like a babbling

brook. How the golden halo had formed around her when she'd touched the photo, and that after it had faded, she'd been inside her childhood bedroom. How it had been a nursery instead of the empty room it was now, and that her parents had been there.

"The weirdest part is," she said, her voice barely a whisper, "I was there too. But I was a newborn."

Fedilmid rested his chin on his fist, nodding for her to continue.

When Fable came to the part where Endora showed up at the house, her palms grew clammy. "She wanted to train me to use dark magic."

Fedilmid's eyes widened. He blinked, and his expression relaxed. "I suppose that shouldn't be a surprise. She did plant the *Book of Chaos* in your room at Rose Cottage to kidnap you when you got old enough for your powers to blossom."

"But I thought she wanted to steal my magic. I didn't know she thought I was the same as her. Like I was her little prodigy or something."

Fable pressed her lips together, remembering when the lich had trapped her inside that cold dark mansion. Before their blow out—when Fable and her friends had saved Timothy and escaped—Endora had asked Fable to stay with her. To live with her and learn her craft. But with how quickly her great-grandmother had turned on Fable and threatened to kill Thorn and Brennus, Fable had thought it was only a ruse to lure her into one of the life-draining portraits and to somehow steal her magic.

Fedilmid reached across the desk and squeezed her hand. “Fable, you’re nothing like Endora. You may be powerful in similar ways, but your heart and your choices make you so very different.”

Fable squeezed him back. “Do you really think so?”

“I know so. Remember that white light in your heart I told you about? You’ve always reached for it when using your magic, haven’t you?”

“Yes.”

But what if that doesn’t matter? What if some force inside us can make us bad? Like an evil bloodline. One that your parents recognize in you right from birth.

Fedilmid smiled warmly and let go of her hand. “Then you aren’t anything like your great-grandmother. You’re you, and you’re blazing your own path of truth and light. Don’t forget, you have always defeated her before.”

“Not really. I’ve only ever gotten away from her.”

Fedilmid tilted his head. “When anybody else would have been captured or even killed. You are special, Fable. You will be her undoing, and you will make sure she gets locked away again."

"With your help?"

"With all our help."

Fable's heart clenched, yearning for him to be right. But what if he wasn't? What if she failed them and Endora was not only set free, but she gained even more power?

Or worse, what if something dark inside me makes me join her side? Her gut twisted. *All my selfish feelings about wanting Thorn to stay, and the way I get grossed out about Timothy's powers instead of being happy for him—are those dark feelings from Endora's bloodline inside me?*

Fedilmid pointed to her name on the box's metal plate. "Now as for this, I believe these are evocation tokens. I'm amazed your father was able to make them." He chuckled, shaking his head. "He told me he had barely a sliver of magic. Malarky!"

"So you know how these work?" Fable brushed her fingers along the photo. The urge to whisper her protection chant bubbled up inside her, but she held it back, self-conscious of her wayward energy.

"It's sorcerer magic, so I don't know exactly how it works." Fedilmid drifted to the wall behind them, scanning the shelves filled with dusty old books. "But your parents must have infused these objects with memories for you. The spell of evocation brings them to your mind as if you are plunked inside that moment." He placed a hand over his heart. "Oh, how wonderful. That memory of you as a baby . . . It must have been quite the experience for you."

Fable thought of her mother holding the baby to her chest, cooing softly. *Why did Endora have to interrupt? Why did she have to tear my parents away from me at all?*

"Aha!" Fedilmid pulled a thick volume with a teal-blue cover from the shelf and set it on the desk. He opened it to the table of contents, ran his finger down the list, then flipped to a page titled *Evocation Tokens*.

He pursed his lips as he read. "Did you say or do anything specific when you touched the photo the first time? It says here each item needs a code to unlock the memory. That way, they will only work for the right person."

"A code?" Fable remembered the chant—the one she'd used several times before to create the magical shield around herself and her friends. She'd let it overtake her the first time she'd touched the picture. "It must be that song Aunt Moira and I use for our protection spells. How would my dad know about that though? Did he have that kind of magic too?"

"If he did, I'm not sure he knew about it," Fedilmid replied. "When I met him, he and your mother were being chased by undead. They didn't have a protective shield then." He gestured at the box's contents. "How many tokens are there?"

"There are a few things in here, but I've been afraid to touch any of them."

"Now that we know the spell works, why don't you take a look?"

Feeling braver, Fable took the photograph and set it on the table. Beneath it, she found a dried purple flower pressed between clear plastic, a gold cufflink with an M engraved on it, a grey stone the size of Fable's fist, and a plastic yellow star she recognized from her baby mobile in the memory.

At the bottom of the box lay a braided leather bracelet with red and orange feathers woven within it. Fable picked it up, and like with the other items, the urge to chant pushed at her lips. She held her tongue, admiring the bright feathers, and lay the bracelet in the golden evening sunbeam on the desk. Her breath hitched as the feathers caught the light, shining like fiery jewels.

Fedilmid adjusted his glasses. “Those look like phoenix feathers. I wonder where your parents got them.”

“A phoenix? Like the bird we’re looking for?”

“Yes. Strange indeed.” He flourished his hand over the table’s contents. “All these objects must hold some meaning for the evocation spell to stick. I imagine each one has a special memory your parents saved for you.” He looked at her with misty eyes. “I’m so glad they left this for you. And that you found it.”

Fable felt lightheaded, and her magic whirled inside her. She pushed it down, fear mingling with her desire to dive into each memory right away. That first one had brought bitterness along with its sweet moment. What other secrets were in these tokens?

“I’m going to call Carina to ask her about this,” Fedilmid said. “As a witch, I don’t feel comfortable encouraging you to use this sorcerer magic without the proper precautions. Carina should be able to tell us what to do.”

“You’re going to call Carina?” Fable asked. “Could you ask her if she found out anything more about the Blood Star and Gaea?”

He chuckled. “It’s only been a couple days since we saw her. I’ll ask, but I imagine she hasn’t gone to the university yet." He paused. "You know, I've been meaning to talk to you about your studies."

"My studies?"

He peered at her over the flat rim of his glasses. "You'll be starting school this fall here in Mistford."

"Right." Her aunt had told her as much last week, but Fable had put no thought to it. Aunt Moira couldn't homeschool the children forever. She had to find a job. Since they were moving here permanently, she'd enrolled Fable, Timothy, and Brennus for public school in Mistford.

Fedilmid leaned both hands on Nestor's desk. "Algar and I will be returning to Tulip Manor, so I won't be able to mentor you with your magic anymore."

The words hit Fable like a punch in the stomach. She couldn't imagine anybody else taking on her mentorship. She thought of Fedilmid's patience. His kindness. His wisdom. She was going to lose all of it.

"Who's going to help me, then?" A ball of dread formed in her chest. "Not Aunt Moira. Please don't say Aunt Moira." Guilt pinched her, but training with her aunt would never work. Aunt Moira had always suffocated Fable's magic. In fact, she'd hated it for most of Fable's life.

What if my flames erupt again? She'd never trust

me to control them. Even with the Blood Star. She'll make me hide my magic again!

"Fable." Fedilmid clasped her shoulder, and his soothing energy washed over her. "Deep breaths. It's going to be okay."

She sucked in a breath, leaning in to Fedilmid's calm emotions.

"Your aunt is a better witch than you give her credit for," he said. "However, she will be busy looking for a job and figuring out the situation with Stirling. We both agreed that working with another sorcerer—someone whose magic comes from within, like yours—would be the best choice."

Fable gave him a stiff nod, not daring to speak. How could anybody else compare to Fedilmid and his teaching? Aside from Thorn and Brennus, he'd been the first person to truly believe in her abilities. Who'd nurtured her magic instead of smothering it. He'd taught her *everything.*

"After our visit to Skyview Tower, I was thinking about Carina. Of course, you two should get together to see if you're a good match first. What do you think?"

"Carina?" Fable asked. "Does she even have magic? She doesn't seem that powerful. And she's way more interested in sciences like astronomy."

"All astronomers have at least a pinch of magic," Fedilmid replied. "Do you think somebody without it could read the stars the way she and Antares do? She has more than most, though. As a strong sorceress, she could have worked for the ministry or become a teacher. But she chose astronomy."

"If astronomers have magic, why can't Nestor mentor me?"

"He's one astronomer with only a pinch." Fedilmid winked. "Besides, he's a wizard. His pinch comes from books, not from within."

Fable lifted her chin. "Has Carina ever had to defend herself or her loved ones from somebody trying to kill them?"

Fedilmid gave her a sideways look. "You'd best not judge Carina too quickly. If you'd rather not work with her, perhaps your aunt could find the time, after all."

"No." Fable dropped her chin, relenting. "I'll meet with Carina."

"That's what I thought. Now, pack up your tokens and put them away in your room." He pointed at the telescope at the window. "I believe Nestor and Brennus have plans to use that tonight to go over the maps Carina gave him." He patted his belly. "And all this talk has made me snackish. I saved some room for Alice's homemade bread. Let's go see if she'll share some with us."

"I can keep the memory box?" Fable began to gather the tokens, ignoring the chant humming inside her head. "You don't want to keep it with you until you talk to Carina?"

Fedilmid gave her a wry look. "I think you are more than capable of handling it. We let you keep the Blood Star now, after all."

"The Blood Star doesn't work."

Fable fumbled as she dropped the dried flower into the box, tipping it and spilling its contents across the desk. She let out a squeak, her heart racing, and righted the memory box.

"It's still very important," Fedilmid reminded her, kneeling to pick up the broken piece of glass that had fallen to the floor. He straightened and dropped it inside the box. "I trust you won't try to access the tokens' magic until I give you the go-ahead."

"I won't."

She placed the bloom and the photo in the box as well, then picked it up and made her way to the door. As she led Fedilmid down the hallway, guilt pinched her chest. *How could I have been so rude about Carina mentoring me? More dark thoughts. Is that how Endora would think?*

When they reached the door to her room, she hesitated before going inside. "Fedilmid?"

"Mm-hm?"

"I'm sorry for being disrespectful about Carina. I promise I'll give her a chance."

"Thank you. We will both appreciate it if you give her an honest shot." He leaned his head closer to her. "I will miss being your mentor, Fable. But you'll always be the granddaughter I never had."

He ruffled her hair, and her heart raked against her ribs as he strode towards the stairs. First Thorn was leaving. Now Fedilmid and Algar. This fall, she'd be losing three of the most important people in her life—one of her best friends, and the only men who had been grandparents to her.

Endora's smug voice crept into her mind—*She is like me . . . Without guidance, the darkness will take her too.*

Without guidance. Fable was about to lose her guide. Her anchor. The person who had taught her to control her emerald flames. Before Fedilmid's help, they had flared into a giant wall of fire and burned Brennus's arm. How could they possibly be good?

And in the Oakwrath, they had only obeyed her after she accepted them as part of her magic. But maybe she had obeyed their demands, not the other way around. She'd allowed them to mingle with her white light. With her heart.

What if they were dark magic, and she'd let them gain control?

SEVEN

Strange Murmurings

The mid-morning sunshine warmed Fable's back as she balanced a pail of kitchen scraps and slid open the door of Nightwind's stable. The comforting smell of hay and wood shavings met her nose, mixed with the sounds of the firehawks' soft clucking. Nightwind's stall was empty. When Fable had passed through the yard on her way here, the winged-horse had been standing there with Algar, who'd been fitting him with a leather harness for their trip.

As Fable closed the door behind her, Star stuck her head into the alley from the open stall.

"Good morning, Fable! I sensed your aura headed this way a few minutes ago." She turned her head to the side, examining the bucket with one golden eye. "Are those treats for us?"

"They are." Fable made her way to the stall and glanced inside the pail. "It looks like Alice threw in some basil leaves."

Three of the other firehawks came running from

their straw nest in the back corner and crowded around Fable's legs.

One stretched out her wings. "Basil!"

Another bobbed her head, hopping around Fable's feet. "Oh, yum!"

The other strutted closer to Fable. "Did you know basil boosts your immune system?"

Star flapped her wings, ruffling her feathers. "Ladies! Where are your manners? Give Fable some room."

Fable giggled, enjoying the hens' antics. They backed away, allowing her to pour their goodies into the plastic feed pan on the floor. The smallest of the group remained in the nest, watching Fable with a droopy head. All the firehawks looked similar, with brown feathers and moss-coloured spots. But because they knew each other through their auras—which Star had once explained as the energy around a living creature—they didn't need names and could easily tell each other apart. Star only had a name because Fable had given it to her.

Fable dumped most of the scraps into the feed pan, keeping a few basil leaves and strawberry tops for Star. As the three firehawks crowded around the food, she knelt in the shavings next to her friend and offered her what remained. Star gently took a leaf in her beak, and in a few quick snaps, it was gone.

As the bird browsed the other food in the bucket, Fable gestured at the lone hen in the nest. "Is she okay? She looks sad."

Star glanced up from her meal. "Poor thing. She had an egg she'd been brooding when that horrible zookeeper caught us. Obviously, he made us leave it behind."

"That's awful." Fable frowned, remembering the firehawks' crowded cage at the spring festival. If only she'd reached them before Doug had.

Star rummaged through the pail, then pulled out a strawberry top and brought it to the heartbroken hen. She perked up and took the fruit scrap, and Star strutted back to Fable.

"That was nice of you," Fable said.

"She'll be just fine," Star replied. "In a few days, I'm sure she'll be out hunting for bugs with the rest of us."

"How long do you think you'll stay?"

Star paused for a moment, as if thinking it over. "Until Fedilmid tells us it's safe to return to the Burntwood. I think that's best. He said the warlocks would fetch the other members of our flock to join us here. It's not ideal, but until Endora is secured inside her mansion, I'm afraid she'll be hunting us for that nasty spell. We're lucky to have Alice's and Nestor's hospitality."

"They love helping others," Fable replied. "They took in Aunt Moira and all of us kids, and even let Fedilmid and Algar stay. We've been here for months. We owe them a lot."

Star nibbled at the hem of Fable's dress. "You be safe out there in the mountains, okay?"

Fable stroked the firehawk's back. "We'll be fine. Fedilmid and Aunt Moira have been extra careful since we returned from Stonebarrow. And didn't you say Endora is distracted by Halite right now?"

"Yes," Star replied. "But you never know what she's up to. And that henchman of hers . . . He was acting really strange."

"Doug? Strange how?"

Star shuffled her feet. "Have you ever seen a man so broken he's talking gibberish to himself?" She sighed. "He came into that barn a few nights in a row and kicked out the guards, then paced along the stall aisle, holding his head and whispering. I could only catch bits and pieces, but it was like he was talking to somebody who wasn't there. The poor man sounded terrified, even desperate." She tutted. "It's sad, really."

Fable's stomach clenched as she thought of him curled against a headstone in the Oakwrath Thicket. Endora had forced him to bond to Halite. Even though Fable didn't like the man one bit, she still felt sorry for him.

"Endora made him make a warlock pact with Halite," she told Star. "Maybe he was speaking to her. Maybe the immortals can communicate through telepathy or something?"

"Perhaps," Star replied. "I don't know how warlock magic works. But he looked like a man about to do something bad. He kept repeating that he'd find it—whatever *it* is." She nuzzled Fable's arm. "I hadn't thought about it much until last night, after we spoke. But he could be looking for the Blood Star, don't you think?"

Fable pressed her lips together. Was Halite encouraging Endora and Doug to steal the Blood Star? It made sense. If the Life Tree was dying and she was truly siphoning Endora's magic, could she gain the star's power through the lich?

Timothy's voice echoed through the barn. "Fable!"

She hugged the firehawk, then got to her feet. "I promise I'll be careful. Stay safe here too."

Star bobbed her head. “Goodbye again, dear. I’ll see you soon.”

Fable nodded, then stepped into the barn aisle. Timothy ran up to her, practically bouncing. His long bangs flopped over his eyes, and he pushed them aside. “Hey! Mom sent me to get you. Everybody’s waiting up in the yard.”

Fable started towards the door. “I still have to get my luggage.”

“Thorn brought it down for you. Just the purple suitcase, right?”

“And my book bag.”

She and Timothy walked out into the bright sunshine. When they reached the top of the hill, a familiar bird the size of an elephant greeted them with a squawk. Thora’s yellow and teal-blue plumes rippled in the breeze. Next to the lightning bird, Nightwind looked like a miniature pony—one with a black coat and pristine white wings.

Timothy walked over to the giant bird, and she lowered her neck so he could pet her. “I can’t believe we get to ride Thora and Nightwind again!” he said. “I thought Mom would make us take Fedilmid and Algar’s van.”

Algar marched down the front steps with a suitcase

in his burly arms. Brennus followed him with a bag in each hand.

"The roads are too rough," Algar said.

"And the van's too slow," Brennus added.

They made their way to Thora and began to load the luggage into her harness bags.

Fable looked at the straps on the lightning bird's back, counting the handles for the riders. "Thora can only carry four people. There's supposed to be seven of us going, and there's no way Nightwind can hold three. So someone must be taking the van then?"

Algar finished unbuckling his strap, then gave Thora a pat on her side. "Your aunt's staying here. She and Nestor have another meeting with Sergeant Trueforce—"

"Trueforce? Why?" Fable's back grew rigid. She'd met with the hound-eyed police sergeant before about Endora, and the man hadn't believed a word she'd said. It was as if Endora being free again was too hard for him to even fathom—or care about.

Algar sighed. "Because something has to be done about a lich warlock on the loose, don't you think? That's what the police are for."

"They didn't help us last time Fable talked to them." Brennus frowned.

"That's why the adults are dealing with them," Algar replied. "It stinks, but the sergeant doesn't seem to take kids seriously." He glanced at Fable. "Now don't worry about that, alright? Let us deal with the police. Besides, Moira is staying for another reason too. She has an interview with Mistford's care home." He paused, glancing at the inn with concern in his dark brown eyes. "And honestly, she's the only one who can look after Stirling, anyway."

Fable followed his gaze. Stirling sat in the parlour window, glaring as if happy to see them go. A family of guests crowded around the other window next to his, pointing at the magical creatures.

"Wait." Timothy dropped his hand from Thora's neck. "Does that mean I have to stay behind too?"

"I don't believe so." Algar wiped his hands on his canvas pants. "Why?"

Timothy scuffed his toe in the grass. "Mom always makes me stay behind with her. She thinks I'm a baby."

"She was going over your bag this morning while you were talking to Malcolm." Algar nodded towards the inn. "So let's see what she says. She'll be out in a few minutes."

The old man walked over to Brennus, who was struggling with a hard-shell suitcase. In one swift motion, he took it from the boy's hands and shoved it into the leather sack on Thora's harness.

"Geez." Brennus gave him a sheepish grin. "You're pretty strong for an old guy."

Algar huffed, but his lips quirked with a smile that was barely visible through his grizzled beard. "Thanks to all the wood chopping I do." He poked Brennus's slender arm. "You could use a few more chores."

Fable and Timothy giggled at Brennus's flushed cheeks. He shook his head with a grin, then closed the leather flap of Thora's bag and buckled it.

"In all seriousness, though," Algar said. But instead of completing the sentence, he pulled a golden amulet from his pocket and held it up for them to see.

Fable's breath hitched. She recognized those green flames dancing against the pendant's glass. It was Halite's amulet—the object that amplified her magic and which had opened the portal to the Oakwrath last month. After the kids and the Jade Antlers escaped from Endora and the dragon, Fedilmid had hidden it. If it fell into Halite's claws again, she could use it to escape the thicket and unleash her revenge on the city of Mistford.

Algar handed the necklace to Brennus. "Fedilmid took this out of safe-keeping this morning."

Brennus took the amulet with trembling hands.

"Are you sure you want me to take it? Wouldn't it be better if you or Fedilmid kept it?"

Algar gave him a serious look. "We talked about it, and both of us agreed that this should be your responsibility. But we will help you. Fedilmid has put a tracking spell on it, and before we leave, he plans to enchant it to look like a pocket watch."

Brennus went to put the chain over his neck, but Fable let out a squeak.

"Wait! Remember what happens when you wear it? It makes you want to use its magic. And Halite can sense that."

"Oh, right." Brennus flushed again, then folded the chain neatly and put the amulet in his pocket. "Thanks, Algar, for trusting me."

Algar clasped his shoulder. "You should be the one to destroy it and break the curse on your parents. We'll be there for support, but we believe in you."

Brennus's eyes grew misty. He gave Algar a firm nod, then turned away from him and busied himself adjusting the bag at Thora's side.

The front stairs to the inn creaked as footsteps thumped down them. Aunt Moira and Thorn joined the group with the creatures. Thorn shifted her army-green backpack. Aunt Moira set down a blue suitcase covered with green cartoon aliens, then handed Fable her star-spangled book bag. Fable checked inside to make sure she'd remembered everything. Sure enough, the Blood Star and her parents' memory box lay alongside the *Book of Chaos* and her mother's journal.

"Did you remember to pack a dress shirt, Timothy?" Aunt Moira asked. "Juniper mentioned something about a town feast while you're there."

Fable's curiosity piqued. *A feast?* Thorn had taught her a lot about Folkvar traditions, and Fable couldn't wait to see some of them in person.

Timothy's face brightened. "I still get to go?"

Aunt Moira's mouth pressed into a firm line. "I see Algar already told you the news. Yes, you still get to go. But there are rules."

She put her arm around his shoulder and led him a few strides away. Fable grinned as her aunt pulled a paper from the pocket of her skirt, imagining the list she was rattling off to Timothy—*Brush your teeth morning and night. Make sure to wear clean socks every day. And don't use your magic!*

Thorn approached Nightwind and ran her hand through his silky black mane. He nudged her arm with his velvety nose. Fable joined them and petted the pterippus's neck.

"In only a few hours, we'll get to see your new home," she said, ignoring the ache in her chest. *Though I wish you weren't leaving me.* Her flames flickered inside her, and her chest hitched. *No! I can't think like that. This is a good thing for Thorn.*

Thorn let out an anxious breath. "Yeah. It's hard to believe I'll be living with Juniper in a Folkvar colony soon. I hope they like me."

She took off her backpack and opened it, checking its contents. A bundle of dried herbs hung from its zipper.

Fable pointed at it. "Are you sure you should have that on your bag? You know, because of what Juniper said about how the people there feel about magic."

Thorn snorted. "I'll tell them it's decoration. Or potpourri to mask the smell of animal sweat." She patted Nightwind's shoulder. "No offense." She pulled Fedilmid's speaking-stone out from under her collar. "I'm keeping this on me too. With Orchid heading back into the wilds, I want to stay in touch with her. But for all they know, it's just a pretty necklace."

Fable's stomach pinched, and her flames flickered inside her again. She bit her lip, not sure if Thorn should sneak the necklace into the colony. Aunt Juniper clearly knew about magic items. Even if the other Folkvars didn't like magic, wouldn't they recognize such items too?

But shouldn't Thorn get to be herself? Like she said earlier, they might get used to greencraft and accept it once they know the real her.

Fable gritted her teeth, forcing her flames to retreat. "Did Orchid leave already?"

"Yes." Thorn heaved a sigh. "We said goodbye this morning. I hate that Estar is sending her on another mission when we're supposed to be visiting family. And isn't finding the phoenix a mission too? An important one to help defeat Endora, like Estar supposedly wants?" She scowled, zipping up her bag again. "It's almost like Estar only wants control. Why would the immortals care about Endora if the Ministry of Mistford booted them out of Starfell?"

Fable shifted uneasily. Her friend had a point. But the Jade Antlers had helped them against the lich. "The immortals might have a past with her we don't know about."

Thorn snorted and slung the backpack over her shoulder. "It wouldn't surprise me if Endora messed with them at some point. She has bad ties with everybody."

Algar strode over to them and held out his hand to Fable. "Can I pack that book bag for you?"

"Sure." Fable handed it to him.

As he added it to the luggage in Thora's harness, Fable caught her grandfather's eye in the window. Her stomach knotted as she thought of what Carina had said about the star's destiny.

The mother and child will reunite, and peace will come to Starfell.

If Carina's words were true, then shouldn't Stirling be the one to connect with the Blood Star once it was healed? Shouldn't he be the one to defeat Endora? He'd helped create the star, after all. He'd put the enchantment on it to make sure it only bonded to someone with good intentions.

And, according to the memory she'd seen, he'd turned Endora and her dark magic away before. Surely, he could do it again. She swallowed, trying to push the thoughts away. *We can't put him in danger. I have to fend off the darkness and defeat her myself.*

I only hope I can.

EIGHT

A Ferocious Shadow

Leena Houndstooth stopped at the edge of the trees behind the faded purple inn. She shook her frizzy grey hair from her eyes, then put both fingers to her lips and whistled, calling the dire wolf to her side. His scruffy black head bobbed through the tall grass as he ran towards her. Once he sat at her feet, gazing at her eagerly with his blood-red eyes, she reached into her trouser pocket and pulled out a piece of cheese.

He took it gently from her fingers, then chomped it down in one bite. After swallowing, he whined and nudged her hand with his cold sooty-coloured nose.

“I don’t have any more, Knox.” She glanced at her backpack laying beneath the nearest tree. It wasn’t a lie. She would have to get more food before they set off again. She poked his furry side. “Besides, you’ve been getting too soft living at Endora’s mansion and lazing around her grounds all day. No more treats today.”

He snorted as if she’d offended him.

Through the leaves, the sound of wings beating

met her ears. The lightning bird she'd spotted at the inn rose into the sky with three young teens—one of them clearly a Folkvar with her towering height and blue-grey skin—and the old witch on its back. A pteripus carrying a grizzled man and a young boy followed suit, and they vanished into the clouds above.

Earlier that morning, she'd crouched beneath the inn's kitchen window and overheard some adult voices talking about going to the Folkvar colony in the Windswept Mountains. She'd only heard enough to gather bits and pieces, but the female voice had definitely mentioned a phoenix—the same mythical bird Endora was after.

She glanced at Knox, her stomach churning. "The Folkvar girl—she must be Orchid's sister. So that means these are the people she and Sir Reinhard told me about. The ones trying to heal the Blood Star and fight off Endora."

The hair on Knox's back bristled at the old hag's name, and his lip curled in a snarl. Leena gave his ears a sympathetic rub. She'd seen what it was like for the dire wolves under Endora's foot—sure, they were well fed. And most days, they didn't do much but hang around her sprawling grounds. But when the lich was in a bad mood, the animals caught the brunt of it. Leena had saved Knox from a whipping from one of the undead guards, snatching the weapon from the creature's skeletal hands and breaking its magical handle in two.

Endora's reaction had been terrifying. But saving Knox's hide had been worth it. And when had Endora ever been nice, anyway? After Leena had smashed the glass frame of her prison, she'd been relieved to find her magic still worked. It had only taken a moment to charm the lich into allowing her to live. But not without paying a price—her freedom. Leena tugged her sleeve over her wrist, hiding the twisting vine tattoo Endora had given her. She closed her eyes, blocking the memory of the evil spell Endora had used to mark the tracking magic on her skin.

She might be able to track me, but I still have Brawn. She touched the spot above her heart. *And as long as we're smart, we can do our work within her bounds.*

She ran a hand through her shaggy grey mop of hair, comforted by its presence. It meant that her patron, Brawn, was with her wherever she went. And since Endora was one of Brawn's sworn enemies, her capture had presented an opportunity for him. Through their telepathic link, she'd been feeding the immortal warg information about Endora and her activities, helping him formulate a plan to get rid of the lich for good.

Plus, I helped Orchid and Sir Reinhard save those firehawks, she thought smugly. *And now I have freed Knox from her bloody grip.*

Knox bumped her hand again. She rested it on his head, her mind whirling. "What do you think we should do, my ferocious shadow? Go back and tell Endora what they're up to like she demanded? Or follow Thorn and Fable to warn them about her plan to capture the phoenix?"

Knox tilted his head as if he understood. Endora thought he was an unintelligent beast, but Leena knew better. The creature knew Endora was evil. And with the way he nudged the tattoo on her wrist, Leena was sure he also knew the lich was tracking them.

If we go after them, we could lead Endora straight to them. But just because the hag could always see Leena's whereabouts didn't mean she could sense if other people were there. Leena scratched her chin. Should she go to the inn and speak to someone there about Endora? But she didn't know the owners or if they knew anything about the lich. And it looked liked the adults who were aware of what was going on had taken off with the kids to the colony.

Maybe we should return to the mansion and

convince Endora to send us to scout for the phoenix instead of Doug. Then we could warn the group from Mistford without making her suspicious.

Leena picked up her backpack and slung it over her back, then whistled at the dire wolf. "We'll grab some food, then figure out what to do next. Let's go."

Her feet barely made a sound as she slipped gracefully through the trees. The dire wolf followed her just as quietly. When she came to the back of the stone stable, a foul smell overwhelmed her. She stopped, recognizing the scent of wet dirt and compost.

Doug. She placed a hand on Knox's back. He sniffed the air with flared nostrils. The henchman's disgruntled voice came from the dense trees to their left. She crouched behind a bush and parted the leaves.

Doug and his undead pal stood facing each other, partially hidden by a bushy pine tree. The transporter's face was red, and his eyes drooped with exhaustion. Leena's gut twisted. The hag had forced him to bond to Halite against his will. The dragon must have been calling to him, and Leena was sure Endora would never allow him to respond. She almost felt sorry for the man. She couldn't imagine the pain Halite must be inflicting in his head.

What is he doing here? Isn't he supposed to be on

his way to the Windswept Mountains to look for the phoenix?

The henchman clutched his head with both grimy hands. “I can’t hold ’er off any longer. The pain—I can’t take it no more. Endora’s bad. But that dragon’s worse!”

The undead figure reached out as if to touch him, but Doug twisted away from it. “No. I’m getting that amulet for ’er. I has to, or this’ll never end.” He glared at the guard. “’Twas Endora who forced me ter bond with Halite. It’s ’er fault. You can come with me to the Oakwrath now, or I’ll put yeh down so yeh can’t tell Endora.”

The undead’s shoulders slumped. Leena cocked her head. She’d never seen a guard so animated before. And so defeated. It was almost as if the guard was conscious, but that shouldn’t be possible. Endora’s animated corpses were merely puppets. A result of necromancy, which raised the bodies but not the souls. Endora didn’t have the power to bring souls back to life. Nobody did.

Brown smog poured from Doug’s sleeves. Seconds later, both he and the undead vanished inside it.

Knox licked her hand, and she stood. *Doug’s betraying Endora too . . . Interesting*. With him serving

Halite, he wouldn't exactly be on Leena's side. The dragon wanted Endora to either bend to her will or end up dead, and Brawn's mission for Leena was to vanquish Endora. To make sure she lost her powers and could never hurt anyone in Starfell—or outside of it—again.

Our goals are basically the same, though Brawn's methods may be less brutal than the dragon's. She shuddered, thinking of Halite's old warlock, Ralazar. The word around the warlock circles was that after he confronted Halite in the Oakwrath, the dragon had thrown him into the pit inside her lair. Leena had no idea if he was alive or not. But either way, he wasn't in a good place.

She touched a lock of wolfish hair beside her ear, the wheels in her head turning. "Maybe we could team up with Doug to defeat Endora. But Halite and Brawn hate each other. What leverage do we have to get him on our side?"

Knox yipped, then jumped up on Leena, pawing her necklace.

"Hey, get down!" She pushed his shoulders, then grasped the warg's tooth that hung from her chain—her key to get through the portal in Stonebarrow that led to the Oakwrath Thicket. She was lucky Endora had learned nothing about warlock magic, or the woman probably would have taken it away.

Knox yipped again in frustration, then narrowed his red eyes at her.

"Brawn's key? But why—?"

Halite's key, which is also an amplifier. Rumour had it that Fable had taken it from the Oakwrath last month when she'd escaped by the skin of her teeth. Up there at the inn, the bearded old man had given the teenage boy an amulet. One that had radiated so hard with immortal power Leena had felt it even from her hiding spot a hundred feet away.

She looked at the dire wolf and grinned. "Come on, you old brute. We're heading to the Windswept Mountains."

He cocked his head and whined.

She smoothed the scraggly fur on his neck. "I'll get a messenger bird to bring a note to Endora saying we have a lead on the phoenix. By the time she gets it, we'll already be on our way. She's so obsessed with getting the phoenix's magic, I doubt she'll protest."

Leena rubbed her fingers together, satisfied with the zing of magic they produced. *Besides, if the old hag freaks out, I can always charm my way back into her good graces.*

NINE

Yetis, Cannons, and Pack Donkeys

Fable gripped the leather handle of Thora's harness, Brennus's arms around her waist, as the bird dove into the clouds below them. The wind rushed over her face, making her eyes water. But she didn't mind. Riding the lightning bird differed completely from travelling with Nightwind. Thora's smooth wing beats comforted her, making her feel secure on the bird's broad back. From his seat behind Thorn, Fedilmid let out a thrilled whoop.

Thora dipped lower, bringing them out of the cloud cover she always produced to keep her presence hidden in the air. After spending the last couple of hours in a wall of white mist, it was like the world opened below them. Miles upon miles of white-peaked mountains covered the landscape. Bright blue rivers wound through the craggy grey rock, and lush green valleys dotted the terrain.

Fable's breath caught. She would choose this over taking Fedilmid's rickety old van every time.

Nightwind flew up beside them with Timothy clutching his black mane and grinning wildly. Behind him, Algar gave them a stiff wave while squinting against the breeze, his grizzled black beard flailing around his face.

Thora chirped, then began a slow descent. As they got lower, a small town in a rich green valley came into view. Thatch-roofed houses dotted the area with generous unkempt yards. Vines with pink and purple flowers grew over the walls and along picket fences. They headed towards the town centre, which was an open circle even bigger than Endora's whole estate. A group of white tents reflected the sunlight, surrounded by gardens growing every kind of fruit and vegetable imaginable.

Thora landed gracefully on the dirt road in front of the town circle, taking a few strides to slow and then stop. Nightwind halted next to her, tucking his wings over Timothy and Algar's legs.

Fable slid shakily to the ground and was soon joined by Fedilmid, Brennus, and Thorn. Timothy and Algar followed suit.

"That was amazing!" Timothy said breathlessly. He patted Nightwind's neck. "Thanks for the ride, buddy." Nightwind snuffled his shoulder.

Brennus shielded his eyes with his hand, taking in the sprawling garden and market before them. “Wow. This place is busier than Mistford’s festival markets.”

The area was teeming with Folkvars—some wearing wide-brimmed straw hats and working in the gardens, others wandering arm-in-arm through the market area, browsing the available produce. Aside from Juniper, Fable had never met an adult Folkvar before. A man who must have been at least eight feet tall strode by them towards the market area, reminding Fable that even though Thorn was taller than most human men, she still wasn’t done growing.

Fable took in the market with curiosity. There was nobody shouting out to customers or exchanging money like at the farmer’s market in Mistford. The people here were browsing the market stalls and filling their baskets without anyone watching them closely. A few of them glanced in the Mistford group’s direction, but nobody seemed shocked at the sight of the creatures.

Timothy approached Fable, his gaze fixed on the town circle. “Everybody here is huge! And they aren’t even looking at us. You’d think a bunch of tiny humans and a giant bird would get some attention.”

Fedilmid chuckled as he unbuckled the bag on Thora’s harness. “We’re in the Windswept Mountains now. They probably see unusual creatures often around here."

Brennus scratched his head. "Are humans unusual too?"

Fedilmid gave him a sly look. "Some of them, yes."

Algar joined him and pulled his husband's rainbow suitcase from Thora's bag. "I haven't been in this area for years. But the last time I was here, I saw a wild griffin, and there were rumours of a yeti skulking about."

Brennus's mouth fell open. "A yeti?"

Timothy pushed his bangs from his forehead. "Those are real?"

"As real as the sea serpent in the Bottomless Sea," Fedilmid replied.

Fable swallowed. She knew firsthand that the serpent was real. Or, at least it had been before Endora had battled with it several months ago.

Thorn made her way to the archway marking the garden's entrance. Green vines with purple flowers sprawled over it. She crossed her arms, watching a Folkvar man in the garden closest to them. He wore baggy brown trousers cut off at the knee, and sweat dripped down his blue-grey face as he picked tomatoes off the row of tall leafy plants.

Fable joined her friend. Happy tears brimmed in Thorn's eyes. She pointed to the nearest market stall, where a broad-shouldered Folkvar man was filling his basket with peaches.

"It's just like at home in the Greenwood," she said. "Just fewer trees and more farms. We mostly foraged for things like mushrooms and wild berries, but we grew tubers like potatoes and turnips. And we had a gathering area almost like this one, where people picked up food for their families."

"So, the food is free? How do the farmers make money?"

"They don't need money. Everybody does their part. If it's like the Greenwood colony, some people grow food. Some forage. Some make clothing or build furniture. Everybody contributes to the community and nobody goes without."

"So everybody shares? And there's no fighting?"

Thorn shrugged. "Sometimes people don't get along, but for the most part, it works. The town council organizes the sale of extra goods to people outside the colony. They put the money towards the community for things we can't make or do ourselves. Folkvars make sure everyone is taken care of."

Fable liked the sound of that. A safe community

where everyone looked out for each other. No wonder Folkvars didn't often head out on their own into the rest of Starfell, where danger could lurk around any corner.

Thorn motioned to a log fence on the other side of the sprawling cottages in the distance. It was hard to tell from this far away, but Fable figured it must have been at least twenty feet tall.

"That's for keeping dangerous beings out," Thorn said, moving her finger towards a tower along the fence. "They monitor the skies too. Aunt Juniper is on the town council now, so I'm sure she told the guards that we were coming. That's why they didn't stop us from landing here."

"How would they have stopped us?" Fable asked.

Thorn gave her a sideways look. "If it's like in the Greenwood, anybody flying in who doesn't come down to the gates first would probably be brought down by cannons."

Fable's neck stiffened. "Cannons?"

"The ones in the Greenwood shot nets to bring intruders down at the gate. If the intruders were lucky, they landed in the bushes." Thorn squinted at the towers. "It looks like these guards might have the same kind. But anybody coming here would know to stop. I've never seen the cannons actually used."

A whoosh of air hit their backs, and Fable turned to see Thora and Nightwind taking off into the sky. Fedilmid, Algar, and the boys stood amongst their luggage, their heads bowed in conversation.

A slim Folkvar woman who must have been about seven feet tall came striding under the arch—Thorn's aunt Juniper. She wore trousers and a blue-and-green tunic with several layers of long stone-beaded necklaces. Her auburn hair was woven into a thick braid, much like Thorn's. A surprisingly short Folkvar man trailed behind her, the top of his head barely reaching Juniper's chin. His bright red curls hugged his scalp, and he wore a knife as long as Fable's forearm in a leather sheath around his hip.

That must be Vetch, the ranger Juniper told us about. The man who knows where the phoenix is.

"Thorn! I'm so glad you're finally here." Juniper smiled warmly and pulled Thorn in for a hug. She dipped her head towards Fable, then waved to the others. "Welcome to the Windswept Colony. My house is right behind you." She gestured beyond the group. "As the new manager of the Windswept community gardens, the town was kind enough to put me up right across the street."

Fable glanced over her shoulder to see a quaint

brown cottage surrounded by a yard filled with pink and orange blooms.

Fedilmid came forward and shook her hand. "Thank you, Juniper. The Windswept colony is as beautiful as you said. You'll have to give us a tour. Moira will be sad she missed this."

Juniper tilted her head. "I thought Moira was coming too."

"She had to stay behind for some meetings." Thorn turned her gaze to the Folkvar man. "You're not Vetch, are you?"

His cheeks rounded in a smile. "No, I'm not Vetch. He's a lot taller and leaner than I am, though not near as good-looking." He held out his hand to her. "I'm Buckhorn. Juniper thought you all would need some help on your trip to find the phoenix. Vetch will lead the way, and I'll be your pack donkey."

His gaze caught on Thorn's speaking-stone, and his smile faded. "That's a pretty gem. What's it for?"

Thorn's hand flew to the necklace, and her cheeks reddened. "It's citrine. Right, Fedilmid?"

Fedilmid cleared his throat. "Yes, that's right. A variety of crystalline quartz. It's quite rare."

Buckhorn raised a brow. "And good for aiding communication, right?"

Thorn looked at Juniper, her eyes rounder than the stone itself. “Um—”

“Oh, Buckhorn, stop teasing the poor girl.” Juniper waved him off. “It is a pretty necklace, Thorn.” She leaned closer to her niece and lowered her voice. “But people around here can be suspicious of such things. It might be best if you keep it tucked beneath your shirt.” She turned to Buckhorn. “And perhaps you shouldn’t say things like that so loudly. We want Thorn to feel welcome here.”

Thorn gave her a stiff nod and tucked the stone beneath her collar.

“Sorry, Thorn. It was just a joke.” He shrugged, flashing her a wide grin.

Just a joke? He asked about the stone’s energy. I know the people here don’t like magic, but who could be afraid of a stone with such simple powers? Fable eyed her book bag, which now lay on top of her suitcase. She walked over to it and slung it over her shoulder. She would have to be extra careful to keep its contents hidden while they were here.

Juniper motioned towards her cottage. “Shall we head to my house and get settled before dinner? I made you all a real Windswept feast.”

As if on cue, Brennus’s stomach let out a loud

rumble. "Let me guess—mushroom salad?"

"I see Thorn's been sharing her favourite recipes with you." Juniper let out a hearty laugh. "No, not this time. There are a few salads, and rice and beans as well. Everything was grown right here at the Windswept colony, either in the community garden or my own."

"What about dessert?" Timothy asked. "Is there an ice cream shop here, like the Drippity Cone in Mistford?"

"Will homemade berry cobbler work?" Juniper asked.

Timothy licked his lips. "Definitely."

Buckhorn grabbed Thorn's and Timothy's bags, then walked next to Thorn as they followed the adults and Timothy across the street. Fable picked up her suitcase and fell into step alongside Brennus.

He lowered his head close to hers. "You think Thorn's really going to be happy here?"

"What do you mean? She seems excited."

Brennus rubbed his jaw. "Even after Buckhorn pointed out her speaking-stone? She'll never be able to do greencraft here. And what about Orchid? She's got magic too, now that she's a warlock."

Fable shushed him so Buckhorn wouldn't overhear, but a knot of uncertainty formed in her stomach. Would the Windswept Folkvars accept Orchid? Aunt Juniper had invited her to live here, knowing the teen was a warlock. Why would she do that if there was no chance of Orchid fitting in?

Brennus hissed in her ear. "Be careful with the Blood Star. Don't let any of them see it, just in case."

Buckhorn looked over his shoulder at them, then put his hand behind his back. Snapping his fingers, a purple aster flower bloomed out of nothing between them. With a wink, he dropped it to the ground, then returned his attention to Thorn.

Fable's pulse quickened, and she tugged on Brennus's sleeve and whispered, "Did you see that? Buckhorn has magic too. We'll be fine."

Brennus stepped over the flower, his mouth set in a firm line. In a hushed voice, he said, "I think that was a warning. He's being secretive about it. I wonder what his story is?"

"Maybe we'll get a chance to ask him later." Fable chewed her lip. *Does anyone else here have hidden magic?* She nudged Brennus's side. "Make sure you keep that amulet out of sight for now too."

"Don't worry." He puffed his chest. "Fedilmid and Algar trusted me with this. I won't let them or my parents down. I can't." He patted his jeans pocket.

"Besides, Fedilmid enchanted it to look like a pocket watch before we left."

Fable gripped the bottom of her bag, wondering how long it was going to take to find the phoenix and its magic. The quicker they could do it, the better.

But healing the Blood Star and destroying the amulet wouldn't solve Thorn's problem about fitting in here. Maybe she would find friendship with Buckhorn, but would she have to hide her greencraft like he seemed to?

And will I be allowed to visit her if anyone finds out I'm related to Endora? Besides Juniper, do any of these people know I'm the great-granddaughter of an evil lich?

Her emerald flames hissed inside her as she thought of Endora's words in her parents' memory—*She's just like me.*

She balled her hands into fists, pushing down her magic. *I've lost control so many times. Maybe they'd be right to ban me from coming here. What if I burn someone the way I did Brennus? What if Endora comes after me? Or worse . . . what if her evil bloodline takes over my magic?*

Juniper opened the picket gate in front of her house, and Fable stepped onto the stone pathway that wound through her yard. She would have to worry about the Windswept Folkvars and their views about magic later. First, she had to heal the Blood Star. And hope with all her heart that it would keep her great-grandmother's dark legacy at bay.

A Ranger with Bite

Fable took her seat at the long birch wood table in Juniper's back yard, wedging herself between Brennus and Timothy. Thorn and Buckhorn sat across from her, eyeing the buttery-looking biscuits and colourful bowls filled with different salads.

Flowering rose bushes and hydrangeas surrounded the eating area, with several dogwood trees behind them, all bathed in golden evening light. White lights had been hung throughout the yard, illuminating the shadowed leaves. Fable felt like she'd entered a fairy tale. As if she were Alice wandering into Wonderland, but instead of the Mad Hatter, she got the calm and welcoming Juniper instead.

Through a gap in the foliage created by a stone path, Fable glimpsed Juniper's garden. It was a shame Fedilmid and Algar were missing this—they had gone to meet with one of the town council members Algar had been friends with when he was younger.

Thorn sat straight with her hands folded in her

lap, looking more formal than Fable had ever seen her. She'd re-braided her hair and put on a clean white t-shirt before heading down for supper. The round bump beneath her collar told Fable she'd tucked the speaking-stone away as her aunt had asked.

Juniper bustled through the glass patio doors with a pitcher of iced water. She set it on the table, then took her seat at the head of it.

Buckhorn reached for a biscuit, but Juniper looked askance at him. "Don't even think about it. We don't eat until everyone is here. You know that." She gestured to the empty chair at the other end of the table. "Did Vetch talk to you this afternoon? I expected him to be here by now."

Buckhorn dropped his hand with a disappointed look. "I saw him right before I headed to the market. He was going out to check in with Crocus at the tower on Bromver Bluff. He shouldn't be long."

"My parents had that rule too," Thorn said. "Even when mom made her brambleberry pancakes on Sunday mornings, Dad always made me wait for Orchid to get out of bed first."

Juniper smiled. "That's because your father had a good upbringing."

"So Thorn's dad was your brother?" Brennus asked.

The lines around Juniper's eyes crinkled. "Yes. Oak was my brother. And Aster, Thorn's mom, was my good friend."

Thorn put her elbow on the table and rested her chin in her hand. As if realizing she'd made a mistake, she straightened and nervously tugged at her braid. "They would have loved this place. You always had the best garden in the Greenwood colony, but it wasn't like this."

Timothy's stomach growled loudly. Fable giggled, and Juniper tilted her head.

"Okay, you can all have a starter before Vetch gets here," she said, glancing at the sky. "He's usually here by now. He's been coming over every week at this time to update me about the phoenix." She sighed, motioning at the food. "Green salad only, alright? I made the honey vinaigrette myself too."

"Salad only?" Timothy made a face, and Fable nudged him with her elbow. "I mean, thanks."

Fable shook her head as she loaded his plate, then hers. The dressing smelled sweet and tangy, much like what Alice made at the inn. She glanced at the garden through the trees, wishing the witch could have been there to see Juniper's A-frames covered with beans and peas, and what looked to be a sprawling pumpkin vine taking over the front corner.

Fedilmid will love this. She thought of his once-bursting-with-blooms greenhouse at Tulip Manor. Since they'd been gone for months now, she wondered how it was doing. Fedilmid had a neighbour checking in on it, but she doubted they would give it the care Fedilmid had. Her chest hitched. *No wonder he wants to return to Tulip Manor. He's given up so much to help me.*

"It's important to eat your greens," Juniper said to Timothy, then helped herself to the salad before her. "Tomorrow evening, the colony is having their Lammas festival, so you'll get to eat all kinds of fresh bread then. As a rule, the Folkvars here don't eat any grain from Ostara—the spring equinox—until Lammas, which means midsummer," she explained. "It's considered bad luck to eat last year's grain harvest when new seeds are in the ground. I went by the bakery on my walk this morning, and they were getting all kinds of rolls and breads ready for the feast."

Buckhorn swallowed his mouthful and nodded eagerly. "Clover told me she's bringing honey-glazed baguettes, and her brother was making blueberry bagels. I can't wait!"

Brennus's eyes lit up, and he rubbed his hands

together. "A feast of pastries? Count me in!"

"Do you grow your own wheat too?" Thorn asked. She looked at Fable. "It wouldn't grow in the Greenwood. We used to go to the Buttertub to buy it."

Juniper dabbed her mouth with her napkin. "The climate here is much better than back home for growing crops. I'll give you a garden tour later. You wouldn't believe it, but I've got a ton of sweet potatoes on the vines."

Timothy poked at his salad with his fork. "Did you grow these tomatoes and peppers too?"

"Like I said earlier, almost everything on this table is homegrown." Juniper took a bite of her salad, closing her eyes as if savouring it.

"Except the mushrooms," Buckhorn said. "I brought you those mushrooms last week from the woods out by Moonflower Tower." He looked at Thorn. "That's Vetch's watchtower."

Brennus barked a laugh. "Moonflower Tower?"

Timothy covered his mouth, giggling. "Why does it rhyme?"

Buckhorn gave him a wry grin. "It sounds frilly, but rumour has it, it's haunted."

Fable cocked her head. "Haunted?"

Buckhorn nodded gravely. "By a Folkvar woman

named Moonflower. It's said she climbs the stairs every night, over and over, stuck in a loop of trying to find her lost love."

Thorn frowned. "That's morbid. And sad."

"Sounds spooky," Brennus said.

"Sounds like a place I want to visit." Timothy grinned.

Fable shot him a look, hoping to remind him to keep his necromancy quiet.

Buckhorn chuckled, pouring himself a glass of water. "It's not really haunted, obviously. But Vetch likes that the rumour scares people away from his post." He thumped the pitcher on the table. "That, and the dark forest surrounding it." The glass door swished open, and Buckhorn gestured towards it with his glass. "Ah, speak of the devil himself."

A lean Folkvar man at least a foot taller than Thorn strode to the table. His strawberry blond waves bobbed around his shoulders with his strides, and his canvas pants and beige button-up shirt were stained with dirt and sweat. Several arrow shafts protruded from a quiver on his back, and he had a bow much like Orchid's slung around his shoulder.

"Good evening, Vetch," Juniper greeted him. "I'd like you to meet our guests," she said pointedly.

"Remember? The folks you are taking out to find the phoenix."

"Oh, right." He furrowed his brows. "Hi."

Juniper set down her fork. "Any new updates on the phoenix's activity? Are we still set to go the day after tomorrow?"

"I didn't see it today." Vetch shrugged and put his hands on his hips. "But yeah, if we head out after Lammas, I think we'll find the bird before it burns."

"Hi, Vetch." Buckhorn raised a hand. "Did Crocus say anything about the new axe I brought him? Saffron made it herself, and it's her new design. She said it would chop through wood like a knife slices through butter." He leaned towards Thorn. "Saffron is the blacksmith here. Her work is top-notch. She competed at the fair in Stonebarrow last year and won for the best handmade sword."

Vetch barely gave Buckhorn a glance. "He didn't mention it."

"Oh, that's alright." Buckhorn's cheeks flushed. "Maybe next time I see him—"

"And what are all your names?" Vetch asked tersely.

Fable frowned, feeling bad for Buckhorn. The way Vetch spoke to him made her think she wasn't going to like the ranger much.

"This is Thorn." Juniper smiled tightly and reached out to pat Thorn's hand. "My niece, who will be moving here in a couple of months. And these are her friends from Mistford—Fable, Timothy, and Brennus." She gestured at each of them as she said their names. "I told you about them. Remember?"

He gave them a curt nod. "Er—sorry. I've been busy keeping tabs on that phoenix and the chimera that's been raiding Sage's compost pile. I forgot you all were coming tonight." He ran a hand through his wavy locks, then slipped off his quiver and bow and hung them on the back of the chair at the end of the table.

Before he could sit, Juniper motioned to his bow. "No weapons at the table. You know that."

He narrowed his eyes at her, then gathered his weapons and deposited them on the outdoor bench near the glass doors. He stomped to his chair and sat, then pointed at the bowl of potatoes in front of Fable.

"Can you hand those over?"

She passed him the bowl, and he took it without a word of thanks. This is who would be helping them find the phoenix? He didn't seem interested in meeting them, much less aiding them on their quest. She glanced at Brennus, who moved his gaze to Vetch and made a cringy face, then ducked his head and helped himself to the three-bean dish before him.

Everybody dug in. The clinking of forks and the soft sounds of chewing only accentuated the awkwardness that blanketed the group in silence. Thorn sat stiffly, barely touching her food. Fable wondered if she was feeling alright. She usually ate three times as much as Fable could.

Thorn went to pick up her glass just as Vetch reached for the rolls. He bumped Thorn's hand, sending water splashing down her chest. Thorn grunted and set down the glass, then grabbed her napkin.

"Oh, dung beetles." Vetch's face broke into a lopsided grin. "Guess you shouldn't be so clumsy."

"Vetch!" Juniper snapped. "That's not funny."

"It's only water." His gaze landed on Thorn's shirt, and his eyes widened. "What's that?"

"What's what?" Thorn's voice quivered as she patted her shirt with the napkin.

He squinted. "That stone. It's glistening."

Thorn paused with her hand in mid-air. "Er—"

Vetch pushed back his chair. "It's magic, isn't it? I don't want that thing anywhere near me." He got to his feet and picked up his plate. "Juniper told me you all had magic. But you can't use it while you're here."

Thorn's face paled, and she clenched the napkin

with white-knuckled fingers.

"It's just a speaking-stone." Timothy put down his fork and glowered at the man. "What's your problem?"

"So it *is* magical." The vein in Vetch's neck stood out as he gave Thorn a cold look. "You leave that behind when we head out, or you're not coming. I'll have no magical disasters in my forest."

Timothy scowled. "It's not *your* forest. Besides, how could a speaking-stone hurt anyone?"

"Timothy," Fable said softly, not wanting him to push Vetch further into a rage. Her cousin was right, but the man's waves of anger and disgust spiralled off him like a storm. In her mind, her emerald flames rose to clash with his wild emotions, but she gritted her teeth and held them back.

"I don't know what a speaking-stone does," Vetch said icily. "But magic has never helped Folkvars." He waved a hand at Thorn. "Why would you use it? It's done nothing but hurt us. Look at what happened in the Greenwood to your colony. And according to Juniper, to your parents."

With that, he strode inside with his food. Fable gawked at him through the glass doors as he plunked down at the kitchen island. Juniper rubbed her forehead and closed her eyes, resting her elbow on the table.

Thorn blinked back tears. She set her wet napkin on the table with a shaking hand.

Fable's flames pushed against the seams of her mind, begging to be let loose on that jerk who had hurt her friend. She took a deep breath, struggling to keep them at bay. But the flames flared inside her. Heat swept over her skin. She wiped a bead of sweat from her brow, then clenched her hands into fists on her lap.

Not now. The last thing Thorn needs is for my magic to go off!

Timothy leaned close to her and whispered, "Are you okay? You're all sweaty—"

"I'm fine." Fable spat the words louder than she'd wanted to. Brennus snapped his gaze to hers, his brows knit together. She cleared her throat, slamming the flames down inside her. They relented, simmering at her edges. "We should be asking if Thorn's okay." She looked at her friend. "You didn't deserve that."

Buckhorn picked up his napkin and began to mop up the water in front of Thorn. "I'm sorry for Vetch's rudeness. He can be . . . stressed out sometimes."

Thorn huffed, wiping her cheek with her forearm.

Fable unclenched her fists, testing to see if her flames would spark again. They flickered, but thankfully she managed to keep them under control. She glanced at Juniper. “Why do we have to go with Vetch to find the phoenix? Isn’t there anyone else?”

“He’s the only one,” Juniper said quietly. “The only ranger who can lead you to the phoenix. It trusts him.”

Buckhorn sighed and dropped the wet napkin on his now-empty plate. “Besides, nobody here likes magic. Who would replace him?” He rested a gentle hand on Thorn’s shoulder. “I had to give up my wizard books when I came to live here too.”

Thorn lifted her chin. “You’re not from here?”

“Nope,” Buckhorn replied. “My parents are solitary Folkvars. They raised me in Sandy Ridge, a tiny desert town near the Burning Sands. I came here to meet my extended family and experience life in a colony.”

Thorn sniffed. “I want to fit in here.”

“You will. If I can, anybody can.” Buckhorn gave her a squeeze, then sat in his chair.

“Thorn, dear,” Juniper said. “Vetch’s behaviour is not acceptable. I told him about your greencraft before you came. I don’t know why he’s making a fuss about it.” She gestured at Thorn’s soggy food. “I’ll go speak with him and get you a new plate.”

She scooped up Thorn’s destroyed meal and marched inside.

Brennus leaned over so only Fable could hear him.

"You sure you're okay? Your cheeks are bright red."

"I said I'm fine."

He looked like he wanted to say more, but his shoulders slumped. "Okay. If you say so." He jerked his head towards the house. "I have never wanted to hurt anyone before, but if anybody needs their butt kicked, it's Vetch."

Fable's magic jolted again, but she closed her eyes and drew a breath. As her heart calmed, so did her flames, until they were merely simmering embers. It was the best she could do right now. "I'm not hungry anymore. Timothy, do you want my beans?"

Her cousin stared through the trees at the back of the yard, rubbing the skull on his bone bracelet.

Brennus peered around Fable at him. "Hey, Timothy. If Thorn has to leave her necklace behind, you're going to have to ditch that bracelet too."

Timothy jerked his head to look at them. "No way. What if we run into some of Endora's undead? These help me focus. That guy can't tell us what to do."

"Well," Fable replied slowly. As much as she hated to admit it, Brennus might be right. "If he's going to take us to the phoenix, you might have to."

"So you'll be leaving your book bag behind, then?" Timothy pointed at Fable's bag, then at

Brennus. "And your amulet?"

Fable sighed. "You know we need those. Those items are the whole point of this trip."

Brennus touched his pocket. "Besides, Fedilmid made the amulet look like a pocket watch. It's in disguise."

Timothy frowned at Fable. "Grandpa's not here. We're gathering the ashes to take to him later. Why can't we do the same for your star?"

Fable crossed her arms. "Because we want to use the ashes on it immediately. We don't know how they'll work on the star, so using them right away will be our best shot. You know Grandpa can't handle a hike through the mountains. Fedilmid and Alice both said as long as we get the ashes to him within a few days, they'll still heal him."

Timothy huffed, then returned his gaze to the trees behind them. "There's something dead wandering around this town. I need the bracelet. It helps me zero in on where dead things are."

"And that's exactly why you gotta leave it," Brennus hissed. "We're going into the wild. There's dead stuff everywhere out there. If you're acting twitchy, Vetch might not help us. Besides, whatever you're sensing right now is probably just a dead animal or something."

Timothy's expression darkened. "Dead animals don't wander." He stabbed the food on his plate with his fork.

That's true. Dead animals don't wander. But undead do. Fable looked into the fading light beyond the garden. Softly glowing fireflies hovered around the plants and trees, adding even more enchantment to the yard. The leaves rustled in the wind, but there was no sign of a black cloak or skeletal figure. No, Brennus was right. Something as insignificant as a snail or sea shell could steal Timothy's attention. What made this time any different? They were safe, tucked away here in the valley. Endora had no idea what they were up to.

Tomorrow, they would celebrate Lammas. But not before Fable told Fedilmid and Algar about what had happened with Vetch. They might need him to lead them to the phoenix, but Fable had a feeling the adults would want to have a firm talk with him before they left.

Fable's magic flickered, her embers still smoldering. She bit her lip. *And what is with the intensity of my flames? The darkness Endora talked about—is that what it's like? Is that how it starts to grow inside me?*

ELEVEN

Scorch

Fable sat next to Thorn on the bottom mattress of the bunk bed they were sharing. The full moon shone through the wide window, washing their bedroom in silvery light. The wood-planked walls and forest-green bedding almost made Fable feel like they were camping.

After supper, the kids had helped Juniper clean up, but their disastrous evening with Vetch had hung in the air like smog. Despite Brennus's jokes and Fable's encouragement, Thorn had been quiet and withdrawn the whole time they'd washed dishes. Timothy had asked her if she'd like to lead them in a yoga session in the garden before bed, but she'd simply shaken her head and trudged up the stairs to her and Fable's room.

Now, Thorn sat cross-legged on her bed in her flannel pyjamas, holding the speaking-stone in her palm.

"Are you trying to contact Orchid?" Fable asked.

"No." Thorn closed her fist around the stone. "I better not use this in case someone finds out. Besides,

Orchid is probably in the Oakwrath where it can't reach her." She ran her fingers over the stone's chain. "What's going to happen when Orchid comes here? What are Vetch and the others going to think of a *warlock*? She can't hide that. She has furry ears and literally channels magic from an immortal being."

Fable shifted, tucking her feet beneath her. "Maybe your aunt is trying to ease the other Folkvars into accepting magic. You know, to get them used to it before Orchid arrives. She spoke with Vetch—"

"Which didn't go very well, did it?" Thorn's face fell. "Sorry. I didn't mean to snap at you. And yeah, Vetch apologized to me. But only because Aunt Juniper asked him to. He still had that shifty look like he didn't trust me."

Fable patted Thorn's muscular forearm. She hated that her friend's first experience here was so conflicted. Thorn had been longing to leave Mistford for ages. Her aunt's offer to let her and Orchid live here had seemed like the perfect solution.

And Vetch had to ruin it with his terrible attitude. A spark of irritation lit inside Fable, igniting her flames. As heat rolled down her arms, Fable dug her fingers into her palms. *Stop it! What is with me tonight?* She huffed, tamping down her magic.

Thorn gave her a sideways look. "You okay?"

"Yeah, I'm fine." Fable swallowed. "It's just, Vetch seems like a real jerk. Honestly, I think Buckhorn is afraid of him. Did you see the way Vetch treated him?"

Thorn's brows lifted. "Yeah. Buckhorn does not deserve that." She thumbed the speaking-stone again, tilting her head. "I think he must get what I'm going through. Maybe I should ask him what it was like moving here. Besides Vetch being a total skullcap, he seems happy here."

"Skullcap?"

A faint smile played on Thorn's lips. "It's a poisonous mushroom. In the Greenwood, we used it as a word for bully." She leaned forward and pulled her suitcase out from the under the bed, then opened it and dropped the necklace inside. "I'm tired. We should probably get to sleep so we don't miss Juniper's big breakfast tomorrow. It sounds like it'll be fresh berries and waffles."

"I can't wait." Fable got up and put one foot on the ladder, then gave her friend one last glance. "Are you going to be okay?"

"Yeah. I'm sure things will seem better tomorrow."

Fable climbed the ladder to the top bunk. After snuggling beneath her blankets, she said goodnight to Thorn.

Thorn flicked off the lights, then settled into bed. “Hey, Fable?”

“Yeah?”

“Thanks for listening. I’ll make sure we stay best friends even after I move.”

Fable’s throat thickened. “I’ll make sure we do too.”

She rolled over to face the wooden rail of her bunk. Her book bag hung on the bedpost, and the silver stars caught the moonlight. How would Vetch react to the Blood Star when he found out she had it? She would have to reveal it when they found the phoenix’s ashes. And sure, he might enjoy watching Brennus destroy a magical amplifier. But how was he going to deal with Fable carrying the most powerful spectral star to have ever fallen? Let alone *healing* it?

And the memory box . . . Fedilmid still hadn’t gotten back to Fable with advice from Carina. He and Algar had returned to Juniper’s cottage just as the kids were going to bed. With everything going on, he probably hadn’t even had time to call the astronomer. But Fable itched to use the tokens again, yearning to see her parents and wondering if the items contained memories that would explain her ties to Endora.

Thorn’s soft snores came from the bunk below,

and Fable slipped her bag from the post and pulled it towards her. Trying to stay as quiet as possible, she propped herself up on her elbow and slid the memory box from the bag.

I'll only look at the tokens. Now that I know the song unlocks the memory magic, I can fight the urge to sing it. She gently lifted the box's lid. With only the moonlight to guide her, it was hard to pick out the items. She reached inside, and her fingers met the feathers of the woven bracelet. The chant sprang to her lips, but she clamped them together and dropped the band, her heart pounding.

I shouldn't unlock the memory. Not until Fedilmid says it's okay. She bit her lip, her emotions mingling with her spinning magic. *But what about the photo? That won't be dangerous, right?* She'd woken up from that vision before. And maybe she'd missed something from it. Something that could provide more clarity about what Endora meant by the darkness taking Fable over . . .

Holding her breath, Fable reached into the box again to find the photo. Something sharp pricked her finger. Her magic buzzed. Instead of a yelp, the whispered chant flew from her lips. The golden aura swarmed her vision again. Before she could stop herself, she began to fall.

When she opened her eyes, a blurry vision of a woman in a jewel-toned green dress stood before her. She blinked, and a room with green floral wallpaper came into focus. It and the four-poster bed told her she was in her parents' bedroom at Eighteen Lilac Avenue.

Oh, no. I promised Fedilmid I wouldn't dive into another memory! She looked around for the golden aura, but it had faded. She swallowed the lump in her throat. *Well, I may as well enjoy this while I'm here.*

Her mother stood in front of the closet with her hands on her hips. A baby who looked to be about nine or ten months old sat on the burgundy rug behind her, playing with a stuffed pterippus. Fable's chest warmed. *I guess I loved animals even as a baby.*

Like the last time Fable saw her parents, her mother was solid. So real, as if she stood right in front of Fable and was not merely a memory. Fable approached her, and her hand went through Faari's shoulder. She sighed, wishing her mother could see her too. *But I guess memories don't work that way. It's like I'm inside a movie. She's not actually here.*

"Morton, do you know where my black heels are?" Faari called out, oblivious to Fable's presence. She searched the closet, then picked up a pair of ballet flats with a frustrated sigh.

Baby Fable made a cooing noise, pointing at the shoes. Faari's expression melted. "Did you take them, missy?" she joked. "I didn't think you'd be big enough to steal my shoes until you were a teenager."

Morton rushed into the room, his black curls bobbing around his head. He wore a dark grey suit and was straightening his tie that matched the colour of Faari's dress. With his free hand, he gestured at the shoes dangling from Faari's fingers.

"What's wrong with those?"

"Flats? Are you kidding?" Faari tossed the shoes onto the floor of the open closet. "They aren't formal enough for your dad's retirement ceremony. The Astronomer's Guild is giving him the Skyseeker's Award! I don't want to look frumpy for his big event."

"You never look frumpy." Morton finished fixing his tie, then slid his hand around her waist and kissed her forehead.

"Even yesterday when Fable threw up on my sweatshirt?" Faari giggled.

"Well . . ." Morton rubbed his jaw. "It's better your

sweatshirt than that dress."

"True." Faari's bare feet padded over the carpet as she made her way to baby Fable. She picked up the child and kissed her cheek. "And frumpy's worth it when we get to have you."

Fable moved to the back wall, her magic swirling inside her with mixed emotions. This was her life before Endora had ruined it. Two doting parents. A safe, loving home in Mistford. She turned her head, unable to look at the scene anymore. Maybe these memories were too hard for her. How could she enjoy this, knowing she'd lost so much?

Baby Fable let out a babble, drawing her attention. A string of drool escaped the baby's lips and fell onto Faari's shoulder.

"Oh, darn. Would you take her while I wash this off before it sets in?" Faari asked, holding little Fable out to Morton. "I hope I don't have to change. This is my best dress."

Morton chuckled and reached for baby Fable. As Faari handed her over, Fable's pterippus caught on Morton's cufflink. It tore from her arms and fell to the floor, taking the cufflink with it.

"Oops!" Morton said good-naturedly. He waved Faari off. "Go wash up. I've got it."

She gave him a grateful smile and strode from the room, while Morton set little Fable on the floor.

"Now, where did that cufflink go?" He got on his knees and felt around the carpet with his hands, peering closely at the floor. "It's got to be here somewhere."

The glint of gold beneath the edge of the bed caught Fable's eye at the same time her younger self saw it. The baby's eyes lit up, and she reached for the pointed object with a chubby hand. Without thinking, Fable rushed over and tried to stop her child-self. But just like with her mom, her hands went right through the child. She jerked them back as the baby grabbed the cufflink.

Baby Fable let out a piercing cry and dropped the cufflink. In what seemed like a split second, an emerald flame erupted from the shrieking baby's hands. When Morton rushed to her and scooped her up, the flames sparked and hit him in the chest, sending him toppling onto the bed with Fable in his arms.

"Fable! Stop!" he cried out, covering her hands with his. The flames died out, but the front of his suit was singed black.

The baby's shrieks ceased to a wobbling cry, and Fable's heart shattered. *I burned my father! The same way I burned Brennus at the festival grounds this spring.*

"It's alright, Fable," Morton tried to comfort the

baby. “I’m sorry. I didn’t mean to shout.” He pulled at his blackened shirt and winced.

Faari rushed into the room in a panic. “Morton, are you alright? What happened?” Her gaze caught on his shirt and her whole body stiffened. “Oh, Fable. Not again.”

Not again? Did I burst into flames often?

“It’s okay,” Morton replied softly. He brushed his hands over the sniffling baby’s head. “She didn’t mean it.” He took her palm and turned it over, then gave it a kiss. “She pricked her hand on my cufflink and scared herself. But no harm done. Right, kiddo?”

The baby reached for him, and he pulled her close so she could put her arms around his neck. She nuzzled him, looking as sorry as a baby could for what she’d done.

Faari gave him a stricken look. “Your suit jacket, Morton. Are you sure you’re okay?”

“I’m fine,” he replied firmly. He motioned for Faari to join him on the bed. “It’s my turn to go clean up. I guess I’ll be wearing that purple suit jacket you hate so much.” He gave her a teasing grin.

Faari returned his smile, though it was tight with worry. Baby Fable raised her arms to her mother, and Fable didn’t miss the way Faari hesitated before taking her from Morton.

The golden aura formed around the scene, blurring with Fable's tears. As she fell backwards, they spilled down her cheeks. Her flames simmered at the edges of her mind, as if pleased with her realization.

My own mother was afraid of me . . . because I hurt people. Just like Endora.

TWELVE

Secret Memories

The next day, the kids toured the colony with Juniper, Fedilmid, and Algar. Fable tried to ignore the thoughts of dark magic and Endora's bloodline tugging at her mind, replacing them with delight at the juicy peaches from the orchard, the free-range chickens—of the non-magical variety—that the Folkvars raised for eggs, and the trickling waterfall at the edge of town. The swimming hole below the waterfall was filled with children and adults alike trying to beat the blazing heat, and Fedilmid promised they could go for a swim after finding the phoenix's ashes. They'd even stopped at Clover's bakery to check out the honey-glazed buns she was preparing for the Lammas feast that evening, the sweet smell of which made Fable's mouth water.

Now, she stood with Thorn in Juniper's entryway, waiting for everyone else so they could head to the town circle for Lammas. The late-afternoon sunlight shone through the spider plants in the cottage's front window, creating a warm atmosphere. Fable had put on the nicest dress she'd brought with her—a royal blue sundress that matched her book bag—and she'd done her best to comb her wayward locks into submission. But she still didn't feel formal enough for the event.

She shifted her bag, then glanced at Thorn. The Folkvar girl ran her hands over her floor-length sage-green skirt to smooth the wrinkles, then checked the intricate braids piled on her head for the umpteenth time.

"You look nice," Fable said. "You're going to make a great first impression."

"You think so? This is Juniper's skirt. You don't think it looks funny on me?" Thorn tugged at it, her brow wrinkled with concern.

"Not at all. The colour looks great on you." In fact, Fable had never seen Thorn look so elegant. It was a big disconcerting.

Thorn patted her twisted braids again, then pulled her hand away. A braid drooped to her shoulder, and she glanced at the bobby pin between her fingers in horror, obviously having pulled it out accidentally. She gave Fable a look of distress.

Fable held out her hand. "Here, bend down. I'll fix it."

Thorn handed her the pin and did as Fable asked.

Fable set her bag at her feet and pinned the braid back into place. "Done. Now stop messing with your hair. How come you're so twitchy tonight?"

Thorn straightened and squeezed her eyes shut, then let out a breath and opened them again. "What if Vetch told everyone about last night, about me using greencraft?" She touched her chest where the speaking-stone usually hung. "I feel torn. Like I have to hide a part of myself to fit in here, only something less obvious than blue skin or pointed ears like in Mistford. Magic isn't literally part of me like it is for you, but still, it doesn't feel right."

Fable bit the inside of her cheek. She knew exactly how her friend felt. For most of her life, she'd had to hide her magic in Larkmoor. Even within the walls of her own home, due to Aunt Moira's fear of someone finding out. But it had never worked. No matter how hard she had tried to squelch it, that piece of her always came out eventually. And the more she'd fought it, the bigger the bang when it had erupted.

"Just because you don't create your own magic doesn't mean greencraft isn't part of you," Fable replied. "Look at Fedilmid, Aunt Moira, even the warlocks. Their magic doesn't come from within them either. They channel it in other ways. If you feel drawn to greencraft, then it's part of who you are. And you shouldn't have to hide it."

Thorn closed her eyes and took a deep breath. "Thank you. But I think I *do* have to. For now, at least."

The sound of swishing robes came from the stairs, alerting them to Fedilmid's descent before he even came into view. But instead of his usual blue robes with the star-spangled hem, he wore bright purple ones with intricate green vines embroidered all over them. Tiny white flowers were stitched along the vines, and they glistened with what only could have been a touch of magic.

Fable's mouth fell open. "Fedilmid, your robes! I've never seen you in anything but your blue ones. These are beautiful. But what about the you-know-what?"

He reached the bottom of the staircase and raised a grey brow. "What do you mean?"

Fable glanced down the hallway towards Juniper's room, then back at her mentor. "The m-a-g-i-c. That has to be what's making them sparkle like that."

"What magic?" Fedilmid flourished his hand with a smirk, making the flowers dance along the bell-shaped sleeve as though they were bending beneath a summer breeze.

Fable grinned, and Thorn snickered. Fedilmid

snapped his fingers. The flowers stilled, and their sparkle faded. But even without the shine, they were still stunning.

"Where did you get that outfit?" Thorn asked.

"Oh, this old thing?" Fedilmid straightened his collar. "I haven't worn this robe for nearly fifteen years. Not since the last wedding we attended in Mistford." He gestured at the girls. "You both look wonderful too. Thorn, the other Folkvars here are going to love you. And for more than your pretty skirt and hair."

Thorn gave him a grateful smile. "Thanks."

Fedilmid craned his neck to look up the stairs. "The boys and Algar should come down in a few minutes. Timothy had burrs stuck all over him, so I asked him to change and clean up. He must have been out in the trees again after we got home. That's the second time today."

Fable tucked her smooth hair behind her ear, wondering if her cousin had been investigating whatever was giving off the dead vibrations. He struggled to resist his magic at the best of times, much less in a whole new town that might have unique bones for him to find.

Fedilmid rocked back on his heels, jerking his head towards the kitchen. "Fable, do you have a moment to chat before we head out?"

Her curiosity piqued, Fable picked up her bag and

followed him into the dining area. He motioned at the round table in front of the glass doors, so she took a seat and he sat across from her.

He folded his hands on the table. "This will only take a moment. I wanted to let you know I spoke with Carina this afternoon."

"You did?" Fable asked. "Did she find anything else out about the Blood Star or Gaea?"

Fedilmid shook his head. "She hasn't found any new information about Gaea in particular. She still thinks we should use the star's destiny to heal it—to arrange a meeting between Endora and Stirling." He furrowed his brows, as if unsure of what to think of that. "But since we're going after the phoenix to heal Stirling's memories, she did say to try those first. I think that's wise. And I am hopeful they will work. There's nothing saying they won't."

Fable's jaw tightened. If they could only know for sure, then she would feel so much better. In a way, she wished Carina had never told her about the star's destiny. "I thought astronomy was a form of science. Why doesn't she know exactly what will heal the star?"

Fedilmid clucked his tongue. "Science is always evolving as we learn more. We do the best we can with the information we have, but even astronomers don't know everything. If they did, they wouldn't have a job. But they are always progressing and discovering new things to help the world. And right now, they don't know a lot about the Blood Star or its constellation yet."

Fable sighed. "I guess that makes sense. I just wish they knew more."

"Carina is trying. She's given us what information she has and her prediction based on that." Fedilmid unclasped his fingers and lay them flat on the table. "You're helping her with her research. You should feel good about that."

Fable lowered her gaze to her lap. "But if I fail to heal the star—"

"This isn't all on you." Fedilmid tapped the table with his fingertips. "Your aunt is meeting with the police in Mistford, and from what I've heard, the warlocks are working to stop Endora too. You're not alone in this."

"But I'm the only one who has the Blood Star." A lump formed in Fable's throat. "And if I don't fix it, Endora's going to grow stronger and collect more people on her wall. And whatever else she has planned. No matter how much power she gets, it's never enough for her."

"Power can be addicting." Fedilmid smoothed his hand over his well-groomed beard. "I'm not sure what she wants aside from breaking her deal with Halite and getting her hands on the Blood Star. You'd think raising your powers to cosmic levels would be enough for one person. But I agree, she probably won't stop there. That's why we want the police and the Ministry of Mistford on our side. They have strong sorcerers that can help us."

Fable frowned, feeling queasy. She'd barely heard Fedilmid's last comments about the police. Endora's words about she and Fable being alike circled her mind, drowning out everything else. Her flames flickered to life, and a bead of sweat formed on her brow.

She stared at the table, digging her fingernails into her thighs. "But I'm desperate for the star's power too." Her voice came out as barely a whisper. "Does that make me like Endora? Am I her power-hungry heir?"

Fedilmid's expression grew tight. "Stop comparing yourself to her. You are not her or her heir. The star connected to you because it sensed the goodness inside you—your desire to help others by stopping Endora from her murderous path. The star chose *you*. Don't forget that." He pointed at her chest. "Remember that white light in your heart?"

Fable nodded, her throat too tight to speak. But she couldn't fully believe him. Not after the memories she'd seen. Endora had sensed the dark lineage within Fable as a baby, and she had later hurt her father in a magical tantrum. She'd done that before she could form her own opinions or make her own choices. It had been pure instinct. An instinct that was *dark*.

Shame washed over her as her flames roiled inside her. There was no way she could tell Fedilmid that she'd fallen into another memory the night before, much less one that showed who she truly was—somebody not worth the Fae Witch's mentorship.

She swallowed the horrible thought, but it sat like a rock in her belly. She sucked in a breath to keep her flames at bay, then met Fedilmid's gaze. "Did Carina say anything about the evocation magic? Is it safe for me to use the tokens?"

Fedilmid steepled his fingers, and a delighted smile lit up his face. "She did. They are safe for you to use. There's no way you can get stuck or alter the past like with time travel." He paused. "However, she said you should only do it with someone watching you, in case you fall or hurt yourself while entering the visions. If you'd like, I can sit with you while you try again."

Fable's stomach knotted. *No. He can't watch. What if the next memory shows something even worse? I could say something out loud or start crying when I come out of it. I can't let him see any of this until I figure out exactly what these memories are meant to tell me.*

Why had her parents left her these awful memories? To warn her about the darkness and that it could take her, like Endora had said? What if she turned evil like her great-grandmother and regained the power of the Blood Star? She could hurt everyone she loved. Maybe even kill them.

Her flames roared with her whirling emotions, and she clenched her hands tighter into fists to stop them from emerging.

"Fable, are you alright?" Fedilmid's brows knit together. "I thought you would be excited to work with the memory box."

She jerked up her chin and wiped her forehead. "Um, yes. I'm fine. It's just—it's a lot. Maybe we should wait until we return to the Thistle Plum before I try using the evocation tokens again. I should focus on the phoenix and the star while we're here. Grandpa Stirling is counting on us to get those ashes."

Fable's chest pinched. When her grandfather's amnesia was healed, what would he remember about her as a baby? Had he seen her the same way Endora had?

Fedilmid tilted his head, studying her. After a

moment, he nodded. "Alright. I understand. I imagine it is quite emotional for you to see your parents. But if you change your mind and want to try again soon, let me know. Okay?"

"Okay."

Thundering footsteps came from the hallway, telling Fable that Brennus and Timothy must be ready to go. Juniper entered the kitchen with a bright smile, wearing a skirt similar to Thorn's and a navy-blue lace shawl around her shoulders.

"Should we head over to the Lammas feast? Algar, the boys, and Thorn are waiting in the front yard. We're going to meet Vetch and Buckhorn at the town centre."

Fedilmid caught Fable's gaze. "Are you ready, or would you like a moment to talk more?"

"I'm ready." Fable got to her feet and adjusted her book bag at her side.

Her heart in her throat, she followed the adults from the room, thinking over what Fedilmid had said about choosing good and the white light inside her. *But Endora was good once. She created the Blood Star with her light, and she loved her son.*

At least she did, before she tried to kill him. Her throat went dry. *I can't be like her! If darkness is coming for me, I have to stop it. No matter what.*

The Intruder

A round of applause erupted around Fable. She joined in as Thorn got up from their table and made her way to the front of the tent. The soft glow of the white string lights hanging from the tent poles caught on the Folkvar girl's copper braids. There was a slight wobble in her usual steady gait, but she held her head high as she approached the town councillors at the head table. Fable sat near the refreshments stand with Timothy and Brennus, who both wore button-up shirts and ties instead of their usual T-shirts or hoodies. Fedilmid and Algar clapped politely nearby from their spot with Algar's friends.

Fable peeked around the deep purple, yellow, and orange wildflower centrepiece. The head table had been adorned with a white cloth embroidered with golden sheaves of wheat, and a braided bread the size of a turkey sat in the middle. Juniper sat next to an elderly Folkvar woman with hair as frizzy as Algar's beard, who she had earlier introduced to Fable as Maple. A middle-aged man as short as Buckhorn and with an even rounder tummy sat on Maple's other side, and the leader of the colony, Flint, stood at the end. With a barrel chest and braided blond hair and beard that nearly reached his navel, he reminded Fable of a Viking from her old story books in Rose Cottage.

Thorn approached the council members, looking hesitant, but they all gave her welcoming smiles. She stood with her back to the audience as Flint picked up a microphone. His deep, booming voice echoed across the tent, and the crowd quieted.

"Welcome to the Windswept colony, Thorn. We are happy to take in you and any other Folkvar who escaped the fire that tore through the Greenwood. To celebrate your arrival, we would like you to be the first to break this harvest's bread."

Thorn dipped her head, then rounded the table so she faced the crowd. She took her place behind the bread, and Flint handed her a serrated knife. Taking a deep breath, Thorn sliced through the middle of the loaf, then gave Flint a blank look.

He chuckled and gestured to the end of the roll. "Perhaps you should start at the end, so you can have the first slice."

A murmur of good-natured laughter went through

the crowd, and Thorn's cheeks reddened. She cut off a slice and took a big bite, and the laughter turned to more clapping. Fable caught sight of Vetch standing near the entrance, leaning against a tent pole. Even he clapped along. Despite his serious expression, Fable hoped it was a sign he was coming around to accepting Thorn.

"Thank you, Thorn. To this year's first grain harvest!" Flint picked up his wineglass, which practically disappeared behind his hand, and raised it towards the crowd.

Joyous shouts echoed around the room.

"Happy Lammas!"

"May the next harvest be just as blessed as this one!"

"Time to eat!"

Fable grinned at Timothy and Brennus, and they all clinked their glasses of iced brambleberry juice together. Flint shook Thorn's hand and announced that everybody could dig in. The Folkvars rushed towards the buffet area. Thorn returned to the Mistford kids' table and took her seat next to Fable.

"Good job," Fable told her. "See? You're fitting in perfectly. They're all so happy you're here."

"Yeah, they're even okay with you not knowing how to cut bread," Brennus said with a grin.

Thorn narrowed her eyes at him, and Fable nudged him beneath the table with her foot.

He held up his hands. “I’m kidding. You did great.”

“Yup.” Timothy craned his neck to look at the line of Folkvars waiting for food. “Now let’s get some of those honey-glazed rolls!”

While they enjoyed their feast of every type of bread and baked good imaginable, a band set up on the stage. Soon, folk music played throughout the room, and the dance floor slowly began to fill. Fable tapped her toe to the tune, trying to let go of her worries about the memories and the star. Still, she checked her book bag for the umpteenth time, making sure the ties were firmly closed.

Despite her and Brennus thinking Juniper’s house would be a safe place to leave their magical items, Timothy had insisted otherwise. No matter how much they had tried to reason with him, he’d still worried that something bad could be lurking around the cottage. Fedilmid and Algar had even given the garden a thorough check, and they hadn’t seen a flicker of black cloak or skeletal remains. But Fable hadn’t wanted Timothy to be on her case all night, so she and Brennus brought the items along, anyway.

Brennus straightened his tie and asked Thorn if

she'd like to dance. Thorn gave him a sideways look, as if trying to decide if he was joking.

"Come on," he said. "When do we ever get to go to parties like this? I've never seen any of you dance before."

Thorn shrugged and got to her feet. "Okay. But just to warn you, I don't know how to dance. The Greenwood Folkvars didn't have parties like this. Our get-togethers were more about meditating and giving thanks." She paused, watching the dancers. "This crowd seems like a lot more fun."

"I've been to tons of music festivals with my parents," Brennus said, standing. "Dancing isn't that different from yoga. Only faster."

Thorn raised a brow. "Are you telling me there's a dance move like downward dog?"

Brennus made a face. "Er—maybe follow my lead. Timothy, are you coming?"

Fable glanced at her cousin, who stared out the open tent door with a frown. In the setting sun, the trees cast long shadows over the gardens. She nudged him, and he flicked his gaze to hers.

"What?"

"Brennus just asked if you want to dance with them."

"Not right now." Timothy shook his head, then

looked at the trees.

Fable shrugged at Brennus, annoyance worming its way into the back of her mind. *What is Timothy's deal? If he gives away his necromancy by going hunting for snails or something, it's going to get us into trouble.*

Brennus picked up his canvas tote and handed it to her, then stooped and lowered his voice. "Do you mind watching this? I doubt anyone would take it, but with you-know-what inside it—well, you know. We can take turns dancing, making sure one of us is always here with the bags."

Fable nodded, disappointed that she wouldn't get to dance with him, but he was right. While chances were slim that anyone here would steal their bags, it wasn't worth the risk.

She slung the tote strap alongside her bag on the back of the chair. "Alright," she said, waving her friends off. "Have fun!"

As soon as they started weaving through the tables towards the dance floor, Timothy pushed his chair back and got to his feet. "I'm going outside. I saw Buckhorn slip out, and I want to talk to him."

Fable grabbed his sleeve. "Please don't," she hissed. "What if someone catches you?"

"Catches me what?"

"Looking for bones or whatever it is you're doing," she replied. "Buckhorn seems fine with magic, but he's not from here."

Timothy clenched his jaw and yanked his sleeve away from her. "Am I not allowed to go outside for some fresh air? You're the one saying how safe it is in the colony and nothing bad could be around. And I thought you trusted me now."

Fable dropped her hand, guilt pinching her chest. "I'm sorry. I just don't want us to get Thorn into trouble. So no hopping snail shells or zombie-walking mouse skeletons, okay?"

Timothy rolled his eyes. "I wasn't going to do that. I'll be back in a few minutes. Tops." He strode away through the milling crowd, heading out the tent exit and into the night air.

Fable sighed, resting her elbow on the table and watching the dance floor. Algar and Fedilmid danced on the edge. Well, Fedilmid danced. Algar shuffled stiffly back and forth, clearly only out there at his husband's request. He frowned as Fedilmid let out a whoop. The old witch raised his arms and wiggled his hips, surprisingly limber for his age.

Thorn, Brennus, and a group of teenage Folkvars joined them, cheering Fedilmid on. A girl with stick-straight reddish-brown hair that fell past her waist gave Thorn a high-five. Thorn grinned in a way that Fable had only seen once before, when they had first found Orchid after the sisters' separation.

A twinge of jealousy went through her. She could see why Thorn wanted to move here. The whole tent buzzed with camaraderie, from those on the dance floor to families and friends gathered around tables, eating and smiling and telling stories. As their leader, Flint was making rounds around the room, chatting with everyone. They all seemed to know and treat each other so well. A community filled with support and trust.

Except for magic, that is. They don't trust that.

On the dance floor, the other Folkvar girl bumped hips with Thorn. Thorn threw her hands in the air, laughing. Fable tried to push her jealousy and thoughts about magic aside. *Thorn could change things here. She could open them up to accepting magic, or at least not being afraid of it anymore. And being so close to nature, greencraft could be the perfect introduction.*

The band switched to a new song, and the mahogany-haired girl hooked her arm through Thorn's and guided her through some steps. Fable scanned the tent, looking for Timothy. *He should be back by now*. She bit her lip, thinking about his obsession with whatever vibrations he'd been picking up around the colony. After a few minutes of watching the exit, she decided to go look for him. *Not that I need to babysit him,* she reminded herself. *But some fresh air would be nice.*

Fable drained her glass of juice, then gathered her and Brennus's bags and got to her feet. She glanced at her friends on the dance floor again. Thorn had stopped, standing stiffly and clutching her chest with a horrified expression. The girl moved away from Thorn and stared at her like she had two heads.

Brennus kept dancing, waving at the others as if to distract them, encouraging them to move to the music too. But the girl pointed at Thorn, her eyes wide with fear, and said something. Thorn's expression dropped. She kept her fist closed at her chest, and Fable caught the flash of a gold chain on her neck.

The speaking-stone! She has it tucked under her collar! She must have gone to her room and put it on after our talk at Juniper's. I bet Orchid tried to talk to her. She never remembers to turn it off like Fedilmid taught her. Fable groaned, panic rising inside her. *Why did I have to encourage her to use magic?*

Thorn's eyes flashed yellow as one of the teenage boys began gesturing at her, clearly angry. Fedilmid rushed to her side and put his arm around her shoulders, while Algar stood in front of her, holding up his hands as if to fend off the would-be attackers. Brennus approached the boy, appearing to be trying to talk him down. The boy responded by puffing out his chest and stepping into Brennus's space as if to challenge him.

Fable shifted the bags' straps higher on her shoulder, then bolted towards the dance floor. She had no idea how to help the situation, but she couldn't bear to let it slip out of control for Thorn.

The girl's shrill voice cut through the air. "Thorn has a magic necklace! There's a voice inside it!"

The music stopped. Gasps filled the room, and every head turned to stare at Thorn.

Fable's magic roiled inside her. The whole tent erupted into shouts, and Fable quickened her pace, slipping through the murmuring crowd. But before she could reach the group from Mistford, someone yanked on the bag straps. She stumbled and whirled, clutching to the bags with all her might, and came face-to-face with a familiar greasy-haired man.

Her mouth dropped as people milled past her, not even noticing her or the grimy man in all the commotion. "Doug?"

He smirked, his red-rimmed eyes flashing greedily as he tried again to pull the bags from her grip. "Yeh've got no one ter help yeh now, and yeh can't use magic. Yeh may as well give these up!"

"No!" Fable gritted her teeth, holding the bags to her chest as he yanked on the straps again. She dug her heels to the floor and twisted away from him.

He leaned closer to her and hissed through his stained teeth. "Yeh don't want me ter tell 'em what yeh got, do yeh?"

"Stop!" Fable's flames roared to be let loose, but she forced them down. How was she going to stop Doug without magic? If he stole both the Blood Star and the amulet, Mistford could be destroyed. And Endora wouldn't need her collectors to capture souls any more.

People would die.

Desperately, she kicked Doug's shin. He let out a wobbly cry, letting go of the bags with one hand and holding his leg. He gave her a dark look. "Fine, then. Yeh asked for it." He cleared his throat, looking around. "Oi! This girl, right here! She's got somethin' weird too!"

The closest Folkvars whirled to look at them. Shouts of alarm rang through the air, but she barely noticed. Fury rose within her, fuelling her emerald flames. They whooshed down her arms and blasted

Doug in the chest, knocking him off his feet. As he fell, he yanked her bag to the ground and the ties loosened. The memory box tumbled out. The lid popped open, scattering its contents.

"No!" Without thinking, Fable grabbed the pressed flower at her feet.

Her flames flared again, and the chant flew from her lips before she could stop it. The golden halo formed in her mind, and she began to fall. Before her vision clouded over, she saw Flint's face appear above her with an angry scowl.

The Dark Truth

The soft sound of crying broke through the golden aura. Fable opened her eyes and found herself standing at the window in the living room at Eighteen Lilac Avenue. Her mother sat facing away from her on the worn green couch in the middle of the room, a lamp on the stand next to her the only light aside from the gently smoldering fireplace. Rain thudded heavily against the roof, and the low rumble of thunder sounded in the distance. A sob came from her mother, and Fable rounded the couch.

"Mom?" She knelt next to Faari. Just like the times before, her hand went right through her mother's leg.

Faari cradled her rounded abdomen, which bulged against the fabric of her floral summer dress. She clutched a torn slip of paper in one hand. A tear slid down her cheek as she bowed her head to read, causing brown waves of hair to fall over her face.

"You'll be okay, little one. I'm going to fix this," she whispered, rubbing her belly. "*Optempero* . . . If she won't do it, I'll make her. It's worth it to save you."

Save me? Fable's heart wrenched at her mother's tear-stained face. *What does she mean by that? Why is she so upset? And where's my dad?*

She peered at the paper in her mother's trembling fingers. Scratchy handwriting covered it—*Compulsion Spell. To bend someone to your will, direct your magic to their mind and say the word 'optempero'. Once their mind opens to you, give them your command. If your magic is strong enough, they will have no choice but to obey.*

Fable rocked back on her heels, gaping at Faari. "What is this? What's going on?"

Lightning cracked outside, followed by a loud rap at the door that was almost drowned out by the thunderous boom that followed. Faari pocketed the paper and wiped her cheeks, then got up and opened the front door. Fable followed her to the entrance. Endora, looking as young and healthy as ever, stood in the doorway in one of her typical sleek black gowns.

Fable's chest hitched, and a heavy feeling of dread fell over her. *What is she doing here? I don't want to see this!* She turned to run up the stairs, but was met with a blurred grey barrier on the third step. It was as if a solid wall of smoke had formed to prevent her from leaving.

It's my mom's memory. I can't leave. Fable pressed her hands to her eyes, sucking in a breath as her mother's voice came from behind her.

"Come in, Endora. Morton is visiting his father at Skyview Tower. It's just me."

Fable sat on the bottom step, hugging her stomach as she watched the scene unfold before her.

"Of course he is," Endora said snidely. "He would never allow me into his home. I'm surprised you went behind his back to meet with me."

Faari wiped her cheek again. "Please, Endora. This is hard enough."

Endora pushed past her and strode into the living room, her satin gown swishing over the floor. She stopped in front of the fireplace and swept the room with a disdainful gaze. "Such a cramped, dingy space. Are you sure this is the right environment to raise a child in?"

"I didn't invite you here for snarky comments about our home." Faari leaned against the entryway, crossing her arms.

She invited Endora here? Behind my father's back? But why?

"Then why did you ask me to come?" Endora spun on her heel and looked Faari up and down. She paused, staring at Faari's stomach, and her amethyst eyes grew wide. "You're losing the baby, aren't you?"

Faari looked to the floor, clutching her stomach. "Yes."

Fable gasped and her spine stiffened. Her mind whirled, and her magic thrummed through her veins.

"My doctor confirmed it today, but I could feel her begin to slip away last night. Her magic, her energy—it's dimming." Faari choked on restrained tears. She made her way to the couch and sat down, rubbing her rounded belly.

Endora's blood-red lips pressed together, but she couldn't hide the slight note of disappointment in her words. "And what exactly do you want from me?"

Faari met her gaze. "You have lich magic. You can give life."

"I can *steal* life," Endora corrected her.

"You can save my child," Faari replied. "Your great-granddaughter."

Endora paced in front of the fireplace, her smirk gone. "You realize the price of that, don't you? To take the years of someone's life and give it to another?" She glanced over her shoulder at Faari, her face grim. "It's dark magic, Faari. Darker than you could think possible. Are you sure that's what you want for your *child*?" She tilted her head, her expression shifting to greed. "What would Morton think?"

"I-I know." Faari's voice cracked. Another tear tumbled down her cheek. "He would be angry, at first. But after seeing our baby, after watching her grow, he would understand." She lifted her chin, caressing her stomach. "I will tell him one day. After she's here."

Endora stopped pacing and narrowed her eyes at Faari. "And what do I get out of this?"

Faari frowned. "What do you mean? She's your great-granddaughter. Your family."

"And what good has *family* ever done for me?" Endora snarled, standing before Faari with her hands on her hips. "My son, my grandchildren. They all turned their backs on me. You think I should heal this child and the knowledge of her being alive is payment enough? Another traitor to add to my collection?"

Faari's mouth fell open with a stricken look. "It should be enough."

"It's not," Endora said flatly.

Faari stared at her for a moment, her cheeks growing red. She bit her lip, then took a deep breath and lifted her hand. Shakily, she said, "*Optem—*"

Endora snatched Faari's wrist, scowling. "Do you really think your magic is strong enough to overpower me?"

Fable gasped, covering her mouth. *My mom just tried to use magic on Endora!* She jumped to her feet, wishing she could yank the wretched lich away from Faari. Her flames sparked at her fingertips, but she could do nothing to stop Endora from hurting her mother. This was merely a memory. A terrible past that could never be changed.

Endora twisted Faari's arm, making the woman whimper, then leaned in so their faces were only inches apart. "If you have nothing to offer, I'm leaving. I don't do charity."

She dropped Faari's wrist, then spun on her heel and strode to the door.

"Wait!" Faari swallowed, rubbing her forearm. "You're lonely. We could let you see the baby. Maybe heal our family ties."

Endora turned to face her, an eager look in her eyes. "I'm listening."

"Is there a way to choose the person whose life you will take?" Faari asked.

Endora turned her gaze to the mantle and plucked a purple flower from the vase on the end. "I will have to feed her the life from myself. But I have ways of replenishing it." She paused, spinning the flower in her fingers. "Is this a faari blossom?"

Faari nodded, looking confused. "Yes. But is there a way to take the years from someone *willing* to give them up?"

Who would ever give up their years for—Fable's chest jolted. "No. Mom!"

More tears trailed down her mother's cheeks, but she held her head high. "Just let me have a few years with her to give her what every child deserves—their parents' love."

Endora regarded Faari carefully, her amethyst eyes gleaming in the firelight. She tossed the bloom on the floor. "I will collect payment eventually, and that payment is your life. Are you sure you want to do this?"

Faari wrapped her arms around her stomach. "Yes," she said, more to her baby than to the lich. "I have to do this."

"And what if my dark magic becomes part of her? What if it twists her soul in the womb?"

"It won't," Faari replied firmly. "She's strong. She's good. And Morton will nurture that in her. Love will always overcome darkness. Look at what you and Stirling made together—"

"Do not speak that name in my presence," Endora hissed, her eyes flashing crimson red. "Besides, there is no love there anymore. But believe what you will." She rubbed her hands together. "I'll do it. She is my great-granddaughter, after all."

She eyed Faari hungrily, and Fable's stomach churned. Fable's magic flowed freely throughout her, as if excited over what was about to happen. She hugged herself even harder, wanting to disappear. Wishing with all her heart that this wasn't true. That this had never happened. But as Endora sat next to Faari on the couch, her eyes glowing scarlet, Fable knew it was real.

My mother gave her life for mine. That's why Endora murdered her.

Black smoke emanated from the lich, surrounding both her and Faari. As Faari let out a scream of pain, the golden aura formed around Fable again, and she jerked backwards. But instead of falling into golden light, emerald flames snaked after her, winking out when she hit reality with a thud.

FIFTEEN

Strange Shadows

Fable awoke with sunshine warming her cheeks. She blinked in confusion, her head throbbing with a dull ache. Instead of the white roof of the tent from the Lammas feast, thick wooden rafters lined the ceiling above her. She pushed aside a pothos vine that sprawled over her pillow from the shelf above the bed.

I must be at Juniper's. She frowned, twisting under the thick quilt, trying to remember what happened. Her head throbbed again, clouding her thoughts. She rubbed the back of it and found a lump the size of one of Alice's strawberries.

Memories of the Lammas feast came rushing to her. Orchid contacting Thorn through the speaking-stone. Doug appearing from nowhere. The evocation tokens. The horrible memory within the purple bloom Fable had touched.

I must have hit my head when I fell. Fable pressed her palms to her eyes, trying to ease both the headache and the shame welling inside her. *After I warned*

Timothy not to show his magic, I blasted Doug in front of everyone. We must be in so much trouble with the town council.

And Endora . . . Fable's heart scraped against her ribs. Her mother had asked the lich to save her. She'd been so desperate, she had tried to force Endora with that spell. Fable hugged her chest. Endora's words from the memory came back to her—*I will collect payment eventually, and that payment is your life.*

Her stomach roiled, as if attempting to throw up the vile magic that swam inside her. *The rock slide didn't kill my mom. Endora took her life in exchange for saving mine.* Her emerald flames rolled gently down her arms, for once not flaring with a raging tide of emotions, but as if merely there to prove a point—that Fable had been right before when she thought she'd had darkness inside her. Fable tried to hold them back, but she was too weak.

She remembered Endora's hungry look as she used her magic on Faari, forcing it upon Fable before she was even born. Her mother's cries of pain echoed inside her head.

It wasn't just any power. It was Endora's dark lich magic. It's part of me.

Fable had to get out of there. She shouldn't be

around anyone. It wasn't safe. No wonder Endora had come to Eighteen Lilac Avenue when Fable was a baby, trying to take her under her wing and acting as if she had a right to Fable and her future. In a way, she did.

Fable squinted against the fog in her mind, forcing the flames to recede. Her gut lurched again. She took a deep breath and threw aside the blanket, then swung her bare feet to the hardwood floor. After straightening her dress—the same one she'd worn to the feast—she wobbled to the door and leaned on the handle for support.

Before she could open it, Fedilmid's voice came from the hallway outside. "No, Vetch. It has to be Fable. Nobody else can heal the star."

"I won't have her in my hunting party," Vetch growled. "Did you see that fire she conjured? She attacked that man!"

Juniper's voice cut in. "That man was attacking *her*! And how did he get into the colony to begin with? With our security, no outsiders should be able to get in or out."

"Don't ask me," Vetch replied icily. "I'm not in charge of the guards. Maybe you should ask Thorn or Brennus or Fable. Someone's magic attracted him here."

Fedilmid sighed heavily. "That man is Doug, and

he's a transporter. He has portal magic."

"Great. So now I'll have some wizard who can emerge through thin air chasing us through the mountains?" Vetch hissed. "No. I'm not doing it."

"You know what's at stake." Fedilmid's tone was so firm it was almost menacing. "We have a dragon and a lich to contain. Both of which would destroy this colony merely for entertainment."

Fable flinched at his words. *Is Endora's lich magic going to make me like that?*

"Vetch," Juniper said softly. "Think of Moonflower. You, of all people, know what Endora can do."

Fable's breath caught. Had he lost someone to Endora's horrible frames too? Just how many people had Endora murdered throughout the years? *To gain the magic that now pumps through my veins.* She squeezed her eyes shut.

"Fine," Vetch replied, but he did not sound happy. "But once this is done, that girl goes back to Mistford. She's only passing through those gates once more. On her way *out*."

"Technically, she hasn't passed through the gates. We flew over them," Fedilmid replied with a hint of annoyance. "But that's not the point. Once we get moving, it won't be long until we're out of your hair."

Vetch grunted in reply. Fable padded to her bed and got under the covers, her head still pounding. A moment later, the door swung open and Fedilmid stepped into the room.

"Ah," he said with a smile, almost as if he hadn't just been arguing with a giant Folkvar man. "You're awake. How are you feeling?"

"My head hurts. What happened after I fell?"

He made his way to the bed and pulled up the chair from beside the nightstand, then took a seat. "You bumped your head pretty hard. I think between that and the evocation magic, your poor body couldn't handle it all. You woke up for a few seconds, then passed out again. So we brought you here to rest and heal." He tapped his head. "How's the goose egg?"

"Still sore." Fable rubbed it, wincing.

"It was more like a lightning bird egg than a goose one last night," Fedilmid replied with a slight smile. "I gave you a touch of healing, but I didn't want to overdo it with all that energy bursting at your seams. Do you think you can heal it the rest of the way yourself?"

Fable jerked her hand away from the lump, her pulse quickening. "No!"

She bit her lip, not wanting to say anything more. She couldn't tell him what she'd seen in the memory or that she didn't want to use her dark magic to heal herself or anyone else.

He gave her a look of curiosity. "Alright. If you don't feel up to it, then may I finish the job? We're planning to head out first thing tomorrow. I doubt a headache will do you good on a trek through the mountains."

Fable nodded and let him place his hand on the back of her head. She closed her eyes as a cool wave of energy swept through her, and the pain receded. After she took a deep breath, the cobwebs faded from her mind.

"Thank you." She checked her head, and the lump was gone.

"You're most welcome," Fedilmid replied. "Now, how are you emotionally? With everything that happened—"

"How's Thorn?" Fable asked. "Is she in trouble? They were already mad at her for having the speaking-stone, and then I exploded with magic. What happened on the dance floor? Did Orchid contact her? And Doug! Did you see him? How did he get in? And my memory box—wait, the Blood Star!"

Fedilmid held up his hands, quirking a brow. "One question at a time, please." He crossed one leg over the other and grasped his knee. "First, Thorn will be okay.

Yes, Orchid contacted her. Thorn had forgotten to turn off the speaking-stone. Again." He rubbed his forehead. "I'm afraid the colony isn't exactly as welcoming as she'd hoped it would be. She needs some time, but a talk with a friend would do her some good."

Sadness washed over Fable as she remembered the way the teens had pointed and yelled at Thorn. It wasn't fair. The magic Thorn used was nothing like Fable's. It wasn't dangerous or dark. And what was so wrong with her wanting to keep in touch with her sister?

"Second, I gathered your evocation tokens and bags. The amulet is safe with Brennus, and the memory box is upstairs in your room." He dug into his pocket and pulled out the star. He held it flat in his palm. Its body glimmered in the light from the window, making the crack look even darker and more jagged than usual.

Broken. Just like me.

Fedilmid held it out to her, and she took it with a shaking hand. Without looking at it, she shoved it in the pocket of her dress.

"As for Doug . . ." Fedilmid stiffened at the henchman's name. "I saw him, of course. Right after you fell, he transported away." His lip twitched. "Leaving behind the most repulsive smell, at that. Worse than a billy goat after a swim."

"How did he get in?" Fable asked. "Doesn't the Windswept colony have a method to stop people like him from breaking in?"

"I don't know. Transporters are rare. I'm not sure if the colony thought about them while setting up their security."

"How did he know where to find us?"

Fedilmid uncrossed his knees and gave her a serious look. "I don't know that either. But it's worrisome. Perhaps he was spying on us at Mistford and one of us let our plans slip. We need to be more careful. I'm sure he's waiting outside the colony, watching for us. We will need to use our magical barriers tomorrow."

Fable's chest tightened at the thought of using her magic on her friends. Now that she knew without a doubt her magic was dark, she was terrified it would go off and hurt them. It had in the past. What if it did again? It was stronger now. And lately, her flames had been reacting to every one of her sharp emotions. She rubbed her forearms, frowning.

"Fable?" Fedilmid cocked his head. "Are you alright? Did you hear what I said?"

Fable choked out a breath. She couldn't tell her mentor that she was only alive because of *lich magic*—power that relied on destroying others to give its master life. And in this case, the sacrifice of her mother. What kind of damage could it have done to her soul, her essence, her whole being when she was so small?

She blinked back a tear, then gave Fedilmid a tight smile. “Yes. I understand. But do you really think Vetch will let us use magic on him?”

“Don’t worry about that. Let me take care of Vetch.” He studied her for a second. “Are you sure you’re okay?”

She nodded stiffly.

“Do you mind me asking what you saw in your memory?”

Fable’s jaw clenched. “It’s private. About my parents.”

“Okay,” Fedilmid replied gently. “I don’t mean to pry. But if it’s something tough and you want to talk about it, I hope you know I’m always here to listen.”

“Thank you,” she whispered.

If only it were that simple. *What am I supposed to tell him? That Endora is the only reason I exist? That she tore my mother’s life from her so I could live? That my flames really are dark magic, like I thought all along?*

Fedilmid got to his feet and patted her knee. “When you’re ready, hop up and help Thorn pack up your room.

We're heading out first thing in the morning."

He made his way to the door, then glanced over his shoulder at her. "I meant what I said about being here if you need someone to talk to. Seeing your parents' memories must bring up a whole mix of emotions. But, you know, they'd be proud of you and what you're doing—facing Endora and dealing with the Blood Star. They would be delighted with the person you've become."

Tears sprang to Fable's eyes as he closed the door behind him. Her flames licked at the edges of her mind, reminding her that Fedilmid's words couldn't be further from the truth. He had no idea what lay inside her.

It should be Stirling healing the star, not me. Just like Carina said, it's meant to reunite the mother and child. Not the twisted monster brought into this world by lich magic.

What am I supposed to do now?

Fable went up to her and Thorn's room and found it empty, the sole spider plant in the corner its only occupant. She packed her clothes in a rush, not wanting to be alone with her spinning thoughts about lich magic and how to heal the Blood Star. After shoving her suitcase beneath Thorn's bunk, she made her way out to the backyard to find her friends.

Timothy and Brennus waved to her from the garden, where they were gathering vegetables for the evening meal. Brennus knelt next to a row of lettuce, snipping off the heads with a set of shears. When Fable approached, he wiped the sweat from his brow with his elbow.

"You're awake! How's your head?"

"Yeah, how are you feeling?" Timothy plucked a tomato from the bushy plant before him and tossed it into the basket at his feet.

"Okay," Fable replied, eyeing the basket. "You're going to bruise the tomatoes throwing them like that. Your mom has told you that before."

He stuck out his tongue at her, then looked at Brennus. "She's fine. I guess the fall didn't knock any sense into her like I'd hoped."

Brennus snickered and cut another head of lettuce, then added it to the basket. "But seriously, are you okay? Your eyes did that zombie thing again. And you didn't wake up properly like last time."

"I know." Fable touched the back of her head. "Fedilmid healed my headache and told me what happened. I'm not sure why I didn't wake up."

Brennus balanced on his heels and squinted at her. "I bet hitting your head and having a ton of magic whizz through you might have had something to do with it."

"Yeah, maybe." Fable's gut clenched. *That and the realization that I stole my mother's life.* "Where's Thorn?"

"Talking with Flint." Brennus jerked his head towards the lattice windows of the top floor of the cottage. "Juniper went in there to save her about an hour ago. But they haven't come out yet."

Timothy jerked another tomato from the vine. Fable took it from him before he could toss it and set it gently in the basket. "Let me do that. We don't need to make Juniper upset too with squishy tomatoes."

"She's a lot nicer than Flint," Timothy said.

Fable winced. "Is it that bad for Thorn? I feel awful. I made the whole magic thing so much worse for her."

"Well," Brennus replied slowly. "You're not wrong. But what else were you supposed to do? Endora's henchman attacked you and tried to steal the *you-know-whats*." He wiggled his brows with each syllable.

"I know." Fable bit her lip. "But I heard Vetch say if it weren't for us, Doug would have never come here to begin with. And he's right."

Brennus stood, put the shears in the basket, and wiped the dirt from his hands. “Juniper said the council knows why we are here. They should have known that helping us find a phoenix to save Starfell from an evil lich and a raging dragon would come with some risks.”

“Yeah, but I feel bad for Thorn. When those other kids were yelling at her, it was awful.” Fable glanced at Timothy. “You didn’t even see that. Where were you? What took you so long outside?”

Timothy crossed his arms. “I was looking for the undead creeping around out there. Remember, the one you all told me wasn’t real?”

Fable’s cheeks grew hot. “That undead who’s always with Doug was out there? I’m sorry. You were sensing it the whole time, and none of us believed you.”

He tugged at the leaf of a tomato plant. “You never do.”

“Aw, come on.” Brennus patted his shoulder. “We’re all sorry. None of us thought Doug would find out we were here, but we should have listened to you. We will from now on, alright?”

“Alright.”

“Did you actually see the undead guard?” Fable asked.

Timothy scrunched his nose. “I’m not sure. I don’t

really remember what happened. The undead's pulsing got stronger around the trees, so I went over there. But then, something else came out of the bushes."

Brennus cocked his head. "What was it?"

Timothy's brows knit together. "I can't remember. It's weird. Everything's all blurry. It's like there was a shadow there, but I can't place it in my head. Then, screaming came from the tent, so I ran inside."

Brennus gave him a worried look. "Did you see anybody else out there?"

"Buckhorn," Timothy replied. "But only for a few seconds. He was on his way inside when I passed by him."

"That's weird." Fable pulled a few more tomatoes from the plant and set them in the basket. "Maybe we should talk to Fedilmid about it."

"I don't know. Maybe it was all the sugar going to my head."

"I don't think sugar makes people see weird shadows," Brennus replied.

Timothy rubbed his arm. "It was getting dark and the trees' shadows were huge. Maybe that's all it is."

Juniper's voice rang out through the yard. "Kids! Time to start cooking!" She stood at the glass doors, beckoning them to come in.

"We'll talk about this more later," Fable said, scooping up the basket of vegetables.

The kids made their way to the house and filed into the warm kitchen. Juniper was washing carrots in the sink, her sleeves rolled up to her elbows. Just as Fable set down the basket, Flint poked his head through the doorway. He met Fable's gaze and scowled, making the braided beard below his mouth twitch. Anger emanated from him like heat from a fire.

"Juniper, I'm heading out."

She twisted to look at him, still scrubbing a carrot. "Did you speak with Vetch?"

"I did." Flint grunted. "We came to an agreement. He'll fill you in."

With that, he stomped away, letting the door swing shut behind him. His footsteps retreated, then the front door slammed.

Fable let out a breath, her magic unfurling inside her. She joined Juniper at the sink as Brennus and Timothy left the room to wash up.

She picked up a carrot and began to scrub it under the running tap. "Um, Juniper?"

"Yes?" Juniper rested her hands on the edge of the sink.

Fable dropped her carrot and rubbed her cheek.

"I'm really sorry about last night. I didn't mean to cause trouble for you and Thorn."

Juniper sighed. "How can I be angry at such a sorrowful face?" She dried her hands on the dishtowel hanging from the cabinet door, then put her arm around Fable's shoulders. "It's okay. We'll figure things out with the council. We head out tomorrow anyway, so old Flint will have some time to cool off."

"Is what happened last night going to affect whether I'll be allowed to visit Thorn after she moves here?"

Juniper gave her a squeeze. "Not if I have anything to say about it. But let's worry about one thing at a time, okay? We'll head out tomorrow and find this phoenix. Like I said, it will take a few days, so Flint will have time to think things through. You did nothing wrong. In fact, you protected the people here from that transporter. I told Flint that. Once he's had a chance to think it over, and you've healed the Blood Star to use against Endora, maybe he'll have a change of heart."

Fable nodded, but her throat thickened. *Sure, I helped the colony now. But I'd acted on instinct, without control. What will happen when the lich magic takes over me?*

Should Flint change his mind? Or is he right in keeping me out of here?

An Unlikely Pair

Leena crept through the foliage behind Knox's wagging tail. The dire wolf padded silently along the soft ground, his ears perked and the hair on his neck standing on end. He stopped and let out a low growl, poking his nose through the needled branches before him. Leena crouched next to him, then parted the tree limbs.

In the small clearing before them, Doug sat on the ground with his head between his knees. His scraggly locks fell over his face, and he rocked back and forth, muttering under his breath. One of Endora's undead guards stood behind him. Its lifeless, empty sockets stared right at Leena from beneath the hood of its cloak.

Leena held her breath, watching the undead for a reaction to her presence, but it didn't move a muscle. Well, since it didn't have muscles, it didn't move a bone. Leena relaxed and scratched Knox's ears, her way of silently telling him *good work.* Knox rubbed his head on her shoulder, his tongue lolling out to the side.

She rocked back on her heels, thinking. How was she going to nab the henchman before he transported away? She didn't know how his magic worked, but he had to do something to trigger it. Some sort of movement or whispered phrase.

I better cover every base.

She studied the man. She could probably reach him from here, as long as she could keep the element of surprise. Tensing every muscle, she leapt from behind the bushes and landed on Doug with a heavy thump. He let out a shocked cry, but she rolled him over and pinned his arms to his sides with her knees, then covered his mouth with both hands. His eyes widened as he twisted his head away from her, trying to speak.

She pressed her hands firmer against his lips. "Promise you won't transport away, and I'll let you talk."

He glared at her, then gave her a slight nod.

She removed one hand, and he craned his neck and hissed through his teeth, as if about to mutter a spell. She clamped her hand back down and lowered her head so she was mere inches from his grimy face. "I have a dire wolf with me, and he'll hunt you down no matter where you transport off to. Do not make us your enemies."

As if to accentuate her point, Knox stalked from

the trees and growled menacingly. Despite his curled lips and flashing teeth, his tail wagged slowly behind him. Leena raised her brows. *He's enjoying this way too much.*

Doug relaxed beneath her and nodded again. Leena straightened and moved her hands, but kept her seat on him, still pinning his arms to his sides. The undead behind them remained still as a statue, looking off into the distance.

Some helper. It didn't even try to stop me.

Doug let out a breath. “Yer that girl from Endora's. Come to track me down fer her? I won't go. That beast is in meh head, and I can't block 'er out!”

Leena smirked. “No kidding? You can't block the immortal you've bonded to? I'm shocked.”

He glowered at her.

She sighed. “You can't block the dragon. That's the point of the bond. You're supposed to serve her. I don't know how Endora is doing it.” She paused. “I don't want to haul you off to the lich. I want to make a deal.”

Doug huffed. “A deal? Why should I believe yeh?”

“Because I know what you're after, and I can help you.” Leena paused, wondering how much information she should give a warlock bonded to the dragon. She unclenched her tight jaw. “I'm a warlock too. Not one of Halite's, obviously."

Doug gaped at her. He tried to wriggle free, but she clamped her knees tighter against his sides and pushed on his chest.

"By the looks o' yer hair, yeh must be one o' Brawn's. Halite hates Brawn."

Knox growled again, but Leena shushed him.

"Yes, I'm an Iron Wolf," she said. "But just because our patrons are enemies doesn't mean we have to be. Both of them want the same thing—Endora's destruction."

Doug gave her a wary look. "Halite wants more than that."

"Obviously," Leena replied. "All the patrons have other goals too. But both you and I want to be free of Endora. It makes sense to work together. And by the way," she added dryly, "last night I almost had that little boy entranced to steal the amulet, and I was going to offer it to you. But you had to ruin everything with your clumsy attempt to take it. And from a girl with more power in her pinky finger than you'll ever have."

Doug hissed again. "I am the most powerful transporter in Starfell! That's why Endora keeps me around."

"Great, but that's the only power you have," Leena

replied. "You're lucky that girl didn't blast you into next week."

Doug swallowed, glaring at her. "And how are yeh gonna help me? Halite's gonna eat me alive if I don't get her that amulet. And she'll eat both of us if she gets wind o' me working with one of Brawn's warlocks. Why do you want her to have the amulet, anyway? Won't it help her fight Brawn?"

"She won't fight Brawn. She's going to use the amulet to break through the boundary between the Oakwrath and the rest of Starfell."

Worry wriggled its way into Leena's mind, but she cast it aside. Once the dragon had the amulet, she'd blast right through that mausoleum portal, creating an opening for all the immortals to get through. Then Brawn would finally be free. And Halite would destroy Endora, and the other immortals would be free to stop her from burning Mistford to a crisp. They could find a way to heal the Life Tree, and the immortals could live peacefully in Starfell like they once did.

Leena bit the side of her cheek. At least, that's what she assumed would happen. If all went according to plan.

Doug's brows knit together. "And yeh think that's a good idea? To let the immortals free?"

"That's what they've wanted all along. That's why they have us—to help them get out of the Oakwrath."

"And what do yeh think they'll do with us once they're free? Yeh think they want ter keep giving us magic for nothin'? They ain't all good, yeh know."

"Halite might not be. But Brawn is." Leena gave him a hard stare. "Halite is bound by the immortals' rules. She can't hurt you unless you betray her."

"And how do yeh think she'll view me workin' with one o' Brawn's warlocks?"

"I'll talk to Brawn. We'll make sure she doesn't turn on you."

Leena wasn't exactly sure how. But while the immortals usually let each other deal with their warlocks however they saw fit, they had stepped in before when Halite had gotten out of line. She was sure they'd do it again. Especially if Doug helped her.

"Look," she said. "Instead of fighting Fable and her crew for the amulet, we can do it a much easier way. A way that doesn't doom us to lose."

"I'm listenin'."

"We can befriend them. Earn their trust. Then sneak away with it. With your transporting magic and my charming and memory wiping, we'd make a good team."

His mouth gaped open, revealing brown jagged

teeth. "You can charm people? Why didn't yeh use that on me instead o' wrestling me to the ground?"

"Because this is more fun." She bared her teeth in a wolfish grin.

He glared at her, pressing his lips together.

Ugh. Doesn't he know anything about being a warlock? She shook her head. "Halite would sense you being charmed. You're connected to her, remember? And she knows I have that power. She'd go after Brawn."

"Ah," he replied, furrowing his brow. "But them kids will never trust me. We have a . . . history."

"Then I'll befriend them. You can hide, and I'll find you when I get the amulet."

Sensing Doug wasn't about to transport away, she crawled off him and got to her feet.

He sat up, rubbing his neck. "What's the plan, then?"

Leena jerked her head at the undead, still standing as if rooted to the ground. "First off, you gotta get rid of that. The boy's a necromancer. He'll sense it following them."

Doug gave it a scornful look. "Done. It's been gettin' more and more obstinate. I'm tired o' it anyway." He pointed at it and raised his voice. "Oi, you! Get outta here. Go back to the grave or to Endora's or wherever it is yeh want ter go. I'm freein' yeh."

It jerked its head towards Doug with a sickening crack.

Leena's insides squirmed. "It doesn't have wants, does it? It's only a raised body. No soul."

"I dunno what it has or hasn't. And I don't care." Doug shooed it with his hands. "Git out o' here!"

The creature shuffled off, and Knox let out a whine. Every hair on his body bristled, and he looked to Leena as if asking if she was sure this was a good idea.

That thing's just creepy, like they all are. She shook off her nerves as it disappeared into the trees. *It's not right, raising bodies like that. Endora's got to be stopped, and if we need a dragon to do it, then so be it.*

SEVENTEEN

The Twisted Curse

Fable unzipped the top of the olive-green backpack at her feet and scanned the items inside it for a second time. Thorn stood next to her, reading the checklist her aunt had given them. Juniper's front yard was strewn with supplies—backpacks, sleeping bags, tent poles, and other various odds and ends. Everything they could need for a few days of hiking and camping in the mountains. Juniper had even given Thorn a double-headed axe that stood as tall as her chin, which was propped against Thorn's bag. Even Vetch had approved it. It was another reminder of how dangerous the wilderness could be.

The mid-morning sun bore down on them, and Fable's t-shirt clung to her back. Vetch had assured them the trees would provide cover from the heat, and the temperature would drop the higher they climbed out of the valley. At supper the evening before, he'd told them he had seen the phoenix nesting in a cave to the north of his watchtower. He figured they could get there in one full day of hiking, then wait and watch for the bird to begin its cycle. All evening, he had been straight to the point and avoided talking directly to Thorn and Fable. In fact, he hadn't even looked at them.

Now, he prowled the yard, going over supplies with a grumpy look on his face. Buckhorn trailed after him gingerly, as if trying his best to avoid the man's wrath. Fable sighed, wishing for anyone else to lead them.

Thorn ran her finger down the paper as Fable listed off the items in her backpack. "Sleeping pad. Sleeping bag. Waterproof bag for hanging food. Fleece sweater. Gloves. Water bottle. Sunscreen. Extra t-shirt and shorts."

Fable tugged at the khaki shorts Aunt Moira had bought for her. She preferred her summer dresses, but her aunt had insisted they weren't good for hiking. Fable had decided against reminding her how she had tromped through the Oakwrath Thicket in a dress.

"Oh, and of course, my book bag and the Blood Star." She patted the bag's bulk against her hip, finding a strange mix of comfort and fear in the sharp edge of the memory box.

There would be no experimenting with the tokens on this trip, but Fable couldn't bear to let the box stay behind. As much as its contents scared her, she was even more worried about losing them. They were pieces of her past that she hadn't put together yet. And while she was fearful of what else they would hold, she wanted the full message her parents had left for her. No matter how awful it may be.

Thorn checked the items off the list. "I've got our tent and some rope. I think Buckhorn is taking most of the food." She gave Fable a wistful smile. "You know, I haven't been camping since we met in the Burntwood. And that wasn't exactly fun. But before that, I camped a lot with my parents and Orchid. I miss it."

"Maybe we can go next summer," Fable told her. "After this Endora stuff is taken care of. I bet there are so many great spots around here."

If I'm allowed to come visit you. The evening before, Fable had tried to talk to Thorn about what had happened at the feast. But Thorn had told her she needed time to think. She'd said she didn't blame Fable for using magic, but the way she'd tossed and turned all night told Fable her friend was still upset. Now, Thorn's neck was bare and there was no sign of the speaking-stone or any of the greencraft herbs that had hung from her backpack before.

"There are! Juniper said Merrow Lake is gorgeous. And the Blooming Hills near the orchards have campsites too." Thorn grinned and shoved the pencil into her front pocket. "I know this is a serious trip, but heading into the wilderness to look for a rare magical phoenix is pretty cool."

Buckhorn approached them with his pack, then tossed it on the ground next to theirs. "Have anything extra you'd like me to carry? I still have room on the outside." He gestured to the clips hanging off his bag, which already bulged at the seams.

Thorn raised a brow. "Are you sure? It looks pretty full."

"Oh, I can fit more on the outside." He patted the top of it, then gestured to the package of dried beans Thorn had strewn with her things. "Actually, that'll fit inside it. I can shift a few things . . ." He opened his bag and rummaged around the contents.

Fable and Thorn exchanged amused looks.

"If you're sure," Thorn said.

Buckhorn tugged on the drawstring to open the backpack wide, and the top of an ornate mirror caught Fable's eye.

"A mirror?" she asked, gesturing towards it. "What do you need that for?"

Buckhorn flushed, looking unsure of what to say. After clearing his throat, he patted his tight curls. "Have to make sure my luscious locks stay in place, right?" He chuckled awkwardly.

Fable and Thorn both giggled. Fable hadn't taken the Folkvar man to be vain, but she had to admit, his hair always did look perfect.

"Want to see something cool?" He pulled the mirror from the bag. "I can make it bigger, to see my body—"

Vetch's angry voice pierced the air. "Are you kidding me? Buckhorn! You forgot the dried fruit *and* the roasted almonds? For crying out loud—go see if Juniper has some we can take."

Fable cringed. Vetch stood in front of Juniper's picket gate, glowering at Buckhorn and pointing at the cottage. Fable could imagine steam rolling off his head.

Buckhorn slumped his shoulders and gave the girls an apologetic look. He shoved the mirror in his bag. "Sorry about that. I better go check on the snack situation with Juniper." He started towards the cottage with a tight smile.

Fable leaned closer to her friend. "It'd be a lot cooler if Vetch wasn't guiding us."

"Agreed." Thorn pressed her lips together, giving the ranger a sideways look.

He avoided her gaze and went back to sorting through the pile of dried food and snacks at his feet, murmuring something to himself.

The front door slammed, and Brennus and Timothy strode towards the girls, Brennus slinging his backpack over one shoulder as they walked. Timothy had his on already, the waist belt snug around him. With that and his red ball cap, he looked like one of the wilderness scouts from Larkmoor.

When they reached Fable and Thorn, Brennus tugged on Timothy's pack, making the boy stumble backwards.

"Are you going to be able to carry this for a few days?" Brennus asked with a grin.

Timothy snorted. "I'll be fine. But you might need Thorn to carry yours."

"Nah. She'll already be carrying Fedilmid's." He hooked his thumb over his shoulder, and Fedilmid and Algar came out as if summoned by his words.

Fable gaped at Fedilmid as he strode over to them with his chest puffed out like a proud peacock. He'd swapped his usual robes for trousers that matched Algar's—and seeing how baggy they were, Fable figured they probably *were* Algar's—and a flowy tunic covered with stitched flowers that reminded her of the robes he'd worn to the Lammas feast. He smiled at them from beneath a wide-brimmed straw hat.

"Wow," Timothy said, looking him up and down. "You look . . . different."

"Algar helped me find the right outfit. I couldn't risk ruining my robes." Fedilmid adjusted the strap of his backpack, which looked more fit for a five-year-old child than a man.

Brennus gave him a wry grin. "What's with the bag? Are you packing camping gear or colouring books?"

Fedilmid squinted at him, then grasped his bag's strap and leaned his head closer to the kids. "Don't let looks fool you. You could fit a whole pterippus in here." He caught Fable's gaze. "I'm not about to let Vetch dissuade me from using my magic. I'm a grown witch, after all."

"Besides," Algar added, turning to the side to show off his massive backpack. "I'm hauling most of our things. Tent, camp stove, both sleeping bags."

Fedilmid lifted his chin. "And I have all our hygiene products, books, and my cashmere blanket. I will not suffer on this trip."

Algar shook his head, then looked at Brennus and crooked his finger. "Can you step aside for a minute? I talked to Alice this morning, and she had some news we need to discuss."

"News?" Brennus cocked his head. "What about?"

Algar looked across the yard at Vetch, then back at Brennus. He lowered his voice. “Your parents.”

Fable tilted her head. They hadn’t seen Brennus’s parents since they were in Stonebarrow last month. She had taken Halite’s amulet into their shop without realizing it powered the store’s magical movements. It had shifted right as the kids had tumbled into the street, and they’d had no idea where it had gone. Without the amulet, wherever the shop was, it was stuck.

“My parents? Did the store somehow shift without the amulet?” Brennus waved his hand at his friends. “You can tell me in front of them.”

“Well, no,” Algar replied slowly, running a hand over his beard. “The store didn’t shift. Alice got a message from them.”

“A message? How could they get a letter to a post office? They can’t leave the store. Ralazar won’t let them have a phone. And they don’t have magic like Fedilmid’s flying mail.”

Fedilmid snapped the buckle on his backpack strap and cleared his throat. “Isla sent it with Roarke.”

“Roarke?” Fable asked. *The messenger raven?* “But he works for the warlocks. Why would he go to the Odd and Unusual shop?”

“Ralazar,” Brennus croaked. “He must be at the store.”

"But how?" Thorn asked. "We left him in the Oakwrath. There's no way he could have gotten away from both Endora and Halite."

"I don't know how, but he did." Algar crossed his arms. "And according to your mother's letter, Brennus, he's hiding in the store."

The lines on Fedilmid's forehead crinkled with worry. "And the store isn't only powered by the amulet. It was also created with its magic."

"So?" Brennus asked.

Fedilmid clasped his hands in front of him, giving Brennus a sympathetic look. "If you destroy the amulet, you will destroy the entire store. With them inside it."

Brennus looked thunderstruck. He dropped his backpack to the ground, his hands shaking. "No. How else am I going to break their curse? That can't be right."

Fable reached out to take his hand, but he marched away from them, heading around the cottage towards the backyard. Timothy went to follow him, but Thorn grabbed his backpack to stop him.

"Give him a few minutes to cool off," she said. "I know how he feels. He needs to think for a bit."

Fedilmid sighed. "This is disappointing. For him and for all of us. I had really hoped destroying the amulet would be the answer."

"Is there a way to get the Tanagers out of the store before he destroys it?" Fable asked.

"Perhaps," Fedilmid replied. "We need to talk to his parents to figure out our options. And unfortunately, we don't have time or the means to do so before we reach the phoenix. We're going to have to help Brennus figure out another way to break their curse."

Near the front gate, Vetch shielded his eyes from the sun with his hand and shouted at Fedilmid and Algar. "Where's he off to? We need to get moving if we're going to make it to Baldy Pass tonight. This is no easy hike."

"Give him a minute," Algar shot back.

"We needed to leave like ten minutes ago!" Vetch curled his hands into fists and gestured at the cottage. "And where is Buckhorn? I'm sick and tired of waiting around for people!"

Algar opened his mouth to shout again, but Fedilmid laid a hand on his forearm.

"Let me handle this," he said softly, but his blue eyes were sharp. His head high, he marched over to the ranger.

"That man needs a lesson in manners," Algar grumbled. "Don't any of you kids listen to him when he gets harping like that. He's afraid of people who can use magic, something he can't understand." He took a deep breath. "I'll go see what's taking Buckhorn so long."

He tightened the waist belt of his backpack, then made his way inside the house.

Timothy's lip trembled as he watched the man go. "What is Brennus supposed to do now? The phoenix fire was supposed to save his parents. Not kill them."

"I don't know," Fable replied, her heart clenching. What could he do? This trip was not going as they had planned at all.

What if all this effort was for nothing? If the ashes didn't heal the Blood Star and they couldn't destroy Halite's amulet, this would be a waste of time. Time that could have been spent finding other ways to defeat Endora and break the warlock's curse.

I guess no matter what, we will still heal my grandfather's memories.

Vetch caught her eye over Fedilmid's shoulder, and his scowl deepened. And now, they had a ranger who didn't want to help them in the slightest. In fact, the look on his face told her he wanted nothing to do with them.

Moira Nuthatch entered Nestor's study, holding a steaming cup of lemongrass tea. From the overstuffed armchair in front of the fireplace, Stirling glanced up from his crossword puzzle and gave her a nod in greeting. Rain pattered against the windows, but it was still too warm to start a fire. Moira sighed as she made her way to him, longing for autumn's cooler weather to arrive.

She set the tea on the side table beside Stirling, then patted his shoulder. "Do you need anything else before I head down to help Alice prepare the breakfast buffet?"

Stirling shook his head, balancing the puzzle book on his knee. "I'm fine. You can stop fussing over me."

"I just want you to be comfortable," Moira replied. "If that's all, I'll leave you alone now." She moved towards the door, but Stirling's huff made her stop.

He placed the book and pencil on the table and twisted to look at her. "I'm sorry, Moira. I shouldn't be so sharp with you. There's so much going on, and I forget where I am half the time." He waved a hand before him. "This whole mess with my past and memory . . . I don't even know who I am."

Moira's chest tensed. *He must be so confused. First, I jerk him out of the only home he can remember, then tell him I'm his daughter-in-law and introduce him to his grandchildren, who I then send off to find a way to defeat his evil mother and heal his amnesia. And now, I'm dragging him around to retirement homes in Larkmoor. Of course he's cranky.*

"It's alright, Stirling. I know this is confusing for you. And you're right, it is *a lot.* It would be even for someone with all their memories intact. We'll get this sorted out. Did you like the home we visited today, Mistford Meadows?"

He pressed his wrinkled lips together. "It's alright. For an old folks' home, I guess."

"The apartments were pretty nice with those views of the Shimmering Meadows. And the menu looked great." She tilted her head, adjusting her bun. "And I feel pretty good about my interview. If I get a job there, it would be a perfect fit for both of us."

"Like in Larkmoor, with all those nurses bossing me around and making me eat gelatin salad?" He scowled.

Moira patted his shoulder again. "Mistford Meadows is nothing like Larkmoor Manor. The nurses seem better trained. And Mr. Ling, the man who interviewed me, seemed a lot more compassionate than old Dr. Dumont." She tapped his crossword puzzle on the table. "They even have a puzzle and board game club you might be interested in."

He huffed again, then looked at her out of the corner of his eye. "Thank you for putting up with an old grouch like me. And for caring."

"Of course I care about you. Whether or not you remember it, you are the father of my one true love."

Over the last decade, she'd been so busy raising Timothy and Fable that she'd barely had time to grieve her late husband. But every time she looked at Stirling, she saw Thomas in his smile. In the way Stirling laughed and how he rubbed his chin when he focused.

She blinked back the mist forming in her eyes. "Now, enjoy your tea and your puzzle. If you need anything more, I'll be in the kitchen with Alice."

He gave her a nod. As she made her way towards the door, her gaze landed on Nestor's desk. The books piled high upon it reminded her of the kids, and her heart hitched. She stopped next to it, running her hand over the cover of an astronomy textbook Brennus had been reading before they left for the Windswept Mountains.

She missed them and their silly antics—Brennus's jokes and Thorn's dry wit. Even Timothy and Fable's bickering. And of course they bickered. Not only were they as close as siblings, they had been through a great deal of trauma together because of Endora. The woman who was supposed to be their family—someone who loved them. But she was never that person and never could be. Moira had always known that. So had her husband and Fable's parents, Morton and Faari. They had all agreed to never allow that vile lich anywhere near the kids.

Tears brimmed in Moira's eyes. *And yet, here we are. Thomas, Morton, and Faari gone. Because of her. And me, Fable, and Timothy fighting for our lives, yet again. Fighting for Thorn's and Brennus's lives too. And despite everything these kids have faced, they always choose to do the right thing. To stand by one another. To face these horrible things together.* Moira's chest swelled with pride. They were good kids, and they'd been through more than any child ever should.

She tapped the textbook's cover with trembling fingers. *And they shouldn't have to deal with any more danger*. That's why she'd gone to the Mistford police station that morning to speak with Sergeant Trueforce again. And while he'd brushed her off just as he had done with Fable and Fedilmid, she'd managed to talk the receptionist into booking her a meeting with the chief of police. Tomorrow, she would go above Trueforce's head. And she wouldn't leave until the chief took her warnings about Endora seriously.

Why can't that old woman stay in her mansion and

leave everyone alone? Moira rubbed her temples. *After her nonsense is taken care of, I will make sure all four of the kids have a normal, peaceful life. School, friends, learning their magic, the latest video games—that's all that should be on their minds. They shouldn't be tromping through the wilderness, chasing after some mythical bird, hoping to stop an evil lich and save Brennus's parents.*

Had she done the right thing, letting them go on this quest? She'd talked it over with Fedilmid, Alice, and the others until they were blue in the face. Fedilmid and Juniper had assured her the children would be safe with them and her ranger friend. That there was no way Endora could know where they were.

But the lich always shows up where she's least expected. Look how she appeared in the Oakwrath of all places. Of course, how were the kids to have known she would cast a spell on that amulet and track them there? Moira's throat thickened as she fought to push down her rising panic. *But that's the problem. Juniper and Vetch don't know everything that horrible woman is capable of.*

She pressed her palm to her forehead, trying to soothe her frazzled nerves. It wouldn't do any good to fret now. As much as it scared her, she'd promised to trust Fable and Timothy more. To allow them to grow into their magic and take some responsibility. *And they're with Fedilmid and Algar. They're safe.*

After releasing a breath, she glanced at the floor and caught sight of something grey poking out from behind the desk leg. She knelt to get a better look. A rock the size of her fist lay on the floor behind it.

What's that doing in here?

When her fingers met its rough surface, her magic whirled to life like a brisk breeze around her. Her protection song burst from her lips without a thought. She clutched the rock tighter, her mind whirling, but she couldn't stop singing.

What's happening to me?

A golden aura formed around her. Before she could cry out in alarm, it swarmed her vision, and she toppled backwards.

Mountain Rumbles

Fable stepped into the cool shade of the forest and breathed a sigh of relief. They'd only been on the trail for three hours, and she was already exhausted. The unrelenting sun had borne down on the group the whole time they'd hiked through the meadow from the colony, and the day had soon become unbearably warm. She'd had to focus on holding the magical barrier around them with Fedilmid so they could keep out of sight, which only added to her fatigue. But it was worth it to make sure nobody like Doug would follow them.

Now, she scrambled after Thorn, barely keeping up with the Folkvar girl's long strides. Ahead of them, Vetch paused with his bow in his hands, scanning the sky. Brennus, Timothy, and Buckhorn moved to the shade on the side of the trail, then dropped their packs and sat on the grass. Thorn joined them, but remained standing, and propped her axe against the nearest tree. She grabbed her water bottle from the side of her pack, then took a big swig.

Fable glanced behind her at Fedilmid, who wiped his brow with a polka-dot handkerchief. Beside him, Algar combed his fingers through his damp beard.

"Do you think it's safe to drop the barrier?" she asked, shifting her backpack to ease her aching muscles.

Fedilmid looked behind them at the meadow, then jerked his chin at Timothy. "What do you think, Timothy? I didn't see any signs of Doug or undead creatures there in the open. Do you sense anything?"

Timothy closed his eyes and stretched out his hands. Vetch glared at him, his jaw tight, but he didn't say a word. He hadn't spoken to any of the kids since leaving Juniper's cottage, which was fine with Fable.

"Nothing big," Timothy replied. "Just the usual tingle of little things, like bugs. Definitely no undead."

"How can you tell?" Buckhorn asked, his cheeks as red as Juniper's ripe tomatoes. He clutched the straps of his backpack near his shoulders, slumping over with exhaustion.

"The air. It vibrates differently for different things," Timothy replied. "I can't miss an undead. They give off a cold, heavy pulse that chills me to the bone. Bugs are only little zings." He pointed to the bird skull on his wrist. "This thing helps me tell where—"

Vetch grunted, and Timothy shut his mouth and lowered his arm.

Fedilmid and Algar exchanged a look, then Fedilmid tucked his handkerchief into his front pocket. "I think it's safe now to drop the barrier. At least while we're in the trees. But Timothy, let us know if you sense anything bigger than a jackalope. We can't be too careful."

Timothy pushed back his ball cap. "A jackalope?"

"A rabbit with antlers," Thorn replied.

"Does it have magic?"

"The power of cuteness," Brennus said.

Thorn snorted. "Combined with the power of goring your calves if you aren't careful."

Timothy's eyes widened, and Algar shook his head. He smoothed his hand over his now-tangle-free beard. "As long as we don't corner one, we'll be fine."

Feeling Fedilmid's magic ease away from them, Fable let hers drop. Instantly, weight lifted from her shoulders. "That's better."

"How much farther to your tower, Vetch?" Brennus asked, snapping off a long blade of grass. He spun it in his fingers.

Vetch lowered his bow and gestured up the trail. It wound through the trees, climbing higher and over a snow-covered mountain pass. Mountains loomed on either side of it with steep slopes. "My tower is on the other side of Baldy Pass. Still a few more hours. If we don't get a move on, we won't have time to set up camp before dark."

Buckhorn squinted at the sky. "It's only mid-afternoon. We have plenty of time."

Vetch levelled a sharp gaze at him. "With how long you take to set up a tent, we need to get moving."

Buckhorn's cheeks grew even redder, but he heaved himself to his feet. "Fine. But for the record, I'm not that slow."

"And he has our help," Timothy said.

Vetch pressed his lips together, then started up the trail and didn't look back. The arrows in the quiver on the side of his backpack rattled with his strides.

Fable and Timothy exchanged glances. *What is Vetch's problem? He's supposed to be helping us.*

The boys got to their feet and started after him and Buckhorn, and Fable fell into step with Thorn. Fedilmid hummed cheerfully behind them, letting her know that he and Algar were bringing up the rear. Fable hadn't been sure how Fedilmid would do on such a long hike. Algar was used to walking around the Lichwood foraging and keeping watch for undead guards, but

Fedilmid spent most of his time with his nose in a book or pruning plants in his greenhouse. But so far, he'd been keeping up fine.

The light weight of his magical backpack probably helps. Fable thought enviously of the tiny pack, trying to ignore her aching back.

They hiked up steep switchbacks for what seemed like several hours, and Fable's legs wobbled with every step. She was grateful for the distraction from her usually-racing thoughts. Instead of worrying about the Blood Star or Brennus and the amulet, she had to focus on putting one foot in front of the other without giving up. Everyone was silent as they climbed. Even Fedilmid stopped humming.

When they emerged from the trees, the temperature dropped, chilling Fable's clammy skin. She rubbed her arms as a breeze swept over them. The trail disappeared, covered by a blanket of slushy snow. Thorn stopped beside her and pointed at a purple flower poking out from a high spot where the snow had drifted away.

"That's a crocus. They only grow in cooler climates." She glanced down the path behind them. "We must be getting pretty high. Look, through the trees you can see the valley way below us."

Fable turned around and followed her gaze past

Fedilmid and Algar, who had fashioned walking sticks from fallen tree branches and were poking them into the snow for balance. The lush green valley lay far below them, the log gates to the colony barely visible now. The fluffy clouds in the clear blue sky seemed so low that Fable could imagine Thorn or Vetch touching them.

The snow beneath Fable's feet softened, and she sank a few inches. *How deep is this stuff?* After righting herself, she asked, "Where did Vetch say the phoenix's den is?"

"On the other side of the pass, I think. Near his watchtower." Thorn took a step, her foot slipping through the snow until she was knee deep in it. She poked the snow with the end of her axe, and it sank through it too. She shielded her eyes with her hand, studying the terrain ahead of them. "This snowpack seems loose. With the heat, it must be softening. It's probably ten or fifteen feet deep under the frozen crust. Maybe we should ask Vetch if it's a good idea to cross the pass right now."

"He must have noticed. I don't think he'd want to go up there if it wasn't safe," Fable said, glancing at the ranger. He stood with his back to them, gazing out over the scenery. Brennus, Timothy, and Buckhorn had stopped beside him, balanced on the hard-packed snow and sharing a bag of nuts and dried fruit.

She patted the side of her backpack, wishing she could feel the comfort of her book bag's soft material. But she'd tucked it safely away inside the pack, not wanting it to get in the way or become damaged on the trail. She thought of the broken star inside it, and her stomach knotted. Now that they were getting close to their goal, would it all be worth it? Would they be able to collect the phoenix's ashes for Stirling? And would she heal the star and regain its power?

The image of Endora with her hand on Faari's rounded belly flashed in Fable's mind. *Do I even want this to work? Shouldn't it be Stirling fixing the star by meeting with Endora, like Carina said?*

"Oh, wow!" Thorn's gasp jerked Fable from her thoughts. The Folkvar girl squatted next to a plain-looking yellow flower poking out from the snow on the edge of the up-slope beside them. She set her axe on the rocks and gently touched the petals. "This is hawkweed! My dad used to sharpen his tools with its juice." She gave Fable an excited look. "A single coat of hawkweed juice could make this axe cut through stone or cement with one blow."

"Wow!" Fable leaned closer to take a look.

"That's really cool."

She plucked another flower with a purple cone-shaped head that reminded Fable of lavender. Breathless, she held it up for Fable to see. "I think this is woundwort! I've never seen it before. But my dad told me it repels dark forces and spells cast with malicious intent. Alice told me that was right, but it's really rare."

Buckhorn's voice floated over them. "You mean when these weeds are used for greencraft?"

Fable's stomach churned. Vetch glared at Thorn with his hands curled into fists. He moved towards them, and his feet slid several inches in the soft snow.

Buckhorn took a step away from the man, swaying with the weight of his pack. "Er—sorry. I didn't mean magic. Of course not. That hawkweed must only be really potent . . . juice. With sharpening properties."

Thorn tucked the flower into her pocket, avoiding Vetch's gaze, then picked up her axe with a sigh. "My parents never called it greencraft. But I guess it's the same thing, really."

"I told you. *No magic*." Vetch spat the words.

Thorn lifted her chin. "I didn't use magic. But you didn't seem upset about the barrier we used to prevent Doug from spotting us leaving the colony."

Vetch squared his shoulders, pushing his wavy hair

from his face. "Sometimes you have to pick the lesser of two evils." He jabbed a finger in her direction, gritting his teeth. "And we don't need the barrier anymore, apparently. No more magic. Period."

Fable scowled at him, wishing once again that he wasn't their leader. With Thorn's knowledge and experience in the forest, he would be lucky to have her as a fellow ranger. But he was letting his fear and hate get in the way. How could he have convinced a phoenix to trust him? The bird must ooze magic and power.

Timothy rested his elbows on his knees. "Aren't we finding the phoenix to use its magic? That's the whole point of this trip."

"Again," Vetch barked. "The lesser of two evils. The worst being Endora Nuthatch. If magic is the only thing that can contain her, then unfortunately, we need it for that. But for anything else, I forbid it."

"Now, Vetch," Fedilmid said, leaning on his makeshift walking stick. "Thorn was only talking about a plant and how her father had used it. She didn't break your—"

The snow shifted beneath him. His eyes widened, and he raised a wizened hand, pointing at the pass ahead of them. Fable spun around, and her heart leapt to her throat.

The snowpack moved like a raging river beneath

their feet. A rumbling noise thundered around them, and Fable scrambled over the moving snow, desperately trying to stay on top of it.

"To the side!" Vetch shouted, gesturing wildly to the rocky, snow-free slope to their left.

Thorn grabbed Fable's hand and they ran over the moving snow, slipping and sliding. Brennus's shout behind them made Fable's stomach churn, but she had to keep moving or risk being swept away with the avalanche. When they reached the up-slope, Thorn thrust her onto the shale. She grabbed the nearest rock outcropping and clung onto it with one brawny arm, clutching her axe with her other hand.

Snow and ice sprayed around them, blinding Fable. The roar of the careening slide was like nothing she'd ever heard. Her magic whirled, fighting to be let loose, her emerald flames flaring. She tried to think of something she could do to save them, to save herself, but couldn't. All she knew was the mind-numbing, frantic desire to survive.

Is this how we're all going to die? Who's going to stop Endora now and free Brennus's parents? Is this how frightened her parents had been when they'd died in that rockslide? With her face pressed against the rock, she let out a sob.

After what seemed like hours but was probably only seconds, the noise stopped. Silence surrounded Fable. She lifted her head, pushing away a layer of cold, wet snow. Her T-shirt and shorts clung to her, soaked with water now instead of sweat. Her arms ached, and she let go of the rock and slumped into the snowbank that now covered the slope.

Timothy's voice rang out. "Fable? Thorn? Is everyone okay?"

She opened her eyes and spotted him and Brennus huddled together behind a boulder on the slope above her. Thorn was digging her way out of a waist-deep pile a few feet below Fable, and Buckhorn lay clinging to a tree down near the edge of the forest.

"I'm fine!" she shouted back to him, her voice trembling. She scanned the pristine white landscape, squinting against the sun's reflection. "Where's Vetch? And Fedilmid and Algar?"

"Down here!" Buckhorn's voice was high with panic. "Come quickly. Vetch isn't moving!"

Thorn pulled herself from the snowy hole and slid down to him on her stomach, holding her axe beside her. Fable got to her feet and dropped her backpack, then raced after her friend. Luckily, with her lighter weight, she was able to skid across the top of the snow.

A wall of snow, ice, broken tree branches, and shale had pushed up against the edge of the treeline. Buckhorn had already taken off his pack and was digging furiously into the base. Thorn tossed her axe aside and dropped to her knees to help him. When Fable got closer, she noticed Vetch's limp body, only his torso sticking out from beneath the snow.

Brennus and Timothy skidded to a stop behind her, gasping for breath.

"Is he okay?" Brennus asked between huffs.

"I don't know!" Fable held her cheeks as Thorn and Buckhorn pulled Vetch loose and lay his body flat.

Thorn placed her fingers on his neck, then looked over her shoulder at Fable. "He's alive, but unconscious."

Her heart thundering in her chest, Fable stumbled down to the trio at the base of the mound, landing next to Thorn on her bare knees in the cold snow. Vetch lay between them and Buckhorn. His arm was bent at an awkward angle, and his hair lay flat against his head. His cheeks were so pale he looked like he could be dead, but soft breaths escaped his lips.

Fable lay her hands on his chest and closed her eyes. Electric blue energy pulsed weakly inside him—his life. The soul that a lich like Endora would be hungry to steal. It slowed beneath her hands, fading from the ranger's body.

Is he dying? He can't! Fable barely knew him, but she couldn't let him slip away. Maybe she'd been too hasty with her judgement, never asking about his life or the reason he hated magic. She didn't even know if he had family waiting for him in some cottage in the Windswept colony. Did he have a spouse? Or kids?

Fable took a deep breath, loosening her chest and embracing the white light inside her. She allowed it to move through her and into Vetch, mingling with his energy. She could feel the stream of power moving throughout him, feeding and strengthening his life force. Her light grew so bright in her mind, she was sure it must be shining from every part of her.

But when he sputtered and Fable opened her eyes, there was no white light around her. Only the sunshine beating down on them, reflecting off the snow. Thorn and Buckhorn both let out relieved breaths as Vetch sat up and pushed Fable's hands away from him.

Fable startled at the snap in their connection. He stared at her with wide eyes and pushed his damp hair from his face.

"You're okay," she told him, wiping her hands on her shorts. "I'm sorry I used magic, but I had to—"

"You're a lich," he choked out.

She rocked back, his words hitting her like a punch to the gut. "Excuse me?"

"Only a lich can give and take life like that." He pushed himself to his feet, his arm clearly not broken any longer. Colour rushed to his face. "I should be dead."

Buckhorn raised his hand towards the ranger. "She saved you."

Fable hugged her elbows, horror creeping through her. "I didn't give you life. I could feel your force inside you. It wasn't gone. I helped you heal."

Vetch shook his head, his face drawn. "I was dying. No healer can give life like that."

Before Fable could reply, he stormed away from them, heading down the edge of the snow wall.

Thorn stood, her eyes yellow with rage. She picked up her axe, gripping it with white-knuckled fingers. "That's it. I've had enough of that skullcap and his temper. You just healed him, and that's how he treats you?"

Fable held back the tears pricking her eyes. "Thorn—"

"No! I'm done with his attitude. He says magic hurts people, but he doesn't stop to think about how he hurts them too." She stomped off after him, looking more terrifying than she had in a long time.

Fable let her go.

Vetch's words burned in her mind—*you're a lich.* Buckhorn tried to catch her eye, but she avoided his gaze. Fedilmid had once told her she was the strongest healer he'd ever encountered. Was it because she wasn't simply a healer? Had Endora turned her into a lich before she was even born?

That's not how it works. To gain lich magic, you have to do something evil. Her mouth went dry. *Was it evil to have taken my mom's life? But I didn't have a choice!*

"Fable!" Brennus waved violently in her direction. "Fedilmid and Algar. They're on the other side of the snow wall! I can hear them yelling."

No! She leapt to her feet, sliding through the snow. Her heart thundering, she tried to steady her emotions for Fedilmid and Algar's sakes.

If she truly had lich magic, at least she could use it to help her friends. And if it took years off her own life, then so be it. As long as she didn't steal anyone else's.

Lost Guidance

As Fable ran by Timothy and Brennus, her cousin grabbed her shoulder. “Fable, wait! It’s not safe.”

She shrugged him off and touched the base of the sloped wall of snow with her foot. It loomed at least twenty feet high. She stepped ankle-deep into it, then dropped to her stomach, careful to avoid the broken branches jutting from the snow. After pulling herself a few inches without sinking, she began to scramble up the incline.

Brennus groaned. “Fable, come on. There has to be another way.”

She paused, looking around the pass. The snow wall stretched all the way to either end of it, drifted against the edges of the steep mountain slopes. “How?”

He rubbed the back of his neck, his face drawn. “I don’t know. Be careful, okay?”

“I’m always careful.”

Timothy and Brennus spoke in unison. “No, you aren’t.”

Murmured shouts that sounded like Algar came from the trees on the other side of the snow wall. Fable pushed harder, scrambling as fast as she could go. Crusted snow, broken twigs, and rocks stung her hands. By the time she reached the top, her whole body burned, but her only fear was for her elderly friends.

She lay on her stomach at the top, then grasped a branch of one of the trees the snow had wedged against and peered down. About twenty feet below her, Algar sat with his back against a boulder, holding Fedilmid's torso in his arms. Both their packs lie on the rocky ground nearby, covered with dirt and debris.

Fedilmid moaned, and relief swept over Fable. *They're both alive.* She'd read about avalanches in the Windswept Mountains in her schoolbooks. Glancing at the snow-covered mountains around them, she realized how lucky they were that only the snow on this pass had loosened—probably because of the hot sun and the group's weight on top of it. Had a whole mountainside come barrelling down, she was sure they'd all be dead.

Fable gripped the tree branch tighter and called down to them. "Are you hurt?"

Algar glanced up at her. His frizzy beard formed a halo around his face. "I'm fine! But Fedilmid had a good tumble. I think he broke his leg."

Fedilmid pushed against his husband's chest, trying to sit up. "It's not too bad!"

"Would you lay still?" Algar rumbled. "You're going to make it worse."

Fedilmid collapsed against him, wincing with pain. "You might be right."

"Can you heal it?" Fable asked.

"My healing powers aren't like yours. I can't mend bones." Fedilmid wheezed, then placed his hands on his shin. "I can ease the pain, but that's about it."

Brennus's voice floated up from behind her. "Does it look safe to go to them?"

Fable looked down, studying the other side of the mound. With the way the snow had built up against the trees, it formed a solid wall of uneven snow and broken tree limbs. Her heart thudded in her ribs.

As if reading her mind, Algar raised his hands. "Stay put, Fable! The last thing we need is for you to get injured too."

Fable's throat tightened. She glanced over her shoulder at the boys. "No. I don't know how we're going to reach them. Does Vetch have a phone? The colony must have a wilderness emergency team or something."

"Didn't you see that old corded phone in Juniper's

house?" Timothy replied. "I doubt they have cell service anywhere in these mountains."

Fedilmid shouted, "You're going to have to go on and find your phoenix. Algar and I can make it down to the colony ourselves."

A frustrated tear ran down Fable's cheek. "With a broken leg?"

I can't do this without Fedilmid. He was supposed to be there to help me heal the star. To keep me from going bad. He's my guide!

The snow beneath her shifted, and a crunching noise made her look at the bottom of the mound. Thorn and Buckhorn had joined the boys, both of them looking fraught. Vetch glowered at them from a few feet away, his arms crossed.

"Well?" Fable shouted at the Folkvar man. "What's the plan? You're supposed to be the expert!"

He met her gaze, but he didn't respond.

Algar's voice came again. "Vetch thinks the phoenix is going to turn any time now! You have to push forward. Once Fedilmid eases his pain, we'll make our way to town. Going slow won't kill us, and we have our supplies."

Fable fumbled with the tree branch, her hands numb with cold. "No! We can't leave you in the wilderness alone."

"Do you think Algar has never managed in the wild before?" Fedilmid asked. "Fable, it will be okay. You don't have to look after us."

Fable's gut roiled. She wanted nothing more than to find a way down to heal her mentor. The thought of the two elderly men on their own in the forest gave her goosebumps. What if they came across one of those chimeras Vetch had talked about? All the rangers around the colony carried weapons. Who knew what else lived in these mountains?

"Fable?" Fedilmid called up to her.

She dug her fingers into the tree bark, trying to ease her anxious thoughts. "Y-yes?"

Algar hollered, "For once, could you listen to reason?"

Fedilmid sputtered. "Algar, that's not what I wanted to say! Fable, we will be fine. And you can do this without me. You can heal the Blood Star. With Vetch's help, you can earn the phoenix's trust."

She thought of Vetch's grim face from only moments before and groaned. *He doesn't want to help me with magic. And maybe he shouldn't.*

Thorn's voice met her ears. "Fable!"

Fable turned her attention to the group on the other side. With her back to Vetch, Thorn pulled her speaking-stone from her pocket. “I’m going to contact Orchid. Maybe the warlocks can send a messenger bird for help. Or come here themselves.”

Even from her perch on the snow mound, Fable could see Vetch stiffen. He rubbed his jaw, but said nothing. Thorn faced him, holding up the speaking-stone, and said something Fable couldn’t hear.

Thorn can deal with him. He’s got to accept her magic now. The lesser of two evils, he’d said. What could be more evil than letting Algar and Fedilmid fend for themselves out here? This situation definitely fit into the ranger’s rule.

Fable switched her focus back to the old men. Algar had left Fedilmid propped against the boulder and was digging through his husband’s backpack. He frowned, soon shoulder deep inside a bag no bigger than his forearm.

“Did you think we were moving out here?” He shook his head, then pulled out a polka-dot teacup and gaped at Fedilmid. “When exactly were you planning to have a tea party?”

“Just find the cashmere blanket, please.” Fedilmid placed his hands on his knee, his grey brows furrowing in concentration. “I’m cold, and this magic is taking a toll.”

Algar’s expression softened, and he pulled a

royal-blue blanket from the bag like a magician pulling a ten-foot handkerchief from his pocket.

"Are you okay for a bit? Thorn's getting hold of Orchid," Fable shouted down to them. "They can send a messenger bird to the colony to get help."

"So she did bring the speaking-stone!" Fedilmid grinned and gave Fable a thumbs up. "Smart girl. We'll be A-okay."

Fable's panic eased. She smiled shakily as Algar lay the blanket over Fedilmid's shoulders. He rubbed Fedilmid's back, saying something she couldn't hear.

She cupped her free hand around her mouth and shouted to them again. "I'm going to talk to the others. I'll check in before we leave."

The two men waved her off, and she let go of the branch and began to slide towards the other group on the ground. Now, she believed Fedilmid's words that he and Algar would be okay. They had each other.

Her emerald flames pushed against her, and she forced them aside. But who would help her keep her magic in check now? How could she possibly heal the star without her mentor? And if she was a lich, would it even work?

Maybe the star broke after she connected to it because she was a lich. Because she was filled with dark magic—exactly like all of Endora's creations.

TWENTY

A Dark Surprise

Fable sighed, leaning into the warmth of the campfire as she rubbed her aching calves. She sat on one of the log stumps before it. Because of the avalanche, they hadn't been able to make it all the way to Moonflower Tower. After hiking over the snowy pass for several hours, they'd descended into mud, which had made their trek even more difficult.

When the sun had begun to set, Vetch had brought them to this campground, which was used by the Folkvar rangers when they made their rounds through the forest. Fable and her friends had claimed this spot near the trail, while Vetch and Buckhorn took the other one in the trees nearby. Through the darkness, a flicker of orange light showed they had started a campfire too.

Brennus's voice sounded behind her, and she twisted to see what he was up to. The edge of the firelight cast an eerie glow across her and Thorn's tent, where Thorn was now chatting with Orchid through the speaking-stone. Her axe lay propped against a tree between their tent and the boys' half-erected one.

Brennus balanced the top of the two-person canvas tent with one hand and motioned to Timothy with the other. "Put that pole through the middle hole."

"I am!" Timothy replied, hidden on the other side of the canvas.

"No, you're not. That's the corner, not the middle!"

Fable giggled and called out to them. "Do you need help?"

"No!" both boys said in unison.

With a swishing sound, the tent flopped over, and Brennus scrambled to right it.

Fine then. I'd rather rest, anyway. Fable stretched her sore arms, then peered at the star-dotted sky, trying to pick out the Gaea constellation. *There are thousands of stars up there. How do the astronomers pick out the different lines and shapes? I wonder if Brennus can do that yet.*

She squinted, thinking she'd picked out a shape that could be two hands with their fingers entwined. But she wasn't sure. It could also be two snakes wound together. She tilted her head. *Or maybe it's part of something bigger, like a Folkvar with hair like Thorn's.* She tucked a loose strand behind her ear, wondering if Carina would teach her to read the stars. Her heart hitched at the thought, torn between wanting to get to know her new mentor and mourning her loss of Fedilmid as her guide.

He said I would always be like a granddaughter to him. That means he and Algar will visit. And I'm sure they'll let me stay at Tulip Manor sometimes.

She had more important things to worry about right now, such as finding a phoenix, healing the Blood Star, and gathering ashes for her biological grandfather. According to Antares's timeline, they only had a day or two until the phoenix would cycle. Surely Vetch had a plan to reach it in time.

She held her free hand over the warmth of the fire, breathing in the fresh scent of pine and wondering how they would approach the phoenix's den. She assumed Vetch would have to go inside first to assure it they meant no harm. *What is its den like? Vetch said it was nesting. I wonder why? It's not like it has to lay eggs if it recycles its own life.*

Vetch's firepit sparked in the distance, sending embers floating into the air. The adult Folkvars' silhouettes stood out against the orange light. Fable hugged her elbows, frowning. *Is there any point in asking Vetch about the phoenix? If I go over there, he'll probably leave or avoid my questions with grunts and scowls.*

And after I saved his life!

Fable picked up the stick leaning on the log next to her and inspected its blackened end. Clearly, it had been used as a fire poker by the last campers there, so she jabbed it into the flames. The logs collapsed to ashes, creating a bright flare of light. Heat puffed over her.

Vetch thinks I'm so evil he won't even sit with me. She thought of what he'd said after she healed him—that she was a *lich*. That no normal healer could give life the way she had. *Which is crazy! I didn't siphon away someone else's life for him.* A lump formed in her throat. Even if Endora's dark magic was sewn into the fabric of Fable's being, she would never steal anyone else's life.

Her gaze fell on Vetch's campsite again, which was barely visible between the trees. *But he seemed so sure about it. And my healing magic is different from Fedilmid's. Fedilmid said so himself. Even if I'm not a lich, what if I'm still warped by the lich magic that saved me? What if it's slowly turning me into one?*

Her emerald flames snapped to life inside her. They rolled gently down her arms, but she didn't have the energy to fight them. She bit her lip, remembering the memory that had proven she *was* different. That she had been formed with lich magic. While her mother had been crying and waiting for Endora, she'd had that paper with the compulsion spell in her hands. Had Endora refused to help her, Faari had clearly planned to use the spell on the woman.

Optempero. A spell to bend someone to your will. Fable's magic warmed, as if liking the idea. *If only I could use it on Vetch to make him change his mind about magic.* Her stomach lurched. *No. How can I even think that? Forcing someone to do what I say, even if they don't want to—that's evil, no matter the reason.*

She threw the fire poker to the ground, then held her head in her hands. Her emerald flames simmered around her, engulfing her as tears brimmed in her eyes. *What is going on with me?*

Brennus's voice warmed the cold silence. "Er—Fable? Are you okay?"

She blinked back her tears, then raised her head. He stood next to the fire, eyeing her warily. She swallowed a sob, forcing her flames to recede inside her.

"I'm fine," she said, shaking her wrists to make sure her magic wasn't about to break out again. "Sorry about the flames. They're under control. I . . . I'm just worried about Fedilmid and Algar."

"It's okay." Brennus's expression relaxed, and he sat on the stump next to hers, resting his elbows on his knees. "I'm worried about them too. But Thorn said Orchid told her that Roarke was on his way. And Algar knows how to survive in the woods."

Fable sniffed, looking towards his crooked—though now at least upright—tent. "Where's Timothy?"

Brennus jerked his thumb over his shoulder. "He went to make sure there's no undead creeping around out there."

Fable's spine stiffened. "Alone?"

"Thorn went with him." Brennus shrugged. "Don't worry. Between her axe and Timothy's necromancy, I'm sure they could take on a whole hoard of undead."

Fable grimaced. "Imagining a hoard of undead stalking through this forest does *not* make me feel better."

Brennus chuckled and nudged her with his elbow. "They'll be fine."

He reached into his pocket and pulled out a brass pocket watch. *The amulet.* Fable sucked in a breath, peering at the fire-breathing dragon etched on the front of it. *Leave it to Fedilmid to make its magical disguise a fancy one.* The etching blurred. She blinked, and the dragon dissolved. A dome of green glass replaced it. A second later, it blurred again, and the brass cover returned.

Brennus caught her eye, then rubbed his thumb

over the dragon, making it fade again. "Fedilmid's spell is wearing off. It's been slipping since we reached the top of the pass. I think it must only work when it's near him."

Fable tilted her head. "I guess it doesn't matter, does it? Everyone here knows it's the amulet." She paused, thinking of what Algar had told them earlier that day—that destroying the amplifier would also mean destroying the store, possibly killing Brennus's parents. "What are you going to do with it?"

Brennus's eyes turned glassy. He scrunched his nose in the familiar way that told Fable he was trying to hold back his emotions. "I don't know. I can't burn it and risk hurting my parents." He groaned. "We need more time to figure this out. I should have stayed with Fedilmid and Algar. If I could have talked to Roarke, maybe he could have gone to the shop and told my parents to get out. Then I could throw this thing into the phoenix's fire and be done with it."

Fable shook her head, her heart aching for her friend. "That still wouldn't work. They can't leave the store. You know that. They're magically bound to it."

Brennus threw the glitching amulet on the ground between his feet. His voice cracked. "It's not fair. I've been trying so hard to find a way to break Ralazar's curse. To save them from a life of misery. I thought I had it figured out." He scrubbed his face with his hand. "Why can't we have normal lives?"

Fable looped her arm around his. "I'm so sorry. We *will* find a way to break that curse so you can be with your parents again. Maybe we can ask Carina and Antares. There might be things written in the stars about Ralazar and his curses."

"Maybe." Brennus nudged the amulet with his toe, glaring at it. "But if that's true, why wouldn't Nestor have shown me that already?"

"I don't know. I wish I had the answers for you."

Fable rested her head on his shoulder, and he leaned his cheek against her hair. They sat for a few moments in silence. Brennus's anxiety and grief pulsed around them. Fable's flames pushed against her seams to meet his emotions, but she held them back.

She thought of her mother's spell again. *What if I compelled Ralazar to let them go? I read the spell. I know how to do it.* Bile rose in her throat, and she pulled away from Brennus. *Stop thinking like that! What is wrong with me?*

Crunching footsteps came from the trees behind them, and they both glanced over their shoulders. Thorn, Timothy, and Buckhorn came marching over the dry grass and into the ring of firelight. Timothy held an open bag of marshmallows. He took one out and popped it into his mouth.

"Any zombies out there?" Brennus asked.

Timothy shook his head and swallowed his mouthful. "No. Just bugs and a small prey animal. A jackalope maybe? I tried to find it, but Thorn said we shouldn't wander off."

"She's right. You shouldn't." Fable glanced at Buckhorn, who grabbed a marshmallow from the bag in Timothy's hands. *So now Buckhorn knows about his necromancy. What if he tells Vetch about it? What's he going to think of Timothy's powers with the dead?*

As if reading her mind, Buckhorn gave them all an amused look. "I wish we'd found a skeleton or something that Timothy could make dance around. I've never met a necromancer before."

"You're not afraid of his powers?" Fable asked.

Buckhorn blew through his lips. "You know I'm not like the other Windswept Folkvars. Remember, I grew up with solitary parents and even learned a few wizard tricks."

The tension eased from Fable's shoulders. "Oh, that's right. I forgot. So you won't tell Vetch? I don't want to make him any crankier about us."

Buckhorn pretended to zip his lips. "Promise. And you're right, there's no need to make him even more thorny." He paused. "No offense, Thorn."

Thorn chuckled and clapped him on the back. "None taken. You'll have to show us some of those wizard tricks when Vetch isn't around."

"While we're talking about magic," Brennus said. "Thorn, did Orchid say if Roarke told her where my parents' store is?"

Thorn's brows knit together. "Why would he tell her that? He can't tell her anything he's not directed to."

"Even if Ralazar is holding people against their will?"

Thorn frowned. "The warlocks' rules and codes are complicated. You know that."

Brennus huffed, crossing his arms. "Seems pretty straightforward to me."

Fable slapped her knees. "No bickering, please. I can't take any more grumpiness on top of Vetch's. Can we focus on something else?"

"Like toasting marshmallows," Timothy agreed, shoving another white puff into his mouth.

Thorn gave him a sideways look. "Yeah. Before you eat them all."

Buckhorn wiped his hands together, then jerked his head in the direction of Vetch's fire. "I told Vetch I'd gather some more firewood, so I better do that before he wonders if a chimera dragged me off for dinner." He stretched his arms over his head. "And then I can finally get some rest. I don't know about you all, but I'm beat from today."

"Me too," Timothy replied, stifling a yawn.

Buckhorn went to move past them, but tripped on a raised tree root and fell to his knees, knocking into Brennus. Brennus and his log seat toppled backwards into the dirt, and Brennus let out a loud "Oof!"

Fable leapt up from her log stool. "Are you two okay?"

Buckhorn sat upright, his cheeks flushed. "I'm so sorry! I swear, sometimes I have two left feet."

"It's okay. No harm done." Brennus scrambled to his feet and wiped the dirt from his jeans, then held out a hand to Buckhorn. "Here, let me help you."

Buckhorn took his hand and pulled himself to standing. After apologizing again, he patted his front pocket and strode off into the trees.

Timothy gazed after him, chewing thoughtfully. "How's he going to get firewood without an axe?"

Fable bit the side of her cheek. *And since when*

is he so clumsy?

"He's probably collecting dead fall from the forest floor," Thorn replied.

Brennus picked up the amulet from the dirt and pocketed it, then went to a nearby tree and found a stick longer than his arm on the ground beneath it. He held it out to Thorn. "Speaking of axes, can you sharpen the end of this with yours?"

Thorn took it from him, hefted her axe with her hand close to the curved head, and proceeded to carve the end of it into a point. When she held it up to inspect her work, Timothy stuck a marshmallow on the sharpened end, and then she handed it to Brennus. After the rest of them had gathered a few more branches from the forest floor and had Thorn sharpen them, they all stood around the fire, watching their treats turn golden brown.

When Fable's marshmallow looked toasted, she pulled it from the embers and held the end of the branch in Thorn's direction. "Do you want this?"

Thorn cocked her head, still holding her marshmallow over the red-hot coals in the firepit. "Aren't you hungry? Mine's almost done."

Fable shook her head. "No. Not really."

Thorn shrugged and picked the gooey treat off

Fable's roasting stick with her free hand, then ate it. After licking her lips, she glanced at Fable. "Are you okay? Your face looks pale."

"You're worried, aren't you?" Timothy asked, inspecting his perfectly toasted marshmallow. "You never eat when you're worried."

Fable sighed and leaned her stick on one of the stumps. "Antares said we only had six or seven days to find the phoenix before it burns. Tomorrow is day six. What if we don't get to it in time?"

Thorn frowned, rotating her marshmallow over the coals. "Aunt Juniper has faith in Vetch. We should too. Even if he is a skullcap, he's a good ranger."

Brennus glowered at the fire as he turned his marshmallow. "Do you trust him? He's made his feelings about us pretty clear. He hates magic. Why would he help us with a magical quest?" He pressed his lips together. "I bet he's scheming to ruin our plans. I say we ask Buckhorn where the den is. If he knows, we can ditch Vetch and find the bird ourselves."

Thorn's eyes crinkled with worry as she glanced at Vetch's fire. "He said he wants to stop Endora."

"Why does he care about stopping her?" Brennus pulled his marshmallow from the fire. "Sure, he hates liches. But he's safe in the colony. It's practically a fortress."

Timothy ate his treat, then set the bag and his roasting stick on the log beside him. He wiped his hands on his shorts. "Doug got inside it though, and he works for Endora. He could sneak her in."

Brennus frowned and chewed his marshmallow, then grabbed another from the bag.

"Juniper told me the phoenix trusts Vetch," Fable said. "I think we need him to get into its den. Isn't it the size of Thora? I'm sure it could kill us if we scared it."

Thorn nodded and swung her stick away from the fire. She blew on the marshmallow, her brows knit together in thought. "My dad used to say you can calm a phoenix by singing to it."

"And how many phoenixes did your dad meet in the Greenwood?" Brennus asked.

Thorn ate her marshmallow in one bite and licked her fingers. "None. But the colonies kept in contact. I'm sure someone from the Windswept one told him that."

"What kind of song?" Fable asked.

"I don't know. Probably a lullaby or something soothing."

Brennus snorted. "Maybe 'Happy Birthday', and you have to bring it a cake too."

Thorn rolled her eyes.

A dark shape moved at the edge of Fable's vision,

startling her. She whirled towards it, her magic swirling down her arms with a burst of green light.

"Put your magic away and *sit down*," a deep male voice hissed. Vetch emerged from the trees with an arrow knocked and aimed at the bushes on the other side of the path. He came to stand next to Fable, and she stiffened. The firelight danced across his face. With his jaw set and a bulging neck vein, he looked like a warrior about to kill.

"What are you doing?" Brennus demanded, holding his pointed stick like a sword. A gooey marshmallow drooped off the end.

Thorn grabbed her axe, then widened her stance and held it in front of her with both hands. Timothy tossed his roasting stick to the ground and clutched the bird skull on his bracelet.

"Show yourself!" Vetch shouted, his gaze still trained on the bushes. "I heard you prowling around, spying on these kids. You won't get away."

A low whine echoed through the clearing. A shadow so dark Fable thought she must be imagining it stepped through the foliage. Glowing red eyes blinked from its depths, and Fable recoiled. The creature slunk into the sphere of orange light, its hackles raised, glowering in Vetch's direction.

One of Endora's hounds!

Memories of being chased through the Lichwood by them swept over Fable, and her emerald flames burst forth, dancing from her fingertips. She readied herself to hurl them at the beast.

Thorn raced forward with her axe held high, her eyes blazing yellow. The hound snarled, its white fangs flashing in the firelight and its scraggly hair standing on end. It gnashed its teeth as Thorn approached, and panic shot through Fable.

It's going to attack her! She shot a fiery blaze of magic at the creature, but it darted to the side with a yelp, narrowly escaping her blast.

"Stop!" An unfamiliar woman's voice echoed around them. "That's enough. Knox, heel!"

Knox? That hound has a name?

Thorn halted, her nostrils flaring, still holding her axe up, ready to strike. The hound huffed and sat, watching Thorn with its blood-red eyes.

"Who goes there?" Vetch demanded. "I will shoot if you don't reveal yourself!"

"Calm down, Ranger Boy." A slight woman with scruffy grey hair that reminded Fable of dandelion fluff slipped out from behind a tree. "A bit jumpy, aren'tcha? You might want to lay off the organic mushroom coffee or whatever it is you Folkvars drink."

She went to the hound's side and patted its head. Its ears drooped and it licked her hand. Fable's mouth fell open. *That thing is tame?*

The woman smirked and put a hand on her hip. "Lower your weapons, Folkvars. You can't seriously be afraid of this cute little puppy." She scratched the hound's chin, and it wagged its tail. "We're not here to hurt you. We're here to help."

The Enchanting Newcomer

A cloak of calm fell over Fable, and she took a soothing breath. A comforting breeze cooled her hot cheeks. Her heartrate slowed, and she dropped her arms, allowing her flames to recede. An inexplicable sense of peace rippled through her. She didn't know why, but she felt they could trust this strange woman.

Vetch lowered his bow with a confused look. The yellow faded from Thorn's eyes, and she rested the end of her axe on the ground. Brennus and Timothy both gave the woman affable grins.

"That's better." The woman strode up to Thorn with the hound at her heels. Her wild grey locks barely reached the middle of the Folkvar girl's chest. She took the axe from Thorn's hand. "You won't be needing this, friend. I'm no threat, right?"

Thorn nodded slowly. "Right. You seem nice enough."

Something didn't seem right, but Fable couldn't put her finger on it. Not that she really wanted to.

She hadn't been this relaxed since her days at Rose Cottage, before she knew she had a murderous great-grandmother. With a sigh, she plopped down onto the stump behind her.

"How are you here to help us, miss?" Vetch's voice was soft, even friendly, which was jarring coming from him. He slung his bow over his shoulder. "No offense, but we don't need help. We're on a mission."

Fable stifled a giggle. *No offense? Has Vetch been possessed?* She tried to catch Brennus's eye, but he was looking dreamily at the spritely woman, who leaned Thorn's axe against the tree beside him. She strutted to the fire and held out her hands to warm them.

"You may need more help than you think." She kept her gaze on the fire as Vetch and Thorn joined her. "My name is Leena. And I know you're trying to stop Endora."

"Leena?" Fable's chin jerked up. Her magic sparked, but it only took a second to settle. "Like the Leena who helped save my friend Star?"

Brennus gasped. "The warlock spy?"

Vetch straightened. "The *what*?"

"That must be why you can train that hound." Timothy reached out to pat it, but it sidestepped his hand, moving closer to Leena. "You're one of Brawn's warlocks."

Leena's lip curled in a smile, and she ran her hand along the hound's back. "Knox is not trained, and he's not a hound. He's a dire wolf. I saved him once, and now he's loyal to me. But he's free to go any time he wants to." She paused, peering at Fable intently. "I'm not sure who Star is, but you all seem to know an awful lot about me."

"She's one of the firehawks Endora held captive in her stable," Fable replied.

Thorn ran a finger along the speaking-stone's chain around her neck. "Yeah, my sister, Orchid, said you helped the Jade Antlers with their rescue."

Leena's brows lifted. "Oh! One of those adorable chickens. Yes, I may have persuaded Doug to look the other way while the Jade Antlers went to get them."

Persuade Doug? How? The only person he'd listen to is Endora.

Brennus held up his hand. "*Fire-breathing* chickens, you mean. Star unleashed her fire breath in front of me once." He frowned. "And it was anything but adorable."

Leena's gaze met Fable's. "You're Fable, then. I knew the moment I saw your eyes. You're the spitting image of your great-grandmother, you know?"

Heat shot up Fable's neck. "How do you know—"

"And that means you're Thorn, Brennus, and Timothy," Leena said, gesturing at the three of them. "Star and Orchid told me about you all." She frowned at Vetch. "Who are you?"

Timothy's cheeks flushed. "That's Vetch, the ranger who's guiding us. And Buckhorn's around here somewhere."

Vetch grunted, then narrowed his gaze at Leena. She gave him a sweet smile, and his expression softened. "How can you help us with Endora?"

Leena paced around the fire. Knox followed, his tail wagging. If Fable let herself forget he had glowing red eyes and teeth longer than her fingers, he would remind her of a puppy bounding after its mom.

"Well, for starters," Leena said, "I've been spying on Endora as a servant for a few months now. So I have a lot of inside info about the lich."

Timothy pushed his bangs from his eyes. "How did you stop her from—"

"What kind of info?" Vetch asked.

Leena stopped and looked him up and down. "Info such as the fact that she's coming after the phoenix too. She thinks its magic can break her bond to Halite."

Fable jumped to her feet, her flames swirling to her fingers. Her pulse thrummed through her, blocking every ounce of peace she'd felt before. "She's coming here? When?"

Leena met her gaze and grasped the tooth pendant around her neck. Instantly, Fable's shoulders relaxed. The warlock cleared her throat. "I imagine it'll be soon. I left before I could find out more, but she has that book. You know, the one with everything about Starfell." She fluttered a hand.

"The Magic and Lore of Starfell." Fable slumped onto her seat, remembering what Fedilmid had told her last summer about the book. "It writes the history of Starfell as it happens."

Leena snapped her fingers. "That's right. You're smart, aren't you, little spellcaster?"

Vetch shifted his bow on his shoulder and rubbed his chin. "How can you stop Endora from coming here?"

Leena tugged her sleeve over her wrist and held it with clenched fingers. "I doubt I can outright stop her. According to Orchid, no one besides Miss Fable here can do that. But I can distract her."

"How?" Thorn asked.

Leena examined her fingernails. "I have a certain power. That's all you need to know. I've used it on Endora twice now, and it worked both times. At least, I was able to slow her down."

Fable wanted to ask her what kind of magic could do that, but another wave of soothing energy washed over her, and she completely forgot what she'd been about to say. Leena gave her a cheeky wink, and Fable's chest warmed. She liked Leena. After all, the warlock had saved Star and her flock. She must be trustworthy.

Vetch cleared his throat. "You lived in Endora's mansion?"

"That's what I said."

"Did you see a portrait of a Folkvar woman there?" He flicked his gaze to the fire. "Thicker build with curly blond hair."

Fable's chest tightened. "How do you know about Endora's portraits?"

He averted his gaze. "Today wasn't the first time I looked death in the face."

"I'm sorry." Leena moved to his side, leaving Knox sitting next to the fire, and rested a petite hand on his muscular forearm. "I saw a few portraits with Folkvars inside them, including a female with blond curls. They were all still. Lifeless."

Vetch let out a slow breath, and tears misted his eyes. "I thought as much. Thank you for being honest."

"I really am sorry it turned out that way." Leena

patted his arm, and he leaned in to her touch.

Fable's stomach grew queasy. *So that's Vetch's history. He did lose someone to Endora. That explains why he's still helping us.* Her heart pinched. *No wonder he's so angry.*

Suddenly, her sadness melted, replaced with the same calm energy that had hit her earlier. Her head felt light, and when she looked at Leena, she felt drawn to the warlock. *We can trust her. She must be telling the truth. How else would she have gotten away from Endora without having some kind of strong power?*

Timothy's sleepy voice floated through the air. "Hey . . . Were you at the Lammas feast?"

Leena jerked her gaze to him. "Excuse me?"

He rubbed his head, looking confused. "Your hair. It reminds me of the shadow I saw in the bushes. And I remember feeling all floaty and happy like this—"

"Of course I wasn't there." Leena crossed her arms, her jaw tense. Knox let out a whine, and she put on a forced smile. "The Windswept council has no idea who I am. How would I even get an invitation to one of their biggest annual feasts?"

Brennus shook his head, as if to clear cobwebs from his brain. "Then how do you even know about it?"

Leena's jaw dropped. "I—"

"You *were* there!" Timothy pointed at her. "And you're doing whatever it is you did to me again!"

A crashing noise came from the trees where Leena had first appeared. Knox leapt up and trotted to her side. Vetch knocked his arrow and raised his bow again, and everyone whirled to face the sound.

"Who goes there?" Vetch demanded. "Buckhorn? Is that you?"

Silence hung around them like a foreboding shadow, then another twig snapped.

"Show your face, or I'll shoot!" Vetch shouted, pulling back the arrow.

A voice that sounded like tires crunching on gravel came from the trees. "Don't shoot. Yeesh. Yeh Folkvars aren't as peaceful as I was led ter believe."

Fable's jaw tensed. *Is that Doug? What is he doing here?*

With a few more rustling footsteps, the henchman stepped into the firelight with his arms in the air. His greasy hair hung over his dirt-smeared face, and his knee-length slicker hung off him in ragged tatters. He peeked around his arm at Vetch. "I mean yeh no harm."

"Doug!" Timothy scowled.

Fable jumped to her feet, her magic writhing inside her like a snake, begging to strike out at the man. She flexed her fingers, letting it flare, but gritted her teeth to keep it under control. *No more accidents. If Doug steps a toe out of line, I have to direct it towards him and him alone.*

Brennus gestured at Vetch. "Keep that arrow on him. Doug works for Endora, and he is not a good guy." His lip twisted as he glared at the henchman. "Is Endora here? Is that why you're hiding out there, spying on us?"

Vetch held his arrow aimed at Doug's chest, and Thorn stormed over to her axe and picked it up.

Doug gave Leena a desperate look. "No! I'm with Leena. I left that old bag Endora." He glanced around him as though she were lurking nearby and had overheard him.

Timothy quirked a brow, crossing his arms. "You're with Leena? Yeah right. And where's that undead guard who's always with you? I can't sense him."

"It was no use ter me anymore," Doug replied. "An' she didn't like it, so I sent it off. No idea where it's at, but it ain't with us."

Brennus gave the warlock a questioning look, and Fable's stomach pinched. *Maybe Leena and Doug are working together then. They both live in Endora's mansion. They must have left there with Doug's portal magic. But there's no way they're here to help us! Doug would never go against Endora.*

Leena groaned, rubbing her temples with one hand. "Well, the secret's out. Thanks to you, Dougie." She glared at him. "Yes, he's with me. But if he keeps messing up our plans, he won't be for much longer."

The truth hit Fable like a slap. *How could I have fallen for her lies? That fake charm oozing out of her!*

Her flames flared. Thorn's eyes flashed yellow, and she raised her axe.

Doug covered his head with his arms, cowering. "Stop! I'm not 'ere to make trouble."

Leena held up her hands towards Fable and Thorn. "Wait! It's not what you think. He doesn't work for Endora anymore."

She locked eyes with Fable.

A warm feeling like a hug surrounded Fable, loosening her chest. She let out a breath, and her arms relaxed. *Of course. Leena wouldn't lie. She saved Star, after all.*

"Stop doing that!" Timothy's voice snapped.

"Doing what?" Leena's voice dripped with false innocence.

"Whatever it is you're doing to Fable! What you did to me at the Lammas feast and made me forget."

Leena looked at him, and his eyes drooped.

Brennus gripped Timothy's shoulder, glowering at Leena. "Hey! Stop it."

"Enough!" Vetch barked, turning his arrow to Leena. "I know witchcraft when I see it. Leave the boy alone."

Leena chuckled, tugging at her sleeve. "Witchcraft? I'm no witch, Ranger Boy."

Fable shook her head to clear the fuzzy thoughts floating inside it. Her flames swam within her, as if confused by all her emotions—real or magically induced. She took a step closer to Leena. "What is going on here? Who are you? And what do you really want?"

Leena rubbed Knox's ears and looked at the ground. "We escaped together. Doug, me, and Knox. None of us want to serve her anymore, and we definitely don't want her to get the Blood Star."

"How do we know you're telling the truth?" Brennus demanded. "You just put some spell on us to make us like you. Or something weird like that."

"I only helped you calm down a bit." Leena rolled her eyes. "I didn't want Ranger Boy here to shoot Knox." She paused. "Or me, for that matter."

Doug straightened, his hands still above his head.

"She's right. The lich made meh do things I never wanted ter do. And now I have this dragon screamin' in meh head all day and night. I want out. I want Endora ter go down. But she's on 'er way here, and that's bad news fer all o' us."

"And you can slow her down?" Vetch asked, still aiming his arrow at Leena.

Leena lifted her chin. "Yes. Lower that arrow, and let's chat."

Vetch did as she said and jerked his head towards a log on the other side of the fire. "You both sit there, hands on your laps. And no magic. Got it?"

"Bossy, aren't you?" Leena replied, but she went and sat on the log with Doug. Knox padded after her and lay at her feet. The dire wolf looked at Vetch with its crimson eyes and growled, his lip curled to show his fangs.

Fable pulled her magic inside her, but let it smoulder at her seams. *There's no way I'm trusting this warlock. Not when she's in cahoots with Doug. What is it they really want?*

For a split second, her mind turned to the compulsion spell. She could make them talk or even go away. She could force them to do anything she wanted them to. Nausea welled in her stomach. *No. Leena just tried to control my feelings, and that was bad enough. That compulsion spell is even worse!* She clenched her jaw, pushing the awful thought away.

TWENTY-TWO

A Warlock's Bargain

Fable took a seat on the log stool between Thorn and Brennus. Timothy sat on Brennus's other side, watching the warlocks warily. Vetch loomed over the barrel-sized log that Leena and Doug sat on. His bow was now slung over his shoulder, but he twirled an arrow in his hands. Doug looked at it from the corner of his eye, and his head twitched. Leena kept her gaze on Knox, who lay at her feet, clearly ignoring the Folkvar's attempt to intimidate them.

Fable glared at the warlock. Her flames crackled beneath her skin, waiting to be let loose. "There's no point in denying it. You were at the Lammas feast, and you used your power on Timothy and helped Doug attack me. Why?"

Leena pushed her scruffy bangs from her eyes and gave Fable a defiant look. "Oh, give me a break. I didn't help Doug attack you. I didn't even know—" She swallowed. "He was supposed to stay hidden."

Timothy snorted. "Yeah, right. You messed with

my memory. What did you make me forget?"

Leena sighed, fiddling with the hem of her sleeve. "I only asked you to bring Fable outside. I enchanted you to make you more agreeable and sent you inside to get her so you could 'show her something cool'." She looked directly at Fable. "Would you have come outside if Timothy had told you some strange lady was out there asking for you?"

"I probably would have gotten Fedilmid to come with me," Fable replied.

"Fedilmid?"

"My mentor. He's a witch."

Leena rubbed her wrist, and Knox lifted his muzzle and licked her hand. "Well, I didn't think you'd come out, and I wanted to talk to you about Endora. Doug wasn't supposed to get involved." She shot him a disgruntled look. "He stormed in there on his own to get your attention. Clearly, he didn't think it through."

Fable touched her shoulder, grasping for her book bag's strap. But she'd left it in her tent, thinking it would be safe. Now, with Doug here, she wasn't so sure. "He tried to steal my book bag."

Doug gave Leena a nervous glance, shifting his seat. "Er—only ter lure yeh outside ter talk to Leena. I didn't mean ter scare yeh or make yeh pass out or whatever."

Brennus crossed his arms. "I don't believe you. You had to have known the Blood Star was in her bag. You were trying to steal it for Endora."

Doug's face turned beet red, and he rose from his seat, pointing at Brennus. "Look here, yeh little br—"

Leena grabbed his arm and yanked him down beside her.

He straightened his filthy collar, then gave the kids a gruesome smile, showing his brown teeth. "I wasn't after that stupid rock."

"Listen." Leena leaned her elbows on her knees, stroking Knox's head. "We want nothing to do with Endora. I never truly worked for her. Orchid told you I was a spy, right? And you trust Orchid."

Thorn shifted, furrowing her brows.

"And Doug is tired of her abuse," Leena continued. "Once she figures out we've both betrayed her, she's going to come after us. You know that as well as we do."

Knox let out a low whine, leaning into her hand.

She gave him a loving look. "Plus, I let one of her dire wolves free. In her mind, that means I stole him. She will want revenge, and there's no way I'm going to let her trap me again."

She caught Fable's eye, and that now-familiar

comfort settled over Fable. Fable dug her fingers into her palms, letting her flames burn away Leena's power. Instead of warm fuzzies, hot sparks of anger filled her chest.

"Stop using your magic on me! This is why I think you're trying to trick us. You won't let us make up our own minds; you keep trying to sway us into liking you."

Leena's eyes widened. She ran a hand over her head, flattening her poufy hair and letting it spring up again. "Look, I'm sorry. I'm only trying to make this easier to swallow. I know it must be hard to trust anyone who's worked for Endora." She drew a deep breath. "Nobody else has done that, by the way."

Fable glowered at her. "Done what?"

"Broken through my enchantment the way you did. Not even Endora could do it."

Fable bit her lip, for once grateful for the raw power of her magic. She hadn't directed her flames to burn through Leena's spell, but she certainly didn't mind that they had.

Leena gave Fable an earnest look. "We can leave if you want. But Endora is on her way, and we *can* help you. We want to help you, because it helps us too."

Vetch tapped the arrow against his thigh, his brows so close together they touched. "You still haven't told us how, exactly. Get on with it or leave."

Leena smirked at him, smoothing her sleeve. "You are cantankerous, aren't you, Ranger Boy?"

He scowled at her, gripping his arrow with white-knuckled fingers.

Leena chuckled in reply. "Calm down. I'll *get on with it*, as you so kindly requested." She looked at Fable and her friends. "As you all know by now, my powers involve enchanting people to soothe them and sway them to be friendly towards me. I can also fog people's short-term memory."

Thorn crossed her muscular arms. "That's not right, erasing people's memories."

"I don't erase memories. That's not how it works—"

"She makes your thoughts blurry," Timothy said, avoiding Leena's gaze. "Like the images are all shadows, and you aren't sure what happened."

"That's horrible," Fable said, thinking of her memory box. Could someone like Leena change those memories? Hope flickered inside her. *Maybe they aren't accurate . . . Maybe Endora had someone tamper with them.*

Leena rubbed her wrist, frowning. "I can't adjust memories that already exist. I can only alter ones with me in them, and it has to be done in the moment."

"So while you were enchanting me, you were also making sure I'd forget it." Timothy clenched his hands into fists.

"I was merely confusing you."

Timothy scoffed. "Because that's so much better."

"Is there a point in all this?" Vetch growled. "You can't make Endora forget about the phoenix. How is her being nice to you going to help us?"

Leena pressed her lips into a firm line. "When she shows up, I will enchant her. Calm her down. Then Doug can transport her away. Dump her off in the Deepwood Swamp, and he can *poof* away before she even knows what happened." She paused, looking at Doug. "Oh, or maybe in the Oakwrath for Halite to deal with."

Doug gaped at her. "I ain't goin' near that dragon!"

"How do we know you won't turn on us?" Brennus asked. "I can't trust any good feelings I have for you."

"It's up to you." Leena shrugged. "I don't want her to have the Blood Star. I don't want her severing her ties to Halite. The Lifetree is leeching the magic from the immortals, and rumour has it, Halite is stealing Endora's. If Halite bleeds every ounce of magic from her bones, that is good for all of us."

Except then Halite is more powerful. Fable looked between Leena and Doug, unsure of what to think of this plan. If Leena was being honest and she wanted to help them, it could work. But Doug? He'd hunted them for almost a year now. He'd stalked them through Mistford for Endora. Chased them through the library. Even spied on them in Stonebarrow. Why would he be any different now?

The man winced, holding his temples. Leena patted his shoulder. "Just answer Halite. It's okay."

"I can't lie to that dragon," he choked out. "If she knows I teamed up with one o' Brawn's . . ."

Fable and Brennus exchanged glances. *Halite. Endora forced Doug to bond with her. Maybe he really is rebelling against the lich.*

"What's in it for you?" Vetch asked. "You must want something in return for helping us."

"Aside from Endora going down, there's something you have that Brawn wants." Leena flicked her gaze to Brennus. "Something from the Oakwrath."

Brennus touched his pocket, his eyes widening.

She gave him a wry grin. "Yes, boy. You know what I'm talking about."

Everyone turned their gazes to Brennus.

Halite's amulet? Why would Brawn want that? Fable's magic pulsed. That didn't make sense. Brawn could make his own amplifier; he didn't need hers.

Unless he wants to hold something against the dragon. The Oakwrath Thicket had its own set of rules, and the immortals had inner politics even the warlocks weren't aware of. At least, not until they were tasked with a mission like obtaining an enemy's amplifier.

Brennus lifted his chin, holding his hand over his pocket. "No. I won't give it to you. I need this. Destroying it might be the only way to save my parents. Ralazar cursed them. They're bound to his shop."

Vetch took a step back, clutching his arrow. Fable wondered what must be going through the man's mind. After all this talk of magic, would he abandon them? Or would he hold up his promise despite being surrounded by the thing he hated—or feared—most?

"Ralazar's Odd and Unusual Shop . . ." Leena chuckled, leaning towards him. "Ralazar created it with Halite's amplifier. If you burn that amulet in the phoenix's fire, you'll burn the store and everything inside it. If your parents can't get out, that'll include them."

Brennus's cheeks flushed. "We don't know that for sure."

"*I* know that for sure," Leena replied sharply. "That's how amplifiers work. Tell me, does this amulet have dancing flames within its glass? Brawn's bracelet held his grey smoke. When it was tossed into the Bottomless Sea and fed to Moranda, her stomach acid destroyed it." She slammed a fist on her knee. "Everything the Iron Wolves had built with it was destroyed in a rain of acid. Our underground lair in Stonebarrow. The spy equipment we'd planted in the Mistford Ministry." She took a shaky breath. "Our travelling hut, with the warlock Dagmar inside it. So yes, I know exactly what will happen when you toss that amulet into the phoenix's flames."

Brennus looked like he was about to throw up. Fable's heart pinched. That was all the confirmation they needed. Brennus couldn't destroy the amulet. At least, not without finding a way to get his parents out of the store first. If that was even possible. And it certainly wasn't going to happen before the phoenix cycled.

"There has to be another way to break Ralazar's curse," Timothy said, his voice cracking. "You're a warlock. How can we free Brennus's parents?"

"Couldn't Brawn do it?" Thorn asked. "Aren't immortals more powerful than warlocks?"

Leena scratched Knox's ears, sighing. "If it were that simple, wouldn't your Jade Antler friends have gotten Estar to do it already?"

Brennus clasped his hands in front of him. "What if

I found out what curse Ralazar used? Could you figure out more about it?"

Leena gave him a curious look. "And how are you going to find that out? Nobody knows where Ralazar is, but he's probably in some pit Halite would use for a prison. Even if you could find him, how would you convince him to tell you?"

"Never mind how," Brennus replied. "I know where he is. He's hiding from Halite in the shop with my parents."

What is he doing? Fable touched his forearm. *He can't be thinking about confronting Ralazar! What if the warlock trapped him too?* "Brennus . . ."

Leena's brows lifted, and she let out a short laugh. "Interesting. I wonder how he got away from her in the Oakwrath." Her eyes glinted with excitement. "If you found out exactly which curse he used, I could probably figure out how to break it. Where is the shop right now? How are you going to get there?"

"Doug." Brennus levelled his gaze at the transporter, who blinked at him sleepily.

"What?"

Brennus jabbed a finger in the man's direction. "You're going to take me to Ralazar's shop."

Doug puffed his chest. "Oh, yeh think so, do yeh?

No way. I wouldn't go near that salamander if meh life depended on it. In case yeh forgot, him and Halite ain't on the best o' terms. Which means him and me ain't either."

Thorn gave him a stern look. "He can't hurt you without Halite punishing him."

"He's already in deep with 'er," Doug replied. "He's not goin' ter care about that. No way. I'm not gettin' cursed by that lizard man."

"He's weak. He looked sick in the Oakwrath, and that battle with Halite must have taken even more out of him." Brennus looked at Leena. "Did Ralazar have magic before bonding to Halite?"

Leena tapped her wrist, thinking. "I believe so, yes. He was a wizard at some point."

A grin spread across Brennus's face. "So Halite is probably leeching his magic too. He's probably not near as dangerous as he was before."

If Brennus is right, this could work. Fable's magic danced inside her. Heat crept up her neck, and a bead of sweat formed on her forehead. But what if he was wrong? What if Ralazar still had the power to hurt him?

She grasped his forearm. "We don't know for sure. Let's wait until after we get the ashes, and then I'll go with you."

"I want to come too." Thorn gestured at her axe. "We can take him together."

Timothy raised his hand. "Me too. You shouldn't do this alone."

Vetch slunk back another step, still gripping his arrow in front of his chest. His expression was unreadable, but Fable was certain he was about to bolt.

"Aw." Leena nudged Doug's side. "Heartwarming. Why can't you support me like that?"

Doug scowled in reply.

"I can't wait," Brennus said. "If I can get them out of the store and return here before the phoenix burns, I might be able to destroy that amulet and get the job done." Brennus took Fable's hand and gave it a squeeze. "I have to do this. These are my parents we're talking about. I can't let them die in that store. Trust me. I'll be alright."

"And Doug will return here in time to get rid of Endora?" Leena asked pointedly.

"I'll send him back immediately after bringing me to the store."

Fable's chest tightened. "Then how will you get back?"

"Doug can come back for me later." Brennus patted his pocket where the amulet lay. "He'll have to if they want the amplifier."

Leena cocked her head, scratching Knox's ears.

Fable gritted her teeth, refusing to let her magic out. The look on Brennus's face told her he was going to do this no matter what. She didn't want him to leave thinking she didn't believe he could. If she'd learned anything from the last few years, it was that her friends' support was life-saving. Without it, she'd never have been able to escape Endora so many times. Maybe knowing that Fable believed in him would give Brennus the same boost.

She gave him a tight nod, unable to speak.

Leena touched Doug's shoulder. "Doug? Your powers are significant, you know that. If you want to sever your bond to Halite and get Endora off your back, this could be the answer."

Doug groaned, scrubbing his face with both hands. "Fine! But this better work." He glowered at Brennus. "Yeh better give us that amulet."

Leena dipped her head. "Thank you, Doug. You won't regret this. I know you're scared of Ralazar, but if you return here quickly after dropping Brennus off, you probably won't even see him." She looked at Brennus. "Are you sure you want to do this?"

Brennus nodded, his jaw tight. "Promise to help me

break Ralazar's curse on my parents. And to give the amulet to Brawn, not Halite."

Leena tapped her fingers together. "A bargain. I like your thinking."

Doug let out a squawk of protest, but Leena got to her feet.

She approached Brennus, holding out her hand palm-up. "Are you willing to bind our agreement? The amulet in exchange for Doug taking you to your parents' store."

Bind it? What does she mean by that? Fable bit her lip. Thorn's brows raised, and she looked nervously between Brennus and Leena.

"And for him to return me to my friends after." Brennus stood and placed his hand above hers.

"And you'll give me the amulet?"

"When I return. That will make sure Doug holds up our end of the deal."

"You can't give it to Ralazar," Leena warned.

"I won't."

Thorn stepped towards them. "Brennus, don't. Orchid told me about warlock agreements. If you break it, you'll have to serve Brawn."

Brennus kept his gaze on Leena. "And if she breaks it?"

Leena flexed her fingers. “Then my bond to Brawn will be severed. I’ll lose my magic.”

Brennus regarded her for a moment, then straightened his shoulders. “Let’s do it.”

“Okay.” Leena raised her voice, still holding out her palm. “Doug will take you to Ralazar’s Odd and Unusual Shop, and once he returns you to our group, you will give me Halite’s amplifier. In exchange, I will help you break the curse on your parents. Agreed?”

Brennus swallowed, then grasped her hand. “Agreed.”

“*Promitto*,” Leena said, her voice barely above a whisper. A silver light burst from their clasped hands, making Fable shield her eyes. It winked out, leaving a trail of grey smoke behind it.

Leena gave him a wolfish smile, letting go of him. “There. It’s done. Are you ready to head out right now?”

Brennus wiped his palm on his shirt. “Yes.”

“Are you sure?” Timothy asked, getting to his feet. “Don’t you need your bag or supplies or—”

“A weapon?” Thorn added, gesturing to her axe. “Something to protect you from Ralazar?”

Brennus touched his pocket and shook his head. “No. I have everything I need. And you need your axe, Thorn. How else are you going to cut down any undead

Endora might bring with her if she shows up?" He gave her a weak grin. "I'll be fine."

Fable threw her arms around his shoulders, her heart thundering inside her. When she'd first met Brennus, he'd been afraid of the shadows in the Lichwood. Even a snapping twig would have startled him. And now he was going to confront the nasty warlock who'd cursed his parents, risking himself to save them from a life of misery. Tears welled in her eyes as he hugged her back.

"I'm so proud of you," she whispered in his ear. "You can do this. I believe in you."

"Back at ya," he replied, squeezing her tighter.

She let him go and took a shaky step back. Leena beckoned to Doug, but he didn't move.

"I dunno." He got to his feet and slipped behind the log. "I know I said yes, but Ralazar—he could curse me too."

Brown smog poured from his sleeves, and Fable's breath hitched. *He's going to leave without Brennus!* She had to stop him. The spell her mother had planned to use on Endora leapt to her mind—*To bend someone to your will, direct your magic to their mind and say the word 'optempero'. Once their mind opens to you, give them your command. If your magic is strong enough, they will have no choice but to obey.*

She rubbed her hands together, calling her magic forth. Her emerald flames swept down her arms, casting a green glow around her. She focused on Doug's mind, willing it to open to her command.

"*Optemper—*"

"Fable!" Leena cried out. "What are you doing?"

Doug's eyes widened in horror, his smog wisping out. Fable's heart clenched, and she couldn't finish the spell. The scene from her nursery rang inside her head. *"Endora kills people," her mother had said. Her dad had given her a sad look. "Is taking away someone's will any better?"*

She lowered her arms, her flames receding. *What am I doing? I was about to force Doug into this, just like Endora forced him to become a warlock!*

"I'm sorry . . ."

Doug ignored her, waving Brennus over. "Git over here. Let's go."

Brennus gave Fable a wide-eyed look. "What were you doing?"

"Let's go. Now!" Doug shouted.

"Go," Leena said. "Before he changes his mind. You're bound now."

Fable looked away from them, tears and shame welling inside her. Brennus strode to Doug's side, and a brown fog engulfed them both. Seconds later, they were gone.

Thorn approached Fable, her face creased with concern. “Fable—”

Leena let out a low whistle. “A compulsion spell? Where’d you learn that, sorceress?”

Fable hugged her elbows, unable to speak the words—that she’d learned it from her mother. Only, her mother hadn’t actually used it.

From the edge of the firelight, Vetch’s steady gaze caught Fable’s. His brow furrowed. He shoved the arrow into his quiver and walked towards his campsite, disappearing into the darkness.

Fable’s stomach lurched. She clutched it, afraid she might throw up.

Vetch must really think I’m a lich now. And maybe I am. Maybe some kind of darkness is building inside me. Why else would I try to cast that kind of horrible spell?

And now, with both Brennus and Fedilmid both gone, she’d lost two of her guides. Half of the people who could keep her grounded. With only Thorn and Timothy left to make her see light, would she whirl out of control, endangering everyone?

Unanswered Calls

Something soft and wet pressed against Leena's cheek, startling her awake. She opened one eye, and Knox licked her face with his rough pink tongue.

"Argh! Stop it!" She laughed and pushed the dire wolf off her sleeping bag.

She blinked, letting her eyes adjust to the sunlight warming her tent. Knox barely fit inside, taking up almost half of the space with his furry bulk. He pawed the zippered door, clearly ready to stretch his legs.

Leena yawned. "Give me a second to wake up, you old brute."

She rubbed her eyes. *Where am I again?* The events of the night before came back to her, and she rubbed her temple. *Baldy Pass. Right. With the Mistford kids, and those Folkvar guys.*

The writhing vines marking her wrist caught her eye, and she frowned. She sat up and found her crumpled black shirt and slipped it on, tugging the sleeve over her wrist to hide Endora's tracking spell. She wondered what the lich was doing right then. Before Leena had left Mistford, she'd summoned Matilda the parrot—one of the warlocks' messenger birds. She'd sent the bird to Endora with a message that Leena and Knox were going to look for a phoenix in the mountains. It wasn't entirely a lie, just a stretch of the truth. Something Leena was good at.

Did I have to trick those kids, though? Guilt pinched her chest. She actually liked them. Especially Timothy, with his skull bracelet and weird necromancy skills. And Brennus, with his determination to save his parents—he was something else. They'd fallen for her fake display of sincerity, but she'd hated lying to them. And that lie hadn't been a mere stretch. Not even a twisted truth. She had deceived them with her story about Brawn wanting the amulet.

To be fair, if Leena offered Halite's amplifier to him, he wouldn't turn it down. To hold the dragon's key to the Oakwrath—something that would also strengthen her powers—would give him the upper hand. But that wasn't Doug and Leena's plan. They were going to give it to Halite. She couldn't tell these kids that she and Doug were plotting to unleash a dragon on their city. What excuse could the two of them give? *Oh, don't worry. We're sure the other immortals will stop her.*

She bit her lip, wondering if she'd thought this plan through well enough.

Knox heaved a sigh, then flopped down next to her, obviously bored with waiting for her to get up.

She rubbed his ears. "Maybe I should try to contact Brawn again." Her patron hadn't answered her calls for over a week now, which wasn't unusual. But it was still frustrating. When he was on a quest, or out with his immortal pals, he rarely replied to her. But still, she could really use his help right now.

"If I could just grab his attention . . ." She lowered her voice to mimic the warg, imagining him puffing his chest with pride. "*Leena, you're a genius! Smarter, funnier, and obviously much more charming than all the other warlocks combined.*"

Knox snorted, looking at her from the corner of his crimson eye.

"You're right. That doesn't sound like him, does it?" She sighed. "He's more like, *Leena, what is going on in that thick skull of yours?*" She paused, grasping the warg's tooth on her necklace. "Still, let's try."

She crossed her legs, then sucked in a breath and closed her eyes. Her mind wandered to the Oakwrath Thicket, picturing its sprawling lilac-coloured vines draping the trees. She envisioned the bull-sized warg greeting her, his scruffy hair streaked with grey, much like hers.

Brawn, are you there?

After a few seconds of silence, the image evaporated. Leena's mind jolted back to the tent. She let go of the tooth, letting her hand slump to her lap. "Well, thanks for nothing." She patted Knox's head. "He's probably on a hunting spree with Validus." The immortals didn't *need* to eat, but that bear was always ravenous, and Brawn loved to hunt.

The kids' voices came from outside the tent. The crackle of breaking branches told Leena they were probably about to start a fire to cook breakfast. "Well, we better get up, Knox." She tapped his nose. "We need to keep our cover about our plans for the amulet. You know, considering Fable can break my enchantments."

She tugged at her sleeve again. Why could Fable break them? Nobody else had been able to. Not even Endora. How could a kid no bigger than a sprite be so powerful?

I'm small too, she reminded herself. Though clearly not as strong as Fable.

Is her magic so strong because she's related to Endora? Can someone inherit that kind of power? I thought you had to do something truly horrible to gain that level of lich magic. Then again, she had no idea how lich bloodlines worked, if that was even a thing.

Her chest tightened. *And that compulsion spell . . . where did she get that?* Leena had never seen it used before. The spell held the same type of magic as her own enchantments, but it was much more powerful. It didn't merely encourage someone to feel a certain way; it forced them to do the spellcaster's bidding. And among enchanters, it was considered taboo. Nobody would ever use it.

Except a lich. She blinked. *That's stupid. She's, what, twelve years old? She's not a lich. And she stopped herself from using it. A lich would never hold back.*

Still, it was strange the kid even knew the spell.

Leena tugged her sleeve over the vine marking again, then got to her knees and unzipped the tent. She gently tapped Knox's nose. "We better get up, my dark shadow. If Endora tracks us down, we need to be ready."

Fable sat on a log stump at the firepit with the memory box open on her lap. The early morning sun peeked over the white-topped mountains around them, slowly evaporating the dew from the grass. Thorn bent over the firepit, creating a pyramid inside it with dried twigs.

Timothy dropped an armload of firewood on the ground beside her. “Yeesh. Buckhorn sure didn’t find much wood last night, and he was gone for over an hour. What was he doing?”

Thorn shrugged and pulled a box of matches from her vest pocket. “He’s no woodsman. And remember, he didn’t have an axe.” She eyed the jagged ends of the branches Timothy had brought her. “Looks like he broke most of these over his knee.”

The smell of pine, dirt, and campfire ashes filled the air, reminding Fable of her time in the Lichwood with Thorn and Brennus the summer before. She hadn’t known then how much her new friends would come to mean to her. They were practically family, just as much as Timothy.

And now, with Brennus gone, it felt like a piece of her heart was missing. A hole that wasn’t there before. Tears brimmed in her eyes. *He did the right thing.* She thought of the way he’d tricked Ralazar in the Oakwrath, throwing the warlock an old necklace instead of the amulet to give them time to dive through the portal. *He’s one of the cleverest people I know. He fooled Ralazar before. He can do it again.*

Timothy slumped onto the log next to hers, his face

sombre. "Do you think Brennus is okay? I thought he'd be back by now."

"By now?" Thorn took a matchbook from her pocket and lit the kindling, then blew on the small flame. "I think it'll take more than a few hours to outsmart Ralazar and get all the information he needs. And he might want some time to catch up with his parents."

Timothy scuffed his toe in the dirt. "I guess. I'm only worried. And where's Doug? I thought he was going to drop Brennus off and return."

"I don't know." Fable balanced the memory box on her lap and rubbed his back. "And I'm worried about Brennus too. But we have to trust him. Fedilmid and Algar do."

"Yeah," Timothy replied. "But I don't feel like they would have let him transport with Doug to Ralazar's shop."

"Probably not." Thorn wiped her hands on her canvas pants, then stood. "But even though Doug is a lowdown rotten fungus, he teamed up with Leena. He wants Brawn to have the amulet. So I think we can trust him to bring Brennus back to us."

Fable's stomach roiled at the thought of putting even an ounce of faith in Endora's old henchman. He'd never shown them any mercy. Not like Arame had.

Endora's previous henchman had warned Fable the lich had been plotting to hurt them, and he'd even helped them escape the mansion.

She tried to swallow her worry and lowered her gaze to the evocation tokens. The bracelet with the phoenix feather lay on top. She ached to touch it, wondering if it held a memory of a phoenix. Maybe it had some advice she could use for the quest that lay ahead of her. She bit her lip, deciding against using it. Vetch was probably on the edge after last night, and she didn't want to push him over it.

The pressed purple bloom lay crumpled next to the bracelet. *Optempero*. She winced. The looks both Doug and Leena had given her after she'd almost cast the spell on Doug had told her they knew what the magic did, and it was bad. They must be aware it could steal someone's will, which was *no better than Endora's lich magic*, according to Fable's father.

A lump formed in her throat. *I thought Endora was terrible for forcing Doug to bond to Halite. How is what I tried to do to him last night any different? What is happening to me?* If Doug hadn't looked so scared, she would have used the spell, just like Endora would have. Her breath caught. *Maybe I would have summoned lich magic. It takes an evil act to become a lich. That's the closest I've ever been to doing something so horrible!*

"Fable?" Timothy prodded her in the side with his elbow. "Are you going to check out another memory? Want Thorn and me to keep watch while you do?"

"No." She snapped the box closed. "Vetch would never be okay with that. I was only looking at the tokens."

Thorn guffawed. She straightened and plunked down on the log across from them. "What do you think he thought of everything that happened last night? He's got no choice but to accept magic around him now."

Timothy giggled. "Did you see his face? I thought he was going to pass out. But he knew he couldn't throw another tantrum. There were too many of us magic casters."

"I can't believe he's letting Leena come with us after she charmed him." Thorn shuddered. "That felt weird, didn't it? With the way you broke her spell, Fable, I don't think she'll use it on us again." She ran her braid through her hands, glancing at Fable from the corner of her eye. "Speaking of spells, what were you doing to Doug right before he left?"

Fable's stomach dropped. She avoided Thorn's gaze, her magic warming along with her cheeks. "It was nothing. Just some spell I heard somewhere, but I couldn't remember it properly."

Her chest ached. She hated lying to her friends. But she couldn't tell them about the darkness building inside her. She had to take control of it and hold it off long enough to get help from Fedilmid. To finally tell him what she'd seen in the memories. If she didn't, who knew what she'd do next?

Timothy rubbed his head. "It didn't seem like nothing. Your flames were all around you. You looked pretty cool."

Fable gritted her teeth. "It wasn't a big deal. I couldn't finish it, anyway."

Thorn and Timothy exchanged worried glances, both of them looking unsure of what to say.

Fable ran her fingers over her name on the box's lid, desperately trying to think of a way to change the topic. "Do you think Leena's trustworthy? I can't decide. On one hand, she saved Star. She seems to want to stop both Endora and Halite. But on the other one, she tricked us. She used a spell to make us like her. And she manipulated Timothy at the feast."

"I'm not sure," Thorn replied. "Orchid likes her. But Leena probably charmed her. That girl's dishonest, and she's good at hiding it."

"Agreed." Timothy nodded. "We better keep an eye

on her, in case she has something weird up her sleeve." He paused. "I like Knox though. I wish I could have a tame dire wolf."

The sound of a zipper met Fable's ears, and she twisted to look at Leena's tent. The flap opened, revealing Leena's poufy grey hair. "She's getting up. Let's talk about something else."

Buckhorn's voice called out to them. "Good morning, sunshines!"

He came striding through the trees from the direction of his and Vetch's camp. Despite being so exhausted the day before, he had a skip in his step now. He was practically glowing, his smile brighter than the morning sun.

Fable opened the book bag at her feet and slipped the memory box inside.

Buckhorn pointed at it. "Hey, what's that?"

"Nothing," Fable replied. "Just something my parents left me."

"Really?" His eyes lit up. "Is it magical?"

Fable tied her bag's strings to secure it and shrugged, annoyed by his prying.

"It's a secret, huh?" He put his hands on his hips, chuckling. "Well, I'm sure it's cool, whatever it is. Anyway, Vetch wants us to meet over at his fire. We need to talk about today's plan."

"Finally." Thorn grunted and got to her feet. She used a stick to push over the kindling pyramid in their firepit so the flame would burn out.

"There's hash browns and beans too," Buckhorn added. "I made enough to share."

"Awesome!" Timothy licked his lips and stood. "Let's go."

Leena and Knox came padding up from behind them. "Is there enough for two more?"

Buckhorn eyed the dire wolf uneasily. "That beast eats vegetarian breakfast food?"

Leena gasped and covered the dire wolf's ears. "Careful, you'll hurt his feelings. And, in fact, he loves vegetarian. He gobbled down a whole hippogriff the other day, so he needs some fibre to balance all that protein."

Fable looked at Knox's sharp fangs, wondering if the warlock was joking or not.

Buckhorn rolled his eyes. "Yes, there's enough. Come on." He started down the path that led to Vetch's campsite.

Thorn and Timothy started after him, and Fable fell into step beside Leena, with Knox in the rear. She glanced at the warlock, taking in her wild grey locks and the tooth pendant on her necklace.

"Why are you staying with us?"

Leena gave her a sideways look, tugging at her sleeve. "Well, it's not for the pleasant company."

Fable raised a brow.

Leena sighed. "Because I said I'd be here when Brennus returns. Besides, I really do want to help. I want Endora to go down just as much as you do."

"And Halite?" Fable asked.

Leena hesitated. "Yes, Halite too. Of course."

"You tricked us."

"Only to gain momentum on my quest—getting rid of Endora. For good, this time. No matter what it takes." She glanced over her shoulder. "Doug better hurry and return to us so he can play his part in our plan to zap her away. What could be taking him so long?"

Fable's stomach clenched. What did Leena mean by *getting rid of Endora*? Halite had taught her that the immortals could be brutal. Did the warlock mean to kill Endora? If casting a compulsion spell was wrong, murdering someone was even more so. Even if that person had taken other lives.

Leena regarded Fable, furrowing her brows. "Isn't that what you want too? To get rid of that old lich?"

"I want to stop her," Fable said. "To make sure

she's confined again and can't hurt anybody else. To be clear, I don't want to *kill* anyone."

Leena gave her an amused look. "So the family bloodline didn't carry on to you." She paused. "I thought . . . That spell you almost used last night—how do you know it?"

Fable stiffened. "That's none of your business." She shifted her book bag on her shoulder, then quickened her stride to catch up with Thorn and Timothy.

She knows there's something wrong with me. That compulsion spell—my mom had mentioned that Stirling gave it to her. Why did he have it?

Maybe the family bloodline *had* carried on to Fable. Had Stirling needed to fight this darkness too? Was that why he'd stopped talking to his mother before Fable was born? She needed to talk to him before this darkness seeped into her even deeper.

Her flames simmered in the pit of her stomach, and panic rose to her chest. For the first time, she wondered what had set Endora on her evil path. Maybe her great-grandmother hadn't wanted to become a lich, but something inside her had burned to come out—just like the darkness in Fable. Did that mean she was doomed to succumb to it and become a lich, like Endora had?

She swallowed, her heart racing. What if she never

got a chance to heal her grandfather? What if she did something evil first . . . and passed the point of no return?

Weird Vibrations

Before Fable even stepped into Vetch's campsite, she breathed in the savoury smell of fried beans and potatoes, and her stomach growled. Once she and her friends reached the fire, they were greeted by a cast-iron pan overflowing with hash sitting on a log over the smouldering coals in the firepit.

Vetch squatted beside his already-packed backpack, checking the pockets and the quiver of arrows leaning against it. Buckhorn went to his pack and pulled out a stack of bamboo plates and a cloth bag filled with wooden forks, then took them to the fire and began to load them with food.

"You're all up. Finally." Vetch straightened and strode over to the group. "We lost a lot of time because of that avalanche yesterday. We have to get moving." He peered through the trees at their campsite, his brows furrowed. "And none of you have packed up your tents yet."

"Let them eat first." Buckhorn handed Fable a plate

and fork. He gave Vetch a pointed look. "At least while you're going over everything we're doing today."

Fable sat next to Thorn on the log bench by the fire and balanced her plate on her thighs. Buckhorn passed out the other plates, then Leena and Timothy sat across from them with Knox at Leena's feet. She scraped some of her hash on the ground for him, and he licked his chops. Fable dug in, revelling in the buttery flavour.

"What is the plan for today, then?" Timothy asked between bites. "You haven't told us anything about this phoenix or where its den is."

Vetch ran a hand through his waves, then pulled up a stump and took a seat. "I know, and Buckhorn made a good point that if I expect us to reach the phoenix today, I should tell you what we need to do." He cringed, as if Buckhorn talking common sense into him had been painful.

"You've been leading a group of kids through the Windswept wilderness blind?" Leena snorted a laugh. "You've got to be kidding me."

Timothy swallowed his mouthful of food. "He doesn't like us."

"That's not true." Vetch's cheeks reddened. "It's just, you have magic. And that can be dangerous."

"Yikes." Leena pointed her fork at him. "You're

hanging with the wrong crowd, if that's how you think, Ranger Boy."

"Will you stop calling me that?" Vetch scowled at her.

"You're a ranger, aren't you?"

"Yes. But I'm not a boy. I'm a man."

Leena lowered her utensil, looking thoughtful. "That's a fair point . . . Ranger Man."

Vetch groaned and scrubbed his face with his hand. "Anyway, we had some other adults with us yesterday, but they got separated by an avalanche." He caught her look of alarm and waved her off. "They're fine now."

Fable's now-full stomach pinched. "Well, we think so. Thorn contacted Orchid, and Orchid sent for help."

Vetch cleared his throat. "So last week, the phoenix was gathering supplies for its nest—"

"What kind of supplies?" Timothy asked. "Does it use twigs and grass like regular birds?"

Vetch shook his head. "No. It's the size of an elephant. It rips up small trees and shrubs, hippogriff feathers, bear or yeti fur, or hair from the manes of chimeras."

Timothy dropped his fork on his plate. "Cool!"

Vetch nodded with a look of pride. "It is cool. Phoenixes are amazing creatures. I'm not sure how old this one is, but from its size, it must be on its third or fourth life cycle. And according to Fedilmid, the astronomers think it's going to start another one any day now."

Fable jabbed at her hash. "Today, tomorrow, or the next day."

"Er—right." Vetch rubbed his neck. "I don't put much stock into their *predictions*," he rolled his eyes, "but it looks ready to cycle soon. It's been nesting, and its feathers are molting."

Thorn leaned forward and grabbed the spoon from the pan, then splatted another helping of hash onto her plate. "What do you mean, you don't put much stock into the astronomers' predictions?"

"They use mag—" He gritted his teeth. "Even the astronomers say their science is not precise, don't they?"

Fable bit the side of her cheek. He was right. Even Nestor had said that to her before. But still, did he have to treat them with such disdain? From what Nestor and Fedilmid had told her, if it weren't for the astronomers' studies and gathering of magical stars, Mistford's harvests would never thrive the way they do now. The moon-and-sun-clock tower wouldn't exist. And they wouldn't be able to predict drastic weather events like storms or tornadoes. Their jobs were important for the well-being of Starfell and its residents.

Vetch pointed to a mountain ridge jutting above the treeline. "The phoenix's den is up there. My tower is on the way, on that point below the ridge. If you squint, you can almost see it." He paused. "We need to stop there to gather supplies to climb the ridgeline. There's a trail up the slope, but there are steep sections. We'll need toe grips for our boots, rope, and helmets. I have them all stored at the tower."

"You think we're going to reach the den by tonight?" Thorn asked doubtfully.

Vetch shrugged. "If we get a move on, yes. There's a patch of trees at the top near its den where we can camp tonight."

Fable gazed at the ridgeline in the distance. It seemed so far away, and no matter how hard she squinted, she couldn't see Vetch's watchtower. Her palms grew clammy at the thought of climbing the steep shale surface. They were safe with Vetch, right? Or were they? Yesterday, he'd led them straight into an avalanche.

What if Endora is up there waiting? We could be walking right into another one of her rockslides . . .

She glanced at Leena, who gave her a comforting nod.

It's okay, Leena mouthed. *We got this.*

Fable didn't know if Leena was somehow charming her again or not, but she felt better knowing the enchantress would be with them. *Her powers work on Endora. She'll be able to help us. If we can trust her.*

They finished eating in awkward silence, Fable mulling over everything they had to do that day. Her bones ached, her muscles were stiff, and they still had so far to go.

What would happen when they found the phoenix? Would it allow them to wait near its den until it burned? Juniper had said it trusted Vetch. But would it feel safe to cycle with four strangers and a dire wolf nearby?

After setting her dishes into the cloth bag Buckhorn held out for everyone, she fell into step beside Timothy. They moved up the path towards their campsite, stepping over raised roots and lumpy ground.

"Do you need help packing up Brennus's things?" Fable asked her cousin, her throat dry at the thought of her friend stuck in that shop with Ralazar. She could only hope that he was safe and making a deal or getting more information from the warlock about the curse. At least he had the amulet with him. It should give him bargaining power, even if he intended to give it to Leena.

"Nah, he didn't have much. Buckhorn said he could

carry Brennus's sleeping—" Timothy stopped and grabbed Fable's arm, pulling her to a halt next to him.

Her breath caught. "What is it?"

"Shh!" He furrowed his brows, then placed his hand over the skull on his bone bracelet and closed his eyes.

Fable's spine tingled. *What does he sense?* The serious look on his face indicated it must have been more than a jackalope.

After a few seconds, he opened his eyes and gazed through the trees, sweeping his bangs off his face. "There's something out there. It's weird though. It feels like an undead, but it's—different."

Fable squirmed, her skin tingling. "How?"

"The throbbing I feel from it is heavy and slow, like an undead. But it feels warmer." Timothy shuddered. "Like it died recently, and somebody raised it right after."

Fable stared at him, her tongue stiff. "So another necromancer must be nearby? Someone like Endora who raises armies of undead?"

Timothy's cheeks paled. "I don't know for sure. It just feels weird. I wish Malcolm were here to help me figure it out."

Fable grabbed Timothy's shoulders and spun him

to face her. “Leena said Endora was looking for the phoenix, remember?”

He pushed her arms away. “I know! But I don’t sense an army. I sense *one*.”

“How can you tell?”

“Her whole army would overwhelm me. Remember in the Oakwrath? I didn’t need this to sense them.” He held up his wrist, pointing at the skull. “I couldn’t get away from their throbbing.”

Fable looped her arm through his and started dragging him towards their tents. “Okay,” she said, more to herself than to him. “So maybe it’s not her. But if it is, Leena’s with us. She can enchant Endora. And I’ll shield us again while we hike to Vetch’s tower. Then you can check again and see if you feel anything there.”

Timothy nodded. “I hope I’m wrong and it’s only some weird magical creature out here or something.”

Fable’s magic thrummed. “Me too. The last thing we need right now is Endora coming after us.”

Fable trudged along the wide, well-worn trail through the pine trees beside Thorn, her feet aching. Timothy and Leena were chatting behind them, the pep in their voices making Fable clench her teeth. How could they not be tired? They'd been hiking up switchbacks for over two hours. Her calves ached with every step, and her knees wobbled.

The magical barrier shimmered every time they stepped out from the trees' shadows. Ahead of them, Vetch marched along outside the shield with his bow by his side. He'd felt safe not using it, seeing as he travelled this trail often. Should someone be watching, he wouldn't seem out of place. Buckhorn scrambled after him, his pack bulging even more than before with Brennus's things. It looked ready to burst at the seams.

Knox slipped through the trees alongside Fable, his head lowered and his ears perked. Leena had instructed him to keep watch for wildlife or other dangers. The way he crept silently like a shadow made Fable's hairs stand on end. No matter how friendly he seemed, she couldn't help but wonder if he was one of the beasts that had chased her and her friends through the Lichwood last year.

As they'd gone higher out of the heavily treed valley, the trail had transitioned from mud to rocks. Vetch's tower loomed through the pine trees ahead of them on the up-slope of the ridge, the sunlight reflecting off its tin roof that poked above the branches.

Fable glanced over her shoulder at Timothy. “Do you sense anything undead?”

He touched his skull bracelet, and his stride faltered. After a few seconds, he shook his head. “I don’t think so. Just some zings and zaps of bugs and other small animals.”

Leena peered over his arm at the bracelet. “That’s so cool how you can sense them. They give me the creeps, but they give you the literal chills.”

“Usually,” Timothy replied. “But recently, I felt something warm.”

Leena made a gagging face, then laughed. “Gross! What was it?”

Timothy frowned. “I don’t know.”

Fable cringed at the thought of something freshly risen sending warm pulses to her cousin.

Vetch halted at the edge of the trees before Moonflower Tower. Its wooden frame creaked in the wind, and the trail behind it wound even higher onto the bare mountain ridgeline. He held up his hand, and they all stopped behind him. His back stiffened. A breeze whipped through the branches, stirring Fable’s magic.

Buckhorn peered around Vetch’s shoulder. His voice came out as a squeak. “What is *that*?”

"What?" Fable asked, pushing ahead to Vetch's side. She kept the barrier in place, afraid of what might be waiting for them.

A pile of orange and purple feathers the size of Thora lay sprawled on the shale in front of the watchtower. Fable blinked, confused, then noticed the crooked wing and the red stains on the rocks beside it.

She gasped. "The phoenix! Is it dead?"

"I don't know." Vetch's voice was laced with worry.

Fable began to rush forward, but she'd only gone one step when Vetch held out a hand to stop her.

"Wait. Whatever hurt her might be hiding." He took his bow from his back and knocked an arrow, then glanced around the clearing.

Fable clutched his forearm. "Let me use my shield on you. It'll make you invisible."

"And have you all shuffle in here with me to keep it intact?" Vetch shook his head. "I have my bow. I'll be fine."

"I'm going with you," Thorn said, lifting her axe.

He shrugged, then crept into the clearing, holding his bow in front of them. Thorn slipped through the barrier and went with him, mimicking his soft steps. Fable held her breath, but nothing happened. No bear or chimera burst from the surrounding woods. No Endora or undead guards appeared in the clearing.

The Folkvars reached the phoenix, and Vetch lowered his bow. Thorn stood behind him, facing the trees with her axe at the ready. Vetch touched the phoenix's side, and it shuddered. A look of relief crossed his face.

"It's alive, but unconscious," he called out. He looked directly at Fable. "I think its injuries are magical."

Magical? Fable's stomach knotted, and her magic hummed inside her. *How does he know that? And who, besides Endora, would attack a phoenix with magic?*

TWENTY-FIVE

The Truth of Song and Light

Fable rushed towards the phoenix lying next to the tower, white light igniting in her chest. The broken wood braces near the top told her the bird must have crashed into it. Luckily, the support beams seemed to be unharmed. The wind whipped over the clearing, rattling through the tower and causing the tall pines to sway. Heavy grey clouds shrouded the early afternoon sun, threatening rain.

Fable stared at the heap of orange and purple feathers matted with blood and dirt that covered the phoenix's body, which was higher than her head. She dropped her backpack near the base of the watchtower's wooden ladder without taking her eyes off the enormous bird. She stepped gingerly around its outstretched wing and its talons longer than her entire leg. Vetch laid his hand on the bird's side, examining a thin gash across its ribs. A blue aura of light clung to the edges of the wound, reflecting from the red blood in neon-blue shimmers.

Fable's gut lurched. "This looks like a mark from

those electric whips carried by Endora's undead," she told Vetch. "I don't understand. Why is the phoenix here instead of in its den, getting ready to cycle?"

Vetch gestured at the broken boards of his tower. "Whoever attacked Embers did it before she got here. There's no way she would have hit the tower if she'd been in good shape."

"Embers?"

Vetch rested a gentle hand above the bird's gash, his face lined with sorrow. "It's a nickname I gave her."

Fable's chest squeezed. *Like the nickname I gave Star*. Obviously, Juniper had been right about the phoenix trusting Vetch. *After getting attacked, her first instinct was to come here. She knew he would help her.* She looked at Vetch with new appreciation. Aunt Moira had always said that people who were kind to animals had good hearts. In Fable's experience, her aunt hadn't been wrong about that yet.

Fable's gaze fell on the bloodstained rocks, and her pulse quickened. "If she dies, won't she be reborn? Isn't that how phoenixes work?"

"No. That only works if they reach the end of their natural life and choose to cycle. They're strong, but they can still die from other causes, like injuries or disease." His voice broke, and he dipped his head.

"Can you heal her?"

"I can try. I don't have a lot of experience with magical injuries, though I accidentally made my dog sick with magic once, and I healed him. Sort of," she replied, remembering when her powers had gone off on Grimm, causing pink bubbles to erupt from his mouth.

He gave her a sideways look, but she ignored it and stepped closer to the phoenix. *Get a grip, Fable. The last thing he wants to hear about is you making an animal sick with your magic.*

After taking a deep breath, she placed her hands above the bird's gash and closed her eyes. Crusted blood met her fingers, but the feathers beneath it felt silky. A thread of fiery orange light formed within the creature, reaching for Fable's magic. She let out her breath, allowing her white light to move with it.

Before the two lights could merge, the phoenix's side heaved. Vetch grabbed Fable's shoulders and jerked her away. Her eyes opened as the phoenix's spear-like talons raked the earth where Fable had just been standing. She stared at the gouged dirt, her chest tight. Her flames roared to life inside her, but she managed to hold them back so she wouldn't burn Vetch. If it hadn't been for him, she would have been shredded along with the rocky ground.

Vetch dragged her further back. The phoenix's eyes opened, revealing golden irises. It let out a strangled cry—something so fierce and wild it reverberated through Fable's skull. A mix between a wildcat and an eagle or a hawk, it was nothing like she had ever heard before.

"Fable!" Thorn rushed towards them, holding her axe. "Are you okay?"

Vetch held up his hand. "Don't come any nearer! The phoenix is already scared. The last thing she needs is some strange girl swinging an axe."

Thorn halted about fifty feet away from them, sliding her gaze from Fable to the struggling phoenix. It let out another squawk as it flailed, trying to get to its feet. Vetch ran to it, holding out both hands.

"Embers," he cooed. "Easy, girl. It's okay."

The phoenix stilled, then rested its head on the ground and huffed, looking at him with one golden eye.

"I'm okay, Thorn." Fable's voice shook. She hugged her elbows, unsure of what to do. She wanted to heal the bird, but would it strike out at her again?

Vetch lay a hand on its neck. "It took me years to get her to warm up to me. I don't know how we're going to convince her to let you touch her."

Fable rubbed her arms, as if that would help keep

her flames inside. "What if you lead me to her? She trusts you."

"Let's try." Vetch reached a hand towards Fable, keeping the other on the bird's thick neck. Fable moved cautiously and took it. His rough fingers squeezed hers. "See, Embers? This is Fable. She's a friend. I trust her. So you can too. She's going to heal you."

He trusts me? Fable's magic perked. *Since when?*

Vetch pulled her a step closer to the phoenix. It let out another terrified scream, which echoed through the valley. Vetch let go of Fable and placed both hands on the bird's head, stroking its feathers. "Easy, girl. You can't scream like that. What if whatever hurt you returns? Let Fable heal you."

Fable's heart sank as she moved away from the bird. "She's not going to let me near her. I don't know what it is, but she's scared of me." *Maybe it senses I'm related to Endora—that I'm made from lich magic.*

Vetch kept his gaze on the bird, still petting her calmly. "She's scared of everyone. She's a wild creature."

Timothy and Leena were now huddled with Thorn, whispering frantically. Knox sat next to them, regarding the phoenix with crimson eyes. Fable wasn't sure if he was wary of Embers or if he wanted to eat her.

Leena nodded at Thorn, then broke from the group and approached Fable. “I can enchant the phoenix,” she said. “My magic can calm her. Make her less afraid.”

“Can you make her friendly to me?” Fable asked.

Leena bit her lip. “I wish. It only works to convince others to like *me*. But still, a soothing effect could ease her fear and let you get near her. Vetch?” She looked at him. “Would you let me try to calm her?”

Vetch looked torn, as if the thought of allowing her to use magic on Embers went against his very core. He glanced at the gash on the bird’s ribs and pursed his lips. “Fine.”

Fable gaped at him. “Are you sure?”

“Just do it,” Vetch growled. “I’m already letting you use magic to heal her. I don’t see how Leena calming her is any different.”

Fable and Thorn exchanged surprised glances. What had changed for him? Had he finally wrapped his head around how Fable had saved him? Or did he feel backed into a corner with no other choice?

Leena gave him a firm nod and flattened her hair. It popped back up, looking even wilder than before. She gazed at the phoenix, and after a moment, the bird’s body stilled and her eyes drooped.

Leena grinned, wiping her hands together. “She’s

practically napping, probably dreaming about being at some kind of bird spa. Try again, Fable."

Fable swallowed the lump in her throat and edged closer to the creature. But as soon as she got within kicking distance, the phoenix raised her head and clacked her beak in warning.

"Easy!" Vetch put his hands on her head again, murmuring to it. Embers relaxed, but kept a watchful eye on Fable.

Fable backed away, stamping her foot in frustration. She directed the white magic in her heart towards the creature, and the dull throb of orange energy told her the bird's life was fading. "It's going to die if I can't heal it."

Thorn shifted, leaning on her axe handle. "There has to be something we can do. Vetch, do you have a first aid kit in your tower? What kind of herbs grow around here?"

Vetch glanced at the tower. "There's not near enough supplies for a wound this big. Besides, the injury's magical." He pressed his palm to his forehead. "She needs real healing. The fast kind."

Timothy ran to Fable's backpack and pulled her book bag from it. After fumbling with the tie, he took out the memory box. "Fable! Remember the phoenix feather bracelet? Maybe it will tell you something."

Fable's throat tightened. Her parents must have encountered a phoenix at some point to get that feather. But would the token even show a memory of that? The one with the purple bloom didn't have her mother picking it. What's saying this memory wouldn't be of something like her father giving the bracelet to Faari? Or Faari purchasing it at a shop? Maybe they actually hadn't met a phoenix at all.

Fable glanced at the bird, who weakly clacked her beak. Her wide eyes had grown bloodshot.

I don't have any other ideas.

Fable marched over to Timothy and took the box from his hands. She looked from him to Thorn. "Will you watch over me?"

"Of course," Thorn replied, thumping her axe. "We won't let anything happen to you."

Fable sat on the ground, holding the box in her lap. Timothy slung her book bag over his shoulder, and Thorn set her axe on the ground. They knelt on either side of her. She opened the box, eyeing the bracelet sitting on top of the other trinkets. Thorn put her hand on Fable's shoulder, and Fable gave it a quick squeeze. Before she could talk herself out of it, she grabbed the bracelet and let her chant burst forth.

The golden aura surrounded her. She caught the phoenix's eye as the world dissolved around her.

Hang on, Embers. I will find a way to save you.

The golden aura shimmered away, replaced by a brilliant orange glow. Fable shielded her eyes, crouching in the sand at her feet. Before her stood a phoenix, the source of the light, which radiated from its feathers and reflected off the stone walls around them. The velvety black sky above them told Fable they weren't in a cave, but in a desert outcropping of beige-coloured rocks.

The phoenix clawed at the ground, throwing back its head and screaming, just like the one at Moonflower Tower.

Fable's breath caught. *It can't see me. It's only a memory.*

Her father slipped into the stone circle. He wore sweat-stained clothes and held his hands in front of him the way Vetch had done at the tower. "I come in peace." He pushed his damp curls from his eyes. It looked as though he'd been walking through the Burning Sands for days in search of the creature.

The phoenix ruffled its feathers, stamping a

talon in warning.

“Please. I need your help. I’ll do anything. Here . . .” Morton slowly reached into his pocket and pulled out a piece of fruit covered with spikey skin. “It’s a dragon fruit. My father said phoenixes like them.”

The phoenix let out a terrifying cry. It echoed around them, and Fable put her hands over her ears.

Morton tossed the fruit to the side. “Okay. No dragon fruit.” He gave the bird a weak smile and dug into the front pocket of his shirt. “What about a flower?” He pulled out a red bloom with crumpled petals. “Chrysanthemum. It guards the threshold between life and death. Put it in your nest to help with your next cycle.”

The bird puffed its chest feathers and cawed again. The orange light emanating from it flared, and it beat its wings.

“Please.” Morton fell to his knees before it. “I’ve been searching for you for days. My wife. She’s in trouble. She made an arrangement to save our precious baby, but she’ll have to pay for it with her life. Only you can save her.”

He knew? Fable’s chest hitched. *How? Did my mom tell him?*

The phoenix squared off against him and stamped

the ground with its sharp talons, clearly trying to drive him off.

Morton slammed his fists to the earth, letting out a sob. “You don’t understand. Faari’s only option was to allow lich magic to heal our child. She even—” He swallowed. “She didn’t use the compulsion spell. She only thought about it out of desperation. Out of the goodness inside her, the desire to use the spell to help our baby. She wasn’t going to use it for her own gain, but for Fable’s. In fact, she gave up her remaining years so Fable could live.” His voice cracked. “And now that Fable is here, I can see she will grow to be just as strong, kind, and caring as her mother. It doesn’t matter that she was touched by lich magic. Her choices will define her, and she is already everything that Endora isn’t—a force for good in Starfell.” He sniffed, wiping his cheeks. “I love them both more than anything I’ve loved before. Please, help me give Faari what she gave to Fable—the chance to live.”

Fable’s throat thickened, and she covered her mouth with both hands. *My mother sacrificed herself for me. You can’t get any more selfless than that. Maybe it isn’t certain spells or magic that make us good or evil, but our intentions behind using them. How we use them. Our choices, as Fedilmid would say.*

"I know you aren't near your cycle yet," Morton begged the phoenix. "But you may have other healing powers that could help me. Please—"

The bird screamed, its glowing feathers erupting with orange flames around it. It let out another threatening squawk and struck at him with its beak.

"No!" Fable cried out, her magic igniting. The flames rolled to her fingertips, ready to blast the phoenix.

But when the bird struck at Morton again, it hit an invisible barrier. Blue light sparked from the impact, illuminating the air between them. The phoenix clacked its beak in frustration.

Fable gasped. *He used the same protection spell I have! Why didn't Aunt Moira tell me he had it too?*

Morton got to his feet, still singing in a clear baritone. It was the same song Fable used to create her barrier. Only now, the words made sense.

"*Light of Starfell, keep us safe.*
May the stars of Gaea know their place.
Hide us from those who would harm.
Protect our souls with this charm.
With the ties of family, both blood and made,
Strengthen this shield so it will not fade."

The phoenix stopped striking at Morton, and its body relaxed. It sat directly in front of him, hiding its talons, and its flames wisped out.

"That's it," her dad said in an awed voiced. "You know this magic. You can trust me."

He reached out to stroke its feathers. The barrier slipped like silk around the creature, enveloping them both in brilliant blue and orange light. The bird heaved a heavy sigh and nuzzled Morton's hand, then opened its beak and trilled. Its song and Morton's mingled together like a beautiful symphony, and a peace settled over Fable that was far more potent than even Leena's magic.

Fable touched her chest. *This is what I have to do. I have to cast my barrier and sing with the phoenix!*

She watched her father petting its neck feathers, and her heart warmed. Much like how Embers trusted Vetch, this phoenix accepted her father too. How did Vetch bond with it without a spell like this? *Maybe he has his own magic he doesn't even know about.*

She moved closer, unsure if she could pierce her father's barrier or not. It hadn't made him or the phoenix invisible, which was odd. *It must be because it's my father's memory. I will see everything he did.*

But just as she was about to slip into the light cast by her father and the phoenix, a shrill cackle slashed through the air. Fable's neck stiffened, and she looked around for the only person such a sound could come from—Endora. Her heart ached at the thought of the lich destroying this moment for her father. Terrified she was about to see Endora kill the bird, Fable scrambled backwards. But with one last look at Morton, she realized he and the phoenix hadn't noticed the lich's interruption. The phoenix plucked a feather from its chest and held it out to Morton, and he took it with a trembling hand.

The cackle came again, and Endora stepped out from behind the stone outcropping nearest to Fable. She wore a brilliant ebony gown with diamond-studded cuffs, but heavy lines creased her face, and the dark shadows under her eyes gave her a haunted look.

Confusion whirled inside Fable, along with her emerald flames. *Why does Endora look old? Is this before she had lich magic? But she had it shortly after I was born.*

Endora gazed at the phoenix and her father, tapping her chin with a pointed black nail. "Oh, sweet child. I heard everything. I know how to tame the phoenix now too."

Her father tucked the feather into his shirt pocket, unaware of Endora's presence.

Fable dug her fingers into her palms, struggling

to keep her flames inside. *I don't understand. Did his shield block him from seeing or hearing Endora? But then I wouldn't be able to see her if this is his memory.*

Endora looked directly at Fable, and her scarlet lips split into a wicked grin. "Thank goodness you brought that memory box with you, or I would have had to torture you for this information."

Before Fable could react, the woman reached her in several long strides. She grasped Fable's wrist, and a piercing scream escaped Fable's mouth.

She's not part of the memory! She's here with me!

She let her flames whoosh from her skin, but Endora held tight. The golden aura formed around them, and Fable began to fall. Endora gripped her arm and went with her, filling Fable's vision with that maniacal blood-red smile.

Sacrifices

Fable jerked awake. Grey clouds filled the sky above her, and she breathed in an unfamiliar smell that reminded her of bitter lettuce. She sat up, blinking in confusion at the watchtower and brushing aside the dirt on her shirt. The feather bracelet, the memory box, and Thorn's purple cone-shaped flower lay next to her. She frowned. *What's going on?*

She rubbed her forehead, trying to clear her foggy mind. Thorn and Timothy lay on either side of her, their cheeks pale and bodies strangely stiff. Timothy clutched the book bag in his rigid hands, and his glassy eyes flicked to hers. Fable's chest hitched. Endora had appeared inside her father's memory! Not as part of it, but as a visitor like Fable. She stared at her stiff companions in horror.

Endora's binding spell! She's here!

Her flames smouldered in her chest. The phoenix still lay slumped beside Vetch's tower, her gently rising side the only sign of life. Endora stood before the bird in that same ebony gown from the memory. She smoothed the tight twist in her grey-streaked hair and glanced over her shoulder at Fable, then crossed her twig-like arms with a smirk on her wrinkled face.

"You're awake, dear great-granddaughter." She sneered, but the crease in her brow gave away her frustration. "How did you escape my binding spell? You should be flat as a board like the others."

Fable swallowed, looking around the clearing for Vetch and Leena. They both lay rigid next to the bottom of the tower ladder—clearly bound by magic and unable to move or speak, exactly like Timothy and Thorn. Knox lunged towards his master, but the chain shackling him to a support beam kept him from reaching her.

Tears welled in Fable's eyes. *No, Leena's not his master. She's his friend. Unlike this horrible lich!*

A full-length mirror with a familiar ornate frame sat propped against the support beam opposite of Knox. Fable frowned. *Where did that come from?*

"I can't have you getting in the way again," Endora snarled. She flicked a hand towards Fable, hurling a blast of crimson light.

Fable's protective song burst from her in the same strange language as usual. Only now, she understood the words. "Light of Starfell, keep us safe!" Her barrier zapped into existence right before the binding spell could reach her, and the red stream of magic fizzled out against it.

Endora's blood-red lips split into a fanged grin, the wrinkles around her mouth causing it to pucker. "Getting quicker, aren't you? You think that shield can protect you? I taught that spell to your grandfather. I know exactly how it works. I may not be able to see you, but I know you're there. I can sense you. We're connected, after all. Through the power of *a mother's love*."

She sent another shot of scarlet magic at Fable. It hit her barrier harder this time with a resounding *crack*. But it dissolved too, leaving Fable unharmed.

Now safely under the cover of her spell, she crouched next to Timothy and pulled the Blood Star from the book bag in his hands. He blinked, and Fable's heart thumped against her ribs. The hollowness in his features reminded her of when he'd been trapped inside one of Endora's portraits in her mansion. Anger boiled inside her. She'd never let that lich hurt him again.

She put a gentle hand on his shoulder, then leaned down and whispered, "I've got this. We'll all be okay." She only hoped those words were true. She put the

Blood Star in her pocket, then got to her feet and raised her voice. "A mother's love? Or is it the lich magic you used to save me?"

Endora's amethyst eyes lit up. "So you know about that. After finding your memory box here, I'd wondered if your dear old parents had left you that one." She paced over the bloodstained ground in front of the phoenix. "Clever, your father using the protection song as the code to unlock them. I had no idea he'd had time to teach it to you before his . . . demise."

Fable's stomach clenched as if she'd been hit. Her mouth dry, she shouted. "How did you get here? And how did you get into my dad's memory?"

Endora smirked and jerked her head towards the feather bracelet at Fable's feet. "Your little trinket there let me in. Like I said, I know the code. That charm is even older than I am."

"But that's *good* magic. How come you can do it?"

"Oh, please." Endora sneered, waving her off. "You think everything is black and white. Good versus evil. Light versus dark. There are shades of grey, child. After all, you wouldn't be alive without the lich magic you loathe so much."

Fable choked back a strangled cry. Her flames slammed against her seams, begging to be unleashed.

But she ground her teeth and held them back. “You didn’t tell me how you got here or how you knew where I was.”

Endora tapped her chin with a coal-black nail. “We have a mutual friend, dear child. He’s been aiding me, since I can’t be away from my mansion for long without, you know,” she said, prodding her lined cheek, “this happening.”

Fable clenched her hands into fists, glancing at Leena. She lay next to the tower, just as stiff as Vetch beside her. *So it wasn’t Leena.* Fable glowered at the lich. “Doug? Where is he?”

“Doug?” Endora’s perfectly-groomed brows raised. “I haven’t seen that blasted fool for nearly a week! He’s gone rogue.” She glared at Leena’s rigid form. “And that girl,” Endora hissed, “a traitor as well. I’d been wondering why she was following that bumbling Folkvar. Now I know the tracking spell I put on her wasn’t wrong.”

Fable glanced at Vetch, confusion clouding her thoughts. *Bumbling Folkvar? She can’t mean Vetch, can she?*

“I should have known the minute I saw her playing with the hounds.” Endora gave Leena’s form a disgusted wave. “No matter. She won’t get down from my wall this time."

Footsteps came stomping down the tower ladder. Buckhorn hit the ground, then turned to face Endora, a licorice whip hanging from his mouth. "Tower's clear, mistress. There's no one else here. But I found some candy."

Buckhorn? Fable's knees grew weak. Friendly, unassuming *Buckhorn* betrayed them? Her voice came out hoarse. "How did you get her here?"

Buckhorn twisted around, a confused look on his face. "Fable?"

"She's here, hiding like a snake in the grass." Endora's piercing gaze landed on her. Clearly, she knew Fable hadn't moved yet.

"How did you bring Endora here?" Fable asked again.

Buckhorn gave a sheepish grin, then gestured to the mirror. "It was simple, really. I have my own kind of transportation magic. It's not as handy as Doug's, but my mirror has a twin. You can move between them. Endora has the other one."

Fable bit back a scream of fury. Buckhorn had been working for Endora all along! Doug hadn't been the one out to hurt her this time. It was the plump, cheery-faced Folkvar right under their noses!

"Why would you help Endora? She's a lich! She'll only hurt everyone, including all the people in the colony."

Buckhorn's expression darkened, and he took another bite of his licorice. "Good. Flint and that council kicked my parents out of the colony for using magic. I had to grow up in that dung heap, Sandy Ridge. The only Folkvar boy in town!" He jiggled the shortened licorice whip. "You know how others treat us out there, like we're dangerous and untrustworthy. My mom asked Flint to let us return after I was born, and he refused. The colony can burn for all I care." He ate the last bite of licorice, then reached into his pocket. "Speaking of which . . ." He pulled out a necklace with a glass dome pendant filled with green flames.

Fable's breath caught. *The amulet!* "Where did you get that?"

Buckhorn shrugged and tossed it to Endora, who caught it with a gleeful look. "I took it off Brennus when I fell at the campfire. It was an easy swap for my old pocket watch."

Fable's stomach roiled, and she fought the urge to throw up. Brennus was in Ralazar's store without the amulet. He had no bargaining power with the warlock. *Maybe that's why Doug hasn't come back to us! What if he found out Brennus didn't even have the amulet and took off?*

"What are you going to do with it?" Fable demanded.

Endora pocketed the amulet, then strode close to the phoenix. "Not that it's any of your concern, but I'm going to destroy it. Isn't that why you're here too? We have the same mission, only a different way of going about it." She tutted, wagging her bejewelled finger. "And you think we aren't alike."

Fable reached into her pocket and touched the Blood Star's jagged crack. Endora must have no idea the bird's ashes might be able to heal it. In fact, she didn't seem to even know it was broken.

Endora regarded the phoenix eagerly. "Now that I know how to tame this beast, I'm going to wake it up and force it to burn."

Fable allowed her flames to roll down her arms, hoping they weren't visible beneath her barrier. She crept over the grass towards the lich and began to circle her. Fable couldn't allow her to destroy that amulet. Her heart cracked open at the thought of losing Brennus, one of her best friends in the world. Of allowing him and his parents to perish inside that horrible shop. She clenched her fists, and a tear ran down her cheek. Endora had already done enough damage by capturing Isla and Bart in one of her portraits, where Ralazar had found them. Fable couldn't let this be the ending to their story.

The compulsion spell . . . Fable's palms grew clammy. *Would it be so terrible to use it to stop Endora? I'd be saving a life. No, four lives—the phoenix, Brennus, and his parents. Maybe even Ralazar and Doug too.* Endora's words from mere moments ago came back to her—*there is no black and white.*

Didn't her father say something like that in the last memory too? That even though the compulsion spell was bad, her mother had only considered it out of her love for Fable. He obviously hadn't thought Faari was evil for thinking about it.

Still, the thought of using it made Fable queasy. *My mom didn't actually use it, though. What if I do, and it's bad enough to turn me into a lich? There has to be another way!*

Desperately, she said, "You can't do that. The phoenix isn't ready."

Endora chuckled. "It doesn't matter. If I push it hard enough, it will cycle."

Embers opened her eyes and gave Endora a terrified look. She raised her head and let out a cry, much weaker this time, and flailed her talons. Endora clasped her hands, looking like a child about to open a Yule present.

She rubbed her boney fingers together. “All I have to do is sing that silly chant, and it’ll let me right in. And then, I’ll make it burn. The flames will destroy the amulet and cleanse that cursed warlock bond from my soul.”

Fable’s gut clenched. What was she talking about? Was she intending to step into the flames to break her bond to Halite? That was crazy! They would burn her too, right?

The ashes. She can use them to heal herself after. Fable’s voice trembled. “You’ll kill her. Don’t.”

“Oh, such drama.” Endora rolled her eyes. “I’m not going to kill it. I’m merely forcing it to cycle early. It’ll only be a little more vulnerable once it reforms. Besides, if it doesn’t make it, it’s still worth it to get that disgusting salamander off my back.”

Was that true? Could she force Embers to cycle early? Panic rose inside Fable, and her emerald flames burst from her hands. The barrier glitched and disappeared, leaving her exposed, and the flames barrelled into Endora’s chest.

Everything happened so fast it blurred around Fable. Endora screamed, her dress erupting into a fiery ball of green and red magic. The phoenix scrambled to her feet with a thunderous cry, then limped towards the trail behind the tower and collapsed in a heap at the edge. Thorn and Timothy leapt up and ran to Vetch and Leena, Thorn scooping up the flower and her axe as she went. She held the flower over the noses of their still-prone companions, and they groggily sat up.

That flower! Thorn said it repelled dark magic. She must have used it to unbind me too. But how? Wasn't she bound?

Endora shrieked again, and the green fire extinguished with a whoosh of air. The smell of burnt hair and fabric filled the clearing, and Endora pointed a blackened finger at Fable.

"I should have done this ages ago, you little brat!" She cupped her hands together, forming an electric orange glow between them. Lightning crackled within it as she spread her hands apart, making the ball of energy bigger. Her shoulders hunched, and her hair loosened from its twist, flailing around her head like Medusa's serpents. Her knees buckled with the effort of holding the raw power, and her bloodshot gaze met Fable's. "It's time to end this, dear great-granddaughter. I allowed you to be brought into this world, and it's time for me to take you out."

Fable's song leapt from her, and the barrier formed

around her. As Endora raised her arms and the crackling ball of power grew larger than the lich herself, a fierce wind whirled around them. Fable had no idea if her barrier was strong enough to withhold the blast. She began to run towards the woods, hoping to make Endora unleash the weapon away from her friends.

But before Endora could attack, an arrow struck the glowing mass, and it flickered. Endora's eyes widened in confusion, and she struggled to maintain hold of the energy. Another arrow struck it, and it exploded with a thunderous boom. The force of it knocked Fable off her feet, and her barrier dissolved.

Reeling, she forced herself upright, holding her head.

Thorn's voice met her ringing ears. "Fable!"

The world tilted beneath Fable's feet. She wobbled, and Thorn's strong arms were suddenly around her.

"You're okay," Thorn said. "We're all okay."

Fable leaned into her friend, breathing heavily. "What happened?"

"Vetch shot Endora's magic, and it worked. It went out!"

"What? But Vetch doesn't have any powers."

"Apparently, hawkweed does have magic," Thorn replied with a grin. She let go of Fable. "I rubbed it on his arrow heads to sharpen them. I figured if it works on axes, it would work on those too. And did you see Endora? Halite must be weakening her. She could barely hold that spell."

"And the woundwort?" Fable asked.

Thorn's smile grew wider. "That worked too! I only pretended to be bound when Endora attacked us. As soon as Timothy hit the ground, I did too. She had no idea I was pretending. One sniff of the woundwort and her spell was broken. Like I said, I'm pretty sure Halite has weakened her a lot."

Fable threw her arms around her friend's broad shoulders, hugging her tightly. "You are a genius, Thorn. Thank goodness I have you." Her chest pinched. *But not for much longer.*

She pushed the thought aside as Thorn hugged her back.

The Folkvar girl pulled away, then hooked her arm around Fable's. "Come on. I think Leena and Vetch have that old lich contained. I dunno what we're going to do with her."

Fable fell into step beside her. "First, we're going to take that amulet."

Endora and Buckhorn sat together on the ground in front of the tower. The others stood over them—Vetch aiming an arrow at them, Knox baring his teeth in fierce warning, Timothy wielding Thorn's axe, which stood taller than his head, and Leena with her hands on their shoulders. Buckhorn gave Leena a flirty smile. Endora stared at the ground, her now-stringy hair covering her face. But she appeared calm. Clearly, Leena was working her magic.

But as Fable and Thorn approached the group, worry wriggled in the back of Fable's mind. It seemed too easy. How could Endora be so weak? Could Halite really have leeched that much power from her? That look in Endora's eyes when she'd conjured that electric orange power—she'd been bent on killing Fable. On taking her out of this world for good.

When Fable and Thorn reached them, Endora lifted her head. Fable went and stood in front of her. Timothy gave Thorn her axe, and they shared a high-five, but Fable couldn't join in the celebration.

Endora glowered at Fable. Her wrinkles had deepened, and there were dark circles under her eyes. The jewels had fallen off her torn, charred sleeves.

And yet, the lich had a sharp-toothed smile on her soot-stained face.

"What?" Fable asked, taking a step back. "You're happy about this? About all the terror you unleashed on us? We're going to make sure you get locked up again. Forever."

Endora jutted her chin, her sunken amethyst eyes gleaming. "No." She pointed at Fable's pocket. "You have the Blood Star. And it's broken."

She let out a cackle, and Fable's magic whirled in response. Heat swept over her. "How do you know that?"

"I created the star!" Endora hissed. "I can always sense when it's nearby, and the lack of energy, of warmth, tells me there's something wrong with it." Her grin grew wider, making her dragon-like fangs even more prominent than before. "And you're planning to use the phoenix's ashes to fix it. See, dear Fable? Like I've always thought, we're so much alike."

Fable's spine stiffened, and her pulse rushed through her veins. "No!"

Thorn strode to Fable's side, jabbing a thick finger in Endora's direction. "She's nothing like you, lich. Her heart is good. It's pure. She only wants to help Starfell."

Endora threw back her head, a cackle escaping her dried lips. "She wants to use the bird's magic to heal the star and gain its power. Which is exactly what I do too."

Fable gaped at the lich, her tongue stiff. The memories her parents had left her—of Endora wanting to train her, of her magic going off on her father, of the lich magic saving her life . . . *Did they leave those memories to warn me that I really am like Endora?*

"That's wrong!" Timothy shouted from behind them. "Fable only wants the star's powers to stop you. To put an end to you murdering innocent people just to extend your own life. Her reasons are selfless, the complete opposite of yours."

Fable's chest warmed, and she touched her pocket where the Blood Star lay. Her father's words in the last memory hit her—*It doesn't matter that Fable was touched by lich magic. Her choices will define her, and she's already everything that Endora isn't.*

Tears brimmed in her eyes. She clenched her fists and met Endora's gaze. "I may have your eyes, but that's where our similarities end. You sacrificed your family, while my mother sacrificed herself for hers. I have her blood in my veins too, and love always trumps hate. I'm nothing like you."

Endora stared at Fable, her purple eyes turning glassy. For a moment, Fable wondered if the lich was going to cry too. But instead, the hag averted her gaze. "None of this matters, anyway. Phoenix fire won't fix the Blood Star. Only I can do that."

TWENTY-SEVEN

The Song of Embers

Heat rushed to Fable's face as she thought of the destiny of the Blood Star that Carina had told her about—*the star will reunite the mother and child, and peace will come to Starfell.* But Endora didn't know her son was still alive. She couldn't have possibly been referring to the star's destiny, could she? Fable glared at the lich, who sat slumped on the ground with that horrible fanged smile. Endora beamed smugly, like she was a cat with a mouse between her paws instead of laying weakened and defeated.

Fable lifted her chin, touching the starry lump in her pocket. "I don't need your help to heal it. I only need the phoenix's ashes."

Endora's smudged brows lifted, and she pushed a charred strand of hair from her face. "You think the ashes of a phoenix have enough power to heal my Blood Star? You're a fool. I created that star. I'm the only one who can fix it."

"We'll see about that," Thorn said, twirling her axe.

Vetch cast the crumpled form of the phoenix a worried look, his bow steadily aimed at Endora and Buckhorn where they sat together on the ground.

Fable levelled the woman with her gaze. "No. You didn't create the star. Your love for your child did, and that's something you've long forgotten."

Endora's eyes widened, and she sucked in a breath. Before she could say anything more, Fable stormed towards the rocky trail behind the tower where the phoenix lay unmoving, sending a silent prayer to the universe that Embers was still alive. Matted feathers lay limp around the creature's body, and long black lashes lined her closed eyes. But laboured breaths escaped her yellow beak, and Fable's chest pinched. She approached slowly, waiting to see if the bird would lash out at her. But Embers didn't wake.

"You poor thing," Fable cooed, crouching next to the phoenix's head. She glanced at the others and caught Vetch's narrowed gaze. She gave him a nod, hoping to convey that she would do her best to save his friend.

She lay her hands on the bird's thick neck and closed her eyes. Embers's orange light barely flickered deep within her body, not flowing like a babbling brook as it should. It throbbed weakly, as if struggling to merely exist. Fable's throat thickened. *She's dying. But I saved*

Vetch from the brink of death. I can save her too.

She took a deep breath, loosening the seams that held back her magic, and forced her white light into the creature's body. She grasped at the orange life thread, but it slipped through her stream of magic like water through a sieve. The harder Fable tried, the dimmer the phoenix's light became.

Sorrow seeped through her bones as she ran her fingers over the animal's once-brilliant feathers. *Why isn't it working?* She glanced over her shoulder at the others. Endora watched her intently through her curtain of tangled hair, a slight curve on her lips.

"You can't save it!" she yelled in a croaky voice. "I leeched its life. I almost had it to the brink of death before it escaped. You can't restore those years. You would have to feed her someone else's life, and you don't have that power. Only liches do, and you're no lich." A slow smile spread over her weathered face. "It's going to die, and there will be no ashes!"

Fable's heart jolted. *My father was right! I'm no lich. I'm everything Endora isn't, just like he said. She took Embers's life, and I only want to give it back. But why can't I? Why won't my healing powers work?*

She got to her knees and rested her head on the phoenix's neck, no longer afraid the bird would wake.

She stroked Embers's soft cheek feathers, letting her tears fall. She cried not only for the broken Blood Star and her grandfather's missing memory, but for Embers too. The phoenix wasn't going to cycle and start a new life. She was going to die. *And all because of me.*

"I'm so sorry." Fable's voice choked. "This is my fault for dragging you into this. When Juniper first told us about you, I never even thought of what would be best for you. If you'd even want to help me. And now . . . you don't deserve this."

The phoenix heaved a sigh, and Fable wondered if she'd heard her. "I wish I could save you."

A hand grasped Fable's shoulder, startling her. Leena huddled next to her and tightened her grip. "There's a way to save her. You can make her cycle."

Fable lifted her head, her magic sparking. "How?"

Leena gave her a hard stare. "Seriously? You know this. That spell you almost cast on Doug—I know what it does. You could use it."

Fable gaped at Leena in horror, pulling from her grasp. "No! The compulsion spell? I can't."

"But it would work," Leena insisted. "Come on, Fable. If you compel her to cycle, she would at least have a chance to live."

Fable's gut clenched. "And then what? Die as soon

as she's reborn because it's too early? She'll be too weak to survive."

Leena jerked her head towards the tower. "You think the rangers won't save her? Get a grip. You can do this." She glanced at the phoenix, whose breath grew even weaker. The bird's eyelids were pale, as if the blood had been drained from her. "It's her only chance."

Fable bit her lip, her mind spinning. *It's not right to take someone's will.* But what other choice did she have? Could saving Embers be an exception, since Fable's intentions were selfless? *But what if she suffers and dies after cycling anyway?*

And what if doing casting that spell is an evil deed? If it is, I could turn into a lich!

Fable jerked away from Leena and threw her arms around the phoenix's neck. Leena let out a frustrated sigh, then straightened and moved away from them. She glanced at Fable over her shoulder. "You're the only one who *can* save her, you know. You're her only hope."

Her heart aching, Fable tried to send her healing powers into the phoenix once more. *I can do this. Fedilmid believes in me. And so do Thorn, Brennus, and Timothy. Even Aunt Moira!* She pushed her magic harder, grasping for Embers's life. But like before, the bird's orange light slipped away like sand through Fable's fingers.

I can't let her die. I have to do something!

Fable opened her mouth to speak, but instead of the compulsion spell, the protection song rang out from her lips.

"*Light of Starfell, keep us safe.*

May the stars of Gaea know their place . . ."

Her magical shield burst from her, creating a dome of shimmering blue light over her and Embers. The bird's eyes fluttered open. For a moment, fear pierced Fable's chest. But instead of slashing at Fable, the bird opened her beak and began to sing. The sweet birdsong mingled with Fable's voice.

"*Hide us from those who would harm.*

Protect our souls with this charm.

With the ties of family, both blood and made,

Strengthen this shield so it will not fade."

They kept singing, and the same peace she'd felt in the last memory of her father and the phoenix in the desert settled over Fable like a warm blanket. Embers lifted her head, nuzzling Fable with her smooth beak. Fable ran her hand over the top of the bird's head and allowed her white light to envelop them both. Embers pulled her talons beneath her and righted herself, then heaved to her feet, towering over Fable.

Kneeling, Fable gazed up at the bird as her feathers cast a brilliant orange light that filled the entire clearing. They both stopped singing, and the protective barrier faded. Embers's feathers burst into flames, but it wasn't a fire that wreaked destruction and death. Instead, the flames danced gently over the bird's body, caressing her like a mother soothing a baby. She lifted her beak to the sky and let out a cry that both broke Fable's heart and sent a whirlwind of joy through it.

Endora's screams echoed around them, but Fable couldn't tear her gaze from Embers. The phoenix stretched her fiery wings, as if waving one final goodbye, then her entire body collapsed into grey ashes. They landed in a pile before Fable, releasing wisps of steam into the air.

Tears pricked Fable's eyes. *She did it! She cycled early, and I didn't have to force her.*

"Thank you," she whispered, burying her face in her hands.

Leena and Timothy rushed to her side. Timothy fumbled with the glass vial Fedilmid had given him and popped the cork. He dipped it into the pile of ashes before them, filling it to the brim.

Leena put her arm around Fable's shoulders. "The

star. Hurry, before the ashes cool!"

Fable took the star from her pocket with trembling fingers. She plunged it wrist-deep into the ashes, willing it to heal with all her might. Her white light flowed from her into the star, and heat tore through her entire body. But when she pulled the star from the ashes and opened her hand, the black, jagged crack was still there.

Her heart shattered. *No. It didn't work! It's like Carina said—*

Endora's gleeful cackle met her ears. Fable jerked her gaze towards the sound. Vetch, Thorn, and Knox all lay sprawled on the grass, and Buckhorn was nowhere in sight. Endora stood hunched next to Buckhorn's mirror, her face wild with wicked joy.

"I told you it wouldn't work!" The lich pointed a crooked finger in Fable's direction. "And now you're hopeless without me."

Fable gaped at her in horror. With one last smirk, Endora stepped through the glass. It shattered behind her, leaving the mirror's frame empty.

Leena leapt to her feet and ran towards Knox and the Folkvars. Bile rose in Fable's throat, and she fought the urge to scream. She clutched the broken star to her chest.

"Now what? The destiny—we can't—"

"Forget her. She's gone," Timothy said, shoving the vial of ashes into his shorts' pocket. He gazed at the remaining pile, and a joyful smile crossed his face. "Look at her!"

A bright orange head the size of an apple popped up through the ashes. Two fuzzy wings emerged. With a wobble, the chick pulled herself free and landed on her rump. She looked at Fable and Timothy with wide golden eyes, then opened her beak and let out a soft peep.

Fable's breath caught. All thoughts of the Blood Star and Endora fled her mind. She shoved the star in her pocket, taking in the wonder before her.

Murmuring voices sounded behind them, and Timothy twisted and waved to their friends. "The phoenix cycled. Come see!"

They all came running, even Knox—with Leena keeping a careful eye on him—and crowded around the ashes.

As they all gasped in awe, Vetch squatted beside Fable. He gave her a serious look, and Fable squirmed. After everything they'd just experienced, was he about to ream her out and tell her to never come back to the Windswept colony?

His expression softened, and he held out a hand for

her to shake. “Thank you. You saved her life.”

Fable’s cheeks warmed, and she tilted her head. She gazed at the phoenix chick, who scratched at the ashes, then toddled closer to them. Her sparse, newly-hatched chick feathers glimmered in the sun, and Fable knew she’d be okay.

She glanced at Vetch and smiled. “Actually, she saved herself. I only gave her a little boost.”

TWENTY-EIGHT

Heart Magic

Fable approached the table in Juniper's garden with a basket of cutlery. Thorn glanced at her from the far end, balancing a stack of plates in her arms. The lights in the dogwood trees around them flickered to life, illuminating the hardwood table and dining area. Fable breathed in the smell of the rose bushes as she began to place utensils in front of each seat. They had only returned to Juniper's cottage the night before, but already, Fable's magic and energy felt refreshed.

"Is Vetch here yet?" Thorn asked, setting down her last plate.

Fable shook her head as she worked. "I haven't seen him, but Juniper said he was coming. You should smell the kitchen right now. Algar is making his root vegetable stew—the vegetarian version, of course—and between that and Aunt Moira's rye rolls, it smells like heaven in there."

"I bet," Thorn replied, smacking her lips. "Hopefully Vetch gets here soon. I want to ask him how Embers is doing."

Fable lay a fork and butter knife at the head of the table. "Me too."

After Embers's cycle, Fable, Thorn, and Timothy had stayed the night with Leena and Vetch at Moonflower Tower. The next morning, Vetch had carefully packed a kennel-sized crate with dried grass and leaves, then used it to take the new baby Embers with them. Since she had cycled early and away from her nest, the rangers would care for her for the next few weeks at their wildlife centre in the colony. Once she was strong enough, they would take her to her den and keep an eye on her as she grew.

When the group had returned to Juniper's cottage, Aunt Moira and Stirling had been waiting. Fedilmid had called her once he and Algar had gotten back safely with the help of a few Folkvar rangers who had hiked up to meet them, and she and Stirling had left the Thistle Plum immediately to greet the kids. After their happy reunion, Fable had healed Fedilmid's broken leg. The witch had then set to work making a poultice with the phoenix's ashes for Stirling. It might take a few days, but slowly, the elder Nuthatch should start regaining his memory.

Thorn pulled out the chair in front of her and took

a seat. "That was really amazing, you know. What you did for Embers. It sounds weird, but when you two sang together, it felt like something changed. Like there was hope again for Starfell and ending Endora's rain of terror."

But the star is still broken. We are back at square one, trying to defeat the lich. Fable swallowed the words, not wanting to break Thorn's positive spirit. She finished setting the cutlery and took a seat next to her friend. "Could you understand the words of my song this time?"

Thorn tilted her head. "No. Why? Could you?"

Fable nodded slowly. "Yes. It's weird, I could never understand it before. But in that memory of my dad and the other phoenix, I heard him sing the words clearly. It was like something clicked in my mind."

"I wonder if that's because of your connection to your dad," Thorn replied. "You're a heart mage. You pick up on the magic of emotions. Last night, you told me he was desperate to connect with the bird. Maybe that strengthened the magic for you."

"I've heard Aunt Moira use that spell before. I couldn't understand her either."

"Yeah. But it sounds like your dad's emotional state was a lot higher than when Aunt Moira has cast the barrier in front of you."

Fable pinched her lips, thinking. "Maybe you're right. I'll have to ask Fedilmid and Aunt Moira what they think."

"Maybe Brennus would know—" Thorn snapped her mouth shut and touched her chest. Tears brimmed in her eyes.

Fable's breath hitched, and she grasped Thorn's hand. "Were you going to say he might know something about the language from his studies with Nestor?"

Thorn nodded, blinking back tears.

"Maybe he does," Fable replied. "When we get him back, we'll ask."

"We don't know where the store is, and apparently Doug has betrayed us." Thorn thumped the table with her fist. "How are we going to save Brennus?"

"I don't know," Fable replied. "But we have to. There's no other option. He's family, and I won't leave him." She wished she was as sure as she sounded. But the thought of Brennus facing Ralazar with no amulet and no way to transport made her gut roil. But they'd find him. And they'd free his parents and somehow get Ralazar locked away too, where he could never curse anyone again.

"I'm with you. And Doug had better watch out if

we ever cross paths again." Thorn bared her teeth, and her eyes flashed yellow.

The swish of the glass door opening caught Fable's ear, and she and Thorn looked at the cottage. Vetch closed the door behind him and strode over to them. For once, he didn't have his bow.

Thorn's eyes faded to their usual moss-green. "Hey, Vetch. Where's your weapon? Did Aunt Juniper confiscate it?"

Vetch shrugged. "No. I didn't see a need for it."

"Are you sure?" Thorn replied. "Fable and I have magic, remember? Don't you need to protect yourself from us?"

Vetch gave her a wry grin, then plunked down into the chair on Thorn's other side. "I deserve that, I guess." He rubbed the back of his neck. "I wanted to tell you both I'm sorry. Which isn't an easy thing for me to do, by the way."

Thorn snorted. "You don't say?"

"Let him finish," Fable said, trying to hide her smile.

Vetch sighed. "I was wrong, okay? You two both showed me that magic isn't evil. Evil people may use it that way, but if it weren't for both of you and your magic, we'd all probably be dead." He pushed his bangs from his eyes. "So what I'm trying to say it, I'm sorry. And thank you."

Thorn thumped his shoulder with her fist. "You're welcome. Does this mean I'm welcome in the colony now? And that Fable will be allowed to visit me any time she wants?"

"I'll talk to Flint," Vetch replied. "I think I can smooth this over. Especially once I remind him how much Moonflower loved that phoenix." His eyes grew misty. "She would have loved to see you sing with Embers, Fable."

"Moonflower?" Fable asked, her chest tight. *He must have named his watchtower after someone. But who was she?*

Vetch swallowed, and his shoulders sagged. "She was my girlfriend and Flint's daughter. We were supposed to get married, but she went missing about six years ago. She and another ranger named Lark found a leather water canteen on the trail. Lark told us it had vines painted all over it. When Moonflower picked it up, there was a flash of light, and she was gone." He scrubbed his face with his palm. "Lark still feels guilty about it. And Flint has never been the same."

"I'm so sorry," Fable said, her voice barely a whisper. "My great-grandmother—she's a monster.

Those objects, they're collectors. That's how she kidnaps people. We're going to put her behind bars again. I promise."

Thorn placed a gentle hand on his back. "Endora killed my parents too. That's why we have to stop her. So she can't hurt anyone ever again."

Vetch gave them both a grateful look, but before he could reply, Timothy's voice carried over the yard.

"The eating area is back here by the garden. Juniper said there should be more than enough food."

A familiar woman's voice joined his. "Are you sure she'll be okay with Knox near the table?"

"Why wouldn't she be?"

Timothy came around the corner of the cottage. Leena and Knox followed him, looking refreshed after their stay at the colony's hostel. They made their way to the table, and Leena gave them all a wolfish smile.

"Hey! I wanted to come say goodbye before Knox and I head out to Stonebarrow tomorrow. Timothy thinks we should stay for supper." She nodded at Vetch. "Hey, Ranger Boy."

He grunted, but Fable could have sworn he smiled for a second.

Thorn gestured to the chair across from her. "You should. We told Aunt Juniper all about you.

She'd love to meet you."

"Why are you going to Stonebarrow?" Vetch asked.

Leena took the chair, and Knox lay in the grass at her feet. His red eyes narrowed, and he snapped at a fly buzzing around him. Leena flattened her poufy hair and leaned back in her chair. "Considering Endora's on a warpath again, I figured Knox and I had better lie low. What happened at the tower was too close for comfort. I have a friend in Stonebarrow we can stay with. Another Iron Wolf."

Fable leaned her elbows on the table. She only knew of one other member of the Iron Wolves—a man who owned the Fog Hollow Inn and had helped Fable and her friends get into the Oakwrath. "Grogan Wolfram?"

Leena flattened her hair again. "The one and only. I forgot, of course you all know him. Orchid told me about your foray into the Oakwrath." She grinned. "Lovely, isn't it?"

Thorn shuddered. "Spikey vines, graveyards, and a murderous dragon? Seeing it once is enough for me." She jerked her chin to Timothy, who stood next to Leena's chair, gazing at the garden. "Timothy sure liked it, though."

"Is that right?" Leena twisted to look at him.

Timothy kept his gaze through the trees, his brow furrowed.

"Earth to Timothy," Leena said.

Fable frowned. "Timothy?"

He flicked his gaze to Fable, then pointed towards the garden. "There's something out there. The pulse . . . it's warm."

Fable's gut churned, and she leapt to her feet. Timothy took off through the trees, and Fable raced after him. The murmured shouts and thumping footsteps told her their friends were getting up to follow. She and Timothy slipped past the dogwoods and into the fading dusk of the vegetable garden. Timothy stopped at the edge and grasped Fable's hand, scanning the area.

"It's so close." He squinted. "There! Behind the tomato cages."

Fable narrowed her gaze. A shadow nearly the size of Thorn loomed behind the bushy plants, then glided towards them as if floating a few inches above the ground. Its black cloak waved in the breeze. Her heart jolted, and her magic roared to life.

One of Endora's undead guards!

She gripped her cousin's hand tighter, tamping down her flames. "Timothy, we need to go—"

Their friends and Knox ran up behind them. Thorn and Leena gasped, and Vetch let out a surprised shout.

"What is *that*?"

"One of Endora's guards," Leena said, placing a protective hand on the dire wolf's head. "My charms don't work on them. They don't have minds or souls."

"Come on, we need to get Fedilmid and Aunt Moira." Fable tugged Timothy in the cottage's direction, her mind racing. She needed to get the adults to cast a protective barrier around the home. She swung her gaze around the edge of the yard, searching for any movement. *Endora must be lurking close by!*

"Stop." Timothy yanked his hand from Fable's. "Look at it. It doesn't want to hurt us."

"What do you mean?" Thorn replied, stepping in front of him and Fable. "Of course it wants to hurt us. It's an undead!"

"Look at it!" Timothy insisted. "It's not a normal undead. Its pulse—it's different from the other undeads'. There's something weird about it."

"All the better reason to get out of here," Leena replied. "I lived with them, remember? I know what they can do. Those whips . . ."

Fable took in her cousin's stubborn expression and willed her heartrate to slow. He gave her a pleading look, and she relented. She peered at the creature, which had stopped only a few feet away from them, its face still hidden beneath its cloak. "How do you think it's different?"

"For starters, if it meant to hurt us, it would have attacked us by now," Timothy replied. "Second, look at its hands."

As if listening to Timothy, the undead held out its hands. Instead of gleaming white bones as Fable had expected, grey skin covered its fingers and seemed to be slowly growing over its palms. Fable grew queasy.

"What in all of Starfell?"

Leena gagged. "That's disgusting. It's rotting. It must be fresh—"

"No." Timothy lifted his chin, staring at the undead with wonder. "Its flesh and skin are growing back."

The undead glided closer, then lowered its hood. Two piercing green eyes stared at them from the white skull. Vetch grunted, looking ready to bolt to the cottage and grab his bow and arrows. Fable covered her mouth with both hands, unable to speak.

How is this possible? How can something undead start to come alive again?

Timothy stepped forward and held out his hand. The undead wheezed, then touched its fingers to his.

Timothy smiled, and it bowed its head.

He glanced over his shoulder at Fable and the others. "See? It's okay. It won't hurt us. I think it wants my help."

Fable bit her lip, shifting uneasily. It was true. The guard didn't appear to be aggressive. It wasn't even holding a whip. But still, how could they trust an undead creature? "Timothy, you can control it, right? If it decides to attack us."

He frowned, patting the undead's arm. "Of course. But it's not going to."

Thorn huffed a breath and turned towards the cottage. "I'm going to get Fedilmid."

"Fable? Thorn?" Aunt Moira's voice rang through the yard. "Where is everyone?"

Fable gave Timothy a serious look. "Bring it with us and keep an eye on it to make sure it doesn't pull anything." She rubbed her forehead. "Your mom is not going to like this."

She pushed by Thorn, Vetch, and Leena and the group made their way back to the dining area with Timothy and the undead at the rear. Fable stepped into the clearing. Her aunt stood next to the table with her arm hooked around Stirling's. The old man hunched his shoulders, fiddling with the bandage on his forehead that held Fedilmid's ash poultice.

"There you all are!" Aunt Moira let out a breath of relief. Her bangles jangled as she gripped Stirling's forearm with her free hand. "Fable, your grandfather remembered something! And it's important."

Wrinkles formed around Stirling's pursed lips. "Come here, child. You've got the Blood Star all wrong."

Fable approached him, shaking her head. Her chest pinched. Does he know the star's destiny—that he'll need to meet with his mother to heal it? "I know. The ashes couldn't heal it. We need Endora—"

"Would you let me speak, kid?" Stirling waved her off, scowling. "We don't need Endora. That destiny Carina told you is correct, but it's not me and Endora who need to reunite. It's you and Faari."

Fable stared at him, thunderstruck. Her throat constricted, feeling like every ounce of air had been forced from her. *That's not possible. My mother is dead! Did Carina read an old destiny? Is there a new one we don't know about?* She looked from Stirling to Aunt Moira, tears threatening to spill. "Does this mean we can't heal the star?"

Aunt Moira, her eyes misty, helped Stirling sit in the nearest chair, then threw her arms around Fable.

"Oh, dear, no. We can." She sniffed and kissed Fable's head. "After all these years, I was sure Faari had died along with Morton and Thomas. But she didn't. Fable, your mother is alive."

Fable's knees buckled, and Aunt Moira gripped her tightly. Her mind fogged with confusion. *My mom's alive? But even if she didn't die in the rock slide, she promised her life to Endora.* She hugged Moira back. "But, how?"

Aunt Moira pulled away, wiping her cheek. "I found a rock—" Her gaze flicked over Fable's shoulder, and her mouth widened in horror. She grabbed Fable and pushed her behind her. "What in Estar's name is *that*? Timothy! Get over here at once!"

Timothy and the undead stood at the opening in the trees behind their friends. The undead pulled up its hood to hide its face, and Timothy tugged its arm. "No, Mom. Look! It's okay. It won't hurt us."

"He can control it, anyway," Leena said with a shrug.

Aunt Moira's face paled, and she opened her mouth to say more, but Stirling held up a grizzled hand. "Trust the boy, Moira. He's more powerful than you think."

Aunt Moira faltered, and Fable grasped her arm. "What rock, Aunt Moira?"

Her aunt tore her gaze from Timothy and the undead. "I-I—" She took a deep breath. "Fedilmid told me about your memory tokens. You must have dropped one in Nestor's study. I found a grey rock there, and when I picked it up, it transported me into that horrible night." She closed her eyes for a moment. "Your mother didn't die in that rock slide. Endora kidnapped her."

Fable's heart pounded against her ribs, and her cheeks grew hot. "Endora kidnapped my mom to steal her life. They made a deal."

"What?" Aunt Moira shook her head, causing a stray lock to loosen from her bun and fall over her face. She pushed it aside. "No. That can't be right."

Leena cleared her throat. "What does Faari look like?"

Aunt Moira glanced at the warlock, her face creased with concern. "Short. Round cheeks. Wavy dark hair." She paused, cupping Fable's shoulder. "A lot like Fable, actually. Why?"

Fable's chest warmed as she thought of her mother's tinkling laughter in the memory of her parents getting ready for Stirling's award ceremony. The woman had practically glowed in that jewel-toned dress. *Aunt Moira thinks we look alike?*

Leena scratched her wrist, then looked at the

undead. The creature pointed upward, and Leena nodded. "That's what I thought too. Fable, I think your mother is alive. I saw her in Endora's mansion, stuffed away in one of the upstairs bedrooms. I was cleaning the room, and there was this portrait with a sheet draped over it. Obviously, I wanted to know who was in it." She paused, her expression softening. "She looked like you. And she was alive. She pressed her hand against the glass. I tried to break it, but you know how tough those portraits are."

"Oh, Fable. We can find her," Aunt Moira said breathlessly. "We can *save* her."

She pulled Fable into another embrace, and Fable let her tears fall. Thorn and Timothy ran to them and joined in the family hug, their warmth and emotions enveloping Fable.

My mother is alive. The memory tokens—they weren't a warning. They were an explanation. Something my parents left to help me defeat Endora. To help me save my mom. It's destiny for us to reunite! And once the Blood Star is healed, we can save Brennus and his parents too. We can put an end to Endora's terror for good!

Aunt Moira pulled a cloth bundle the size of her fist from her pocket, then slipped it into Fable's hand. She lowered her lips to Fable's ear. "When you're ready, this memory is for you. It will explain what happened that night." She gulped. "It won't be easy to watch this, but your parents obviously wanted you to see it."

Fable clutched the cloth-covered rock to her chest, leaning into her family's embrace. With them by her side, she could do anything. All she had to do now was find her mother and Brennus—to make her family and her heart whole.

Endora has no idea what she's up against now.

Follow Fable's adventures in
Starfell Book Six: The Star of Truth.
Coming in 2023!

Want more magical stories from Jessica Renwick? Visit www.jessicarenwickauthor.com and sign up for her mailing list to get your FREE story, *The Witch's Staff*, which was originally published in the *Mythical Girls Anthology* by Celticfrog Publishing.

Authors rely on word-of-mouth.
An honest review on Amazon, Goodreads, or your choice of bookseller would be greatly appreciated.
Only a few words can make a big difference.

GLOSSARY

Aldric – owner of the Magical Menagerie.

Algar Whimbrel (AL-gar WIM-bruhl) – a woodsman; Fedilmid's husband.

Alice Serpens – a witch; owner of The Thistle Plum Inn; Nestor's wife.

Antares Jovian (an-TEH-reez) – an astronomer who works at Skyview Tower; Carina's brother.

Arame (AIR-am) – a portal-caster; Endora's first assistant.

Bart Tanager – a travelling musician bound to Ralazar's curse; Isla's husband; Brennus's father.

Brawn – an immortal warg; patron of the Order of the Iron Wolves.

Brennus Tanager (brEH-nuhs) – Bart and Isla's son; Fable's best friend.

Buckhorn – a Folkvar from Sandy Ridge in the Burning Sands.

Burning Sands – the desert in the far south of Starfell.

Burntwood Forest – forest on the east side of Starfell; previously the Greenwood Forest; where Fable landed when she first left Larkmoor.

Carina Jovian (kr-EE-nah) – an astronomer who works at Skyview Tower; Antares's sister.

collector – a magical item enchanted to transport beings who set it off.

Doug – a portal-caster; Endora's new assistant.

drudger – a non-magical fallen star.

Eighteen Lilac Avenue – Faari and Morton's home in Mistford; inherited by Fable.

Endora Nuthatch (en-DOR-ah NUHT-hatch) – a lich; Morton's grandmother; Fable's great-grandmother.

Estar – an immortal, magical peryton. Patron of the Order of the Jade Antlers.

Evocation magic – the magic of storing memories in objects called tokens.

Faari Nuthatch (FEH-ree NUHT-hatch) – Morton's wife; Fable's mother; deceased.

Fable Nuthatch (NUHT-hatch) – a sorcerer; Faari and Morton's daughter; Moira's niece; Timothy's cousin.

Fedilmid Coot (FEHD-ill-mid) – a witch; Algar's husband; also known as The Fey Witch.

Firdale – mountain town in the far northwest of

Starfell; near Squally Peak.

firehawk – a wild chicken that breathes fire and reads auras; Star's species.

Flint – a Folkvar; the leader of the Windswept Colony.

Fog Hollow Inn – a ramshackle inn in Stonebarrow; owned by Grogan Wolfram.

Folkvar (FOWK-var) – a giant race of people who live in colonies and off the land; Thorn's race.

Gaea (GEE-uh) – the constellation the Blood Star came from.

Grimm – the Nuthatch's loyal mastiff.

Grogan Wolfram – a warlock of the Order of the Iron Wolves; bonded to Brawn; owner of the Fog Hollow Inn.

Halite – the Dragon Queen; an immortal dragon.

Isla Tanager (EYE-lah)– a travelling musician bound to Ralazar's curse; Bart's wife; Brennus's mother.

Juniper – a Folkvar; Thorn and Orchid's aunt.

Knox (noks) - a dire wolf; Leena's friend.

Larkmoor – non-magical town separated from the rest of Starfell by the Windswept Mountains.

Leena Houndstooth – a warlock of the Order of the Iron Wolves; bonded to Brawn.

lich – a magic-caster who gains power by evil deeds; drawn to power to and immortality.

Lichwood – the forest on the west side of Starfell; where Tulip Manor resides.

lightning bird – a large magical bird that can control the elements of the sky.

Maple – a Folkvar; on the Windswept Colony town council.

Magical Menagerie – a travelling circus with magical creatures caught from the wilds of Starfell.

Malcolm Bonekall – a necromancer from Stonebarrow; member of the Order of the Jade Antlers.

Mayor Drabson – the mayor of Larkmoor.

messenger bird – a magical bird that delivers messages from warlocks in the Oakwrath.

Mistford – magical city in the south of Starfell.

Moira Nuthatch (MOY-ruh NUHT-hatch) – a witch; Thomas's wife; Timothy's mother; Fable's aunt.

Morton Nuthatch (NUHT-hatch) – Faari's husband; Fable's father; Endora's grandson; deceased.

necromancer – a type of sorcerer who can control the dead.

Nestor Serpens – an astronomer; owner of The Thistle Plum Inn; Alice's husband; Nightwind's rider and friend.

Nightwind – a pterippus; Nestor's best friend.

Oakwrath Thicket – a dark overgrown forest at the edge of Starfell, past Larkmoor and on the other side of the Windswept Mountains; where the immortals are trapped after being driven out of Starfell.

Opal – an immortal, magical unicorn.

Orchid (OR-kuhd) – a Folkvar; Thorn's sister; a member of the Order of the Jade Antlers.

Order of the Adakite Bears – a warlock order.

Order of the Iron Wolves – a warlock order that Grogan belongs to. Braun is their patron.

Order of the Jade Antlers – a warlock order started by Sir Reinhard to rid Starfell of evil. Estar is their patron.

Piper – an uprooter; lives with the Tanagers.

peryton – a winged deer of magical origin; Estar's species.

pterippus (TEAR-eh-puss) – a winged horse of magical origin; Nightwind's species.

Ralazar – a warlock bonded to the Dragon Queen, Halite.

Roarke – a raven; also a messenger bird.

Rose Cottage – Fable, Timothy and Moira's home in Larkmoor.

sorcerer – a person whose magic comes from

within.

Sir Reinhard – a knight of the Order of the Jade Antlers; a warlock bonded to Estar.

Skytouch Summit – mountain peak in the Windswept Mountains; Halite's original home.

Skyview Tower – an astronomy tower near Mistford.

Skyward University – the astronomy university in Mistford.

spectral – a fallen star with magical properties.

Squally Peak – mountain peak in the Windswept Mountains.

Star – a firehawk; Fable's first friend and guide in Starfell.

Stonebarrow – industrious city in the north of Starfell.

The Buttertub Tavern – a pub between the Burntwood Forest and the Lichwood; halfway between Mistford and Stonebarrow.

Thistle Plum Inn – Alice and Nestor's bed-and-breakfast; resides in Mistford.

Timothy Nuthatch (NUHT-hatch) – Moira and Thomas's son; Fable's cousin.

Thomas Nuthatch (NUHT-hatch) – Timothy's father; Moira's husband; Morton's brother; deceased.

Thora – a lightning bird; friend of the Jade Antlers.

Thorn – a Folkvar; Fable's best friend; Orchid's sister.

Tulip Manor – Fedilmid and Algar's stone cottage in the Lichwood.

undead – corpses raised from their graves by a powerful magic-caster.

uprooter – a small orange lizard from the Burning Sands; can magically entice beings to follow it.

Validus – an immortal, magical bear; patron of the Adakite Bears.

Vetch – a Folkvar; a ranger in the Windswept Colony.

warlock – a person who draws magic from dark forces or beings.

warg – an immortal wolf with moon magic

Windswept Mountains – mountain range that cuts across the west of Starfell.

witch – a person who draws magic from the earth.

wizard – a person who learns magic from books.

Zircon – an immortal, magical rabbit.

Acknowledgements

Thank you so much to all my wonderful readers and the teachers and libraries supporting this series! I love connecting with all of you. You are the heart of Fable's stories.

A special thanks again to my wonderful editor, Talena Winters (without her, these books would not hold the magic they do), my partner and biggest cheerleader of all, Russ, and my close group of friends who have believed in me from beginning!

I hope you all enjoy Fable's next chapters.

Jessica Renwick

About the Author

An avid reader and writer since she was a child, Jessica Renwick inspires with tales of adventures about friendship, courage and being true to yourself. She is the author of the award-winning children's fantasy series, *Starfell.*

She enjoys a good cup of tea, gardening, her pets, consuming an entire novel in one sitting, cozy video games, and outdoor adventures. She resides in Alberta, Canada on an urban homestead with her partner, fluffy monster dogs, a flock of chickens, and an enchanted garden.

You can find her at www.jessicarenwickauthor.com, on Instagram @jessicarenwickauthor, on Facebook, and on Goodreads.

Made in the USA
Las Vegas, NV
17 December 2023

83031567R00236